polychrome

polychrome

a crime of many colours

by Joanna Jodełka

translated by Danusia Stok

STORK PRESS

Published by
Stork Press Ltd
170 Lymington Avenue
London
N22 6JG

www.storkpress.co.uk

English edition first published 2013 by Stork Press
1

Translated from the original *Polichromia* © Joanna Jodełka, 2009
English translation © Danusia Stok, 2013

This publication has been funded by
the Book Institute – the ©POLAND Translation Program

The publisher gratefully acknowledges assistance from the Polish Cultural
Institute in London for its support towards the publication of this book.

Paperback ISBN 978-0-9573912-3-9
ebook ISBN 978-0-9573912-4-6

Designed and typeset by Mark Stevens in 10.5 on 13 pt Athelas Regular

Printed in the UK

To Professor Konstanty Kalinowski
Dear Professor, you were right...

NOVEMBER that year was more like November than ever. Ugliness in all its splendour – as if for show – proud.

Not only had the leaves already managed to fall, they had also managed to blend in with the surroundings, dance with the mud and start the slow process of decaying. Besides, everything had begun to look as if it had decided to disintegrate more vilely than usual.

At least that's what the inhabitants of Great Moczanowo thought and felt.

Evidently the filth they'd once chased away from their village had now returned, since this is where it had come from; they sensed it in the air and beneath their feet again, everywhere; just as they felt everywhere the unimaginable crime which had taken place here and would remain here forever.

They hid and wanted to believe that it was the wind, heavy with rain, and not the ever-present shame which crushed them to the ground, bowed their heads and didn't allow them to go out without reason. Did not allow them to gabble, gossip, grumble either in the shop, on the streets or anywhere. They spoke so quietly they barely heard themselves speak, and the dogs, chained to their kennels, barked less; or maybe that's just what everyone thought.

They were afraid of punishment. Punishment for everything which, barely a month ago, had painted leaves and life in fiery colour.

But what a knot of activity it had been at the time. Everywhere, in homes and by fences, in front of the shop and even by the church – although there a little muted. Half of the sentences had begun with 'apparently', and every detail – carried, so it seemed, by a still summery, warm breeze – had circulated lazily round the neighbourhood, there and back, provoking smiles and joyful spite cut through with a touch of outrage, as if a comma.

People had sighed, rolled their eyes, pulled faces – openly, with satisfaction. A well-known and valued formality. Of course, the prophetic 'it's all going to end badly' had nearly always cropped up, but only as part of the ritual, like an ellipsis without great significance. Because, when it came out into the open, all hell was going to break loose...

Later, contrary to the norm, nobody had said 'and didn't I say so', even the stupidest of peasant women. Because what would that have meant?

For many more years to come, when – out of sheer curiosity – those working at regional administration were asked about it, they mumbled something which was a little unclear and with apparent shame, both the firm believers in God and those who only went to church on special occasions. United as never before.

If then, some thirty years ago, a stranger had by some miracle stopped in the village, he would probably have thought it a touch more sleepy, a touch more depressing, but apart from that much like any other 'ordinary God-forsaken hole'. He wouldn't have discovered that this was precisely what the people thought of themselves, terrified that God had forgotten about them, or wishing He would forget. That if they didn't talk about it, nobody would ask, ever.

But God was on the side of the pessimists again; He was obviously partial to them in these parts. Or perhaps He had good reason.

Because they clearly weren't afraid of Him.

Because it had been a priest – His servant a killer.
Because evil had been conceived.
Such things not even the people forget.

I

ANTONIUSZ MIKULSKI – retired restorer of monuments and buildings – didn't have to get out of bed to see the old apple tree wither outside his window. He didn't feel sorry; the tree was no longer any use. It hadn't produced any fruit for a long time and when it had the apples had been maggoty and sour. He thought the same about himself.

***

Maciej Bartol – commissioner in the Poznań police – had already been awake for several minutes. He felt the day was going to be a scorcher. He wondered whether his ex-girlfriend was going to wear the floral dress today, the one whose straps slipped down so readily. He didn't open his eyes; he didn't want her to disappear.

***

Romana Zalewska – architect – picked up the telephone while still nearly asleep, spoke briefly but to the point, as though she were in the office and not in her own bed, naked. She'd mastered the art to perfection. Fifteen seconds later her head was nestling in her pillow again, free of guilt; she had, after all, worked late into the night.

***

Edmund Wieczorek – retired postman – had been awake for two hours. He didn't want to miss the two students who'd recently moved in on the first floor when they returned. They'd come home at dawn, as usual – not alone. He liked them; they were the only unpredictable cog in the monotonous life of those living in the tenement on Matejko Street. There was something to see.

***

Krystyna Bończak – mother of two boys – was making up another parcel. The prison on Młynarska Street, again. Cigarettes, yet again. She'd prayed and cried through the night, again. She'd fallen asleep in the early hours of the morning and woken up in the morning; still, she was happy the day had already begun. Everything appeared different in the day.

***

The man in strange glasses was putting on a new shirt. He was pleased: he'd just managed to fasten the cuffs – good, they wouldn't reveal his wrists. He approached the window which never opened, and looked out at Warsaw from the height of the thirtieth floor. There was nothing to see during the day.

***

Ksawery Rudzik – real estate agent – woke up earlier than usual and much earlier than needed. He didn't like and, on principle, didn't tolerate wallowing in bed; he'd simply open his eyes and get up. Always, but not this time. He hadn't treated himself to a night in one of the most expensive hotels in Warsaw only to leap out of bed. He was bursting with pride.

As if to reinforce it, he stretched languidly and with pleasure. Only five years ago everything had been different. He'd failed his bar exams for the second time; as usual it was the sons of high-fliers who'd got in but he was nobody's son and very much wanted to change this. Five years of law, five years of hard slog, rotten food and jars from his mother – good but somehow shameful, five years of hope that everything would change, that he'd be able to go to restaurants, dinners and so on.

It had seemed unlikely. It had seemed unlikely even when, for lack of money, he'd started working for a real estate agency, something which he hadn't boasted about too much initially. Until it had become clear, both to him and his employer, that he was damn good at it. Complications didn't put him off – impoverished, greedy beneficiaries who quibbled over unassigned shares in a tenement; couples which, with a flush on their cheeks, had only recently acquired credit for their dream apartment but were now at each other's throats, pulling out their dirty linen and justifying their unjustifiable reasons; opinionated landlords and fussy tenants – he liked all this. He'd stand between them with the expression of one who knew more, who'd solved harder cases. With superiority but also kind-hearted understanding which for years he'd rehearsed in front of a mirror. Law was also proving very useful: magic articles, incomprehensible paragraphs, an appropriately concerned expression seasoned with a loud, sympathetic sigh in the case of taxes, a couple of sentences on the tardiness of courts and cases 'like these' going on for years. All this, thrown in at the right moment, worked wonders.

Yesterday, he'd passed the state exam as a real estate agent. He was one of no more than a few lucky ones. The milieu was closing in: he knew that and it suited him. Why let in new blood? There were enough people there already, the rising economy was not going to last forever, one had to prepare for worse times. He smiled with contentment as he looked down at Warsaw from on high, from a good position.

He wondered a little longer whether to phone Kasia but decided against it. He would have to swap her, too, in the end. A pleasant girl, pretty enough – and he did love her in his own way – but she didn't suit his perfect world. He remembered her showing him the beautiful handbag she'd bought at a bargain price. He'd praised the hideous string object curtly.

He couldn't understand why she didn't notice how it made him sick, how he now hated those cut-price joys, those beautiful cheap handbags and shoes, how he loved the big, ostentatious, brazen golden logos of good brands, how he'd always loved them.

Another visitor also appeared, unwanted in this place, at this moment. His mother. He wasn't going to call her either. The endearment in her voice annoyed him, telling him to look after himself, dress warmly, avoid draughts, and that accent of hers, the turn of phrase which reminded him of where he came from. His lousy surname was enough. His first name wasn't too bad; it could have been much worse – his other grandfather had been called Szczepan.

He quickly chased away any scruples for not visiting his mother, for spending as much on one night in the hotel as would last her a month.

Neither of them understood how little time he had to become someone, that shortly everything would stabilize, that the door to the world he wanted would close soon and everyone would live in pre-determined positions, that he had to hurry, that he could run around tower blocks in sensible shoes and rent apartments to students, but that he had to have shoes which wore down and an expression which showed it didn't matter.

He pondered a little longer, donned a carefully chosen shirt, smiled at the man of success he saw in the mirror and went downstairs for breakfast. He picked a good table (he saw everyone and everyone saw him), helped himself to a small portion of ham and vegetables, not too much; he'd already seen people at various receptions with plates loaded because the food came free. He even tempted himself to a little extravagance in the form of a fruit salad.

He began the ceremony of relishing the moment, the

breakfast and himself – everything was excellent. He just felt he was investing too much energy in the difficult art of appearing natural in a situation which was unnatural to him.

Thoughts about whether he was acting naturally started to grow in strength and could have ended with him spilling coffee and treacherously revealing his natural defects. Fortunately, the man at the next table caught his eye.

He liked to evaluate people; it had become his passion of late, and the accuracy of his judgement had increased his bank account.

The man couldn't have been much older than him; it was only the glasses that added gravitas. They were a bit strange – dark lenses too pale for a pair of sunglasses and yet too dark for corrective lenses; besides, the frames were also neither here nor there, neither old nor new. The dark blond hair had perhaps been well cut three months ago but had now been forgotten about and rested messily on the collar of a boring, grey shirt unfastened to reveal a cord with a gold pendant. The man looked a bit too ordinary to be a guest at a five-star hotel, nor was he a tourist who'd strayed from his group, even less so a sales representative. Most importantly, he was acting naturally. This, Ksawery could sense perfectly well, although he couldn't explain how he'd arrived at the conclusion. The man under observation wasn't interested in his surroundings. He wasn't eating breakfast, or smelling the warm bread rolls; he wasn't starting his day on a pleasant note, wasn't smiling. He was behaving as if he'd found himself at a petrol station and was filling up with the fuel necessary for life, no more. This was how a man behaved eating breakfast standing up at a train station, but not here, thought Ksawery.

It didn't give him any peace. If, for example, the man had entered his office, he, Ksawery, would have raised his eyes from the computer but only for a moment, and immediately pretended he was very busy. He rebuked himself for such thoughts – he had to be careful, had to be alert, the man might be a philosopher but one who had inherited a tenement from his parents, he'd heard of such cases. One could always learn something and he, Ksawery, learned even at moments such as these. As a counter-balance, he praised himself.

He must have watched the stranger for too long because the latter tore his eyes away from his plate, met Ksawery's gaze and without a moment's hesitation bowed in greeting. Ksawery, caught staring, was at first unable to do anything. He didn't get another chance, however, because the stranger calmly continued to eat without looking at him.

And he, too, didn't turn his head in the man's direction. He wasn't proud of himself but quickly found a satisfactory explanation for the awkward situation – a foreigner; our kinsmen always turned their eyes away and pretend to look in the opposite direction.

After breakfast, he walked past reception, asked for his bill to be made ready and a taxi to the airport to be ordered. He knew that the nice woman didn't need any information as to where the taxi was to take him, but it had sounded good and she'd smiled differently somehow; this he'd also rehearsed. He was learning how to make an impression and was improving.

The taxi was of better quality, too – a Mercedes with a neat, tidy and polite driver. Ksawery calmly arrived at the airport, didn't hurry and wore the expression of a man who is not in a hurry. The airplane was even delayed according to plan. Ksawery was sure that he was the only passenger in the departure lounge pleased with the delay and it wasn't at all because he'd barely arrived on time himself. He decided to go to the bar but still couldn't decide whether to grumble a little or order a drink with a large quantity of ice. He didn't decide; he didn't have time.

Behind the glass shelf, which stood on a counter laden with sandwiches, biscuits and slices of cakes, he saw the same man who'd riveted his attention not more than an hour ago in the hotel. He couldn't understand why he kept watching him, why he couldn't make a move, why he felt strange. He was never horrified by coincidences, didn't believe in superstitions and other such rubbish. This was different somehow; he stood and stared, wanted to run away and stay all at the same time. He pulled himself together after a while although he didn't really know after what. He began to observe and listen. This time the man couldn't see him so he had time; he slowly started to calm down, as always when able to focus on the details, one by one, with profound reverence.

The man's voice was deep; he spoke resolutely, not very fast; he could easily have worked for the radio. It took a while for Ksawery to realise, with surprise, that he was speaking Polish as though it were something strange – here in Poland, in Warsaw.

The man no longer looked ordinary although he still wore the same shirt, unfastened so Ksawery could clearly discern a small anchor on the cord around his neck. His hair looked different, too, pulled back and held in place at the top of his head by the glasses.

The stranger was rather handsome. Ksawery wouldn't have been able to judge this himself, no doubt, but saw it very patently in the eyes of the pretty girl serving the man. He recognised the smiles, the fawning. He hated it, although he craved it for himself. To be noticed, remembered.

Hence the pursuit after self-confidence, watches, shirts – all substitutes for something else.

He lost sight of the man for a moment because of a couple of fuming passengers who were seeking information – from anywhere; perhaps that's why they were in the bar. In a split second the nice woman stopped being nice.

He remained glued to the glass display, and the good mood he'd been in this morning melted away like the jelly on the tarts which had the misfortune of not having been swiftly sold. The tarts didn't look good from close up, nor did his reflection in the glass.

He remembered his mother reading something about Leonardo da Vinci, according to whom truly ingenious and beautiful people could only be born from great passion. So he'd been a lost cause right from the start; he hadn't just guessed but known his mother could barely stand his father. He knew very well – he'd heard from the best source possible, his mother.

Now he really did want something to drink – with no ice. He would calm down and soon his thoughts would be back on the right track, true to plan. Perhaps he'd phone the office – that always did the trick.

He'd walked two steps before hearing: 'We meet again.'

He just stared, mouth gaping in surprise no doubt, and felt like a child who, caught red-handed, knows trouble's on the way. But why did he feel like this? He had no idea. So he didn't say anything.

'Sorry for being so direct.' A radiant smile immediately appeared on the stranger's face. 'Just because I remember you doesn't mean you have to remember me. Please forgive me. I'm almost certain we had breakfast together, in the same hotel, that is. Quite a coincidence, don't you think?'

'Could be, although I don't remember.' He had no idea why he'd lied and couldn't say anything cleverer. All he saw was that the curt reply didn't discourage the beaming stranger in the least.

'Please don't be angry that I'm pestering you. You're not the only one I've pestered since yesterday.'

Ksawery hadn't seen him pestering or paying attention to anybody that morning.

'I'm just passing through Poland,' he continued. 'I regret not living here but that might soon change and I'll stay for longer.'

Ksawery didn't have time to ask where the man was from, but his earlier peculiar unease was imperceptibly evaporating, swiftly turning into sincere interest. And his typical, deeply rooted aversion to small talk with compatriots was gradually turning into equally typical, endearing native hospitality extended to foreigners and, eventually, to Poles not born in Poland.

Their conversation, barely begun, was interrupted by a collective groan from a dozen passengers as they heard yet another announcement declaring a further delay of up to forty-five minutes.

They sat down.

'You know, when I watched you this morning, you looked like a million dollars.' The stranger smiled. 'That's a saying, of course. A particularly successful trip to the capital, was it?'

Ksawery was astounded. Watched – how? When? But he replied truthfully about his work, the state exam he'd passed and would, perhaps, have wondered when the man had, in fact, been watching him if it hadn't been for the turn which the conversation had taken.

The following two hours were like honey to Ksawery's ears.

Even the most optimistic script of an intricately planned celebration didn't presume such admiration for himself as he heard from the lips of this foreign stranger. The entire conversation centred on real estate. Ksawery talked a lot, the stranger merely confirmed everything he already knew or had already sensed. How very underrated and still underestimated the profession was in a developing market, what great possibilities it had to offer such a well-educated person as himself, what a good moment it was for development because later there'd be branch offices where someone with experience could make a name for himself or strong local offices which one could open.

For the sake of the conversation, Ksawery also added that he was intending to study estate evaluation – he'd thought about it once and now remembered how well it had sounded. The stranger enthused over the versatility of people in Poland, their desire to educate and better themselves.

They took a long time saying goodbye on landing at Poznań's Ławica airport, hoping that they'd meet soon, which was quite possible considering how the company where the stranger acted as advisor was developing.

Not even the slovenly taxi driver, the dreadful heat or lack of air conditioning in the car could make him angry. He calmly recreated the recent conversation in his mind, basking in turn in the flattery he'd heard and in the analysis of his boundless possibilities.

He also imagined his potential client entering the office and he, Ksawery, loudly joking that commissions were simply falling into his hands. Or maybe something interesting would turn up even sooner, he thought, looking at the parcel he'd promised to deliver. He'd offered to do this when the stranger had told him that he'd promised to deliver it, but wouldn't have time because of the delay. To the parents of a friend who'd died; an old story. Nothing much, just a small parcel of photographs. He'd also promised to add a bunch of sunflowers for the grandmother, which was very important. Ksawery had firmly refused to take money to buy the flowers – a gesture not to say a bonus.

He couldn't remember whether he'd hit upon the idea of relieving his fellow traveller of the small task immediately or only when he'd helped decipher the address in view of making it easier to eventually find the old couple in the future. The address was balm to the ears of the estate agent. An old villa in Sołacz – an expensive area, an expensive street and, even if the house looked as if it were on the point of collapsing, still worth an incredible sum.

An excellent commission – remuneration, he corrected himself. That's what he ought to call it, it sounded better; he recalled the current advice to agents.

If he'd understood correctly, the people to whom he was delivering were the owners of the house and, more importantly, had left no beneficiary. Such people were a rarity and equally rarely, if at all, did they allow in a nosey agent, but with the photographs and flowers... Even a beginner from the office could do a great deal. But he – he could perform miracles. Yes, he'd go there first thing in the morning. He also decided not to tell anyone about it.

Having looked at the same crossroads and the same road workers for the past ten minutes, he was overcome with tiredness. His shirt started to stick to his back and his back to the dirty upholstery; his palms were damp, too – but that was probably due to all the excitement and not the August heat. He took a long time wiping them on the moist tissue he'd taken from the airplane before carefully studying the note he was to attach to the flowers. Flowers, as if a little withered, were painted on the small card. He didn't like them much. In the middle were printed the Latin words *Expecto Donec Veniat* and 'For Aurelia' – handwritten.

He considered it strange but didn't think about it for too long; Latin wasn't his strong point, let alone some words of wisdom. He slipped the note into his wallet, in the compartment where he kept his money, so as not to forget to attach it to the flowers as promised.

In the end, he phoned home, even said something pleasant; after all, he did feel the day was exceptional. He asked what they were having for supper.

And heard – sorrel soup.

The taxi driver who'd just changed lanes saw his passenger's hideous grimace in the mirror. He couldn't stand it and uttered furiously: 'Then find a route yourself. I've no idea how to drive around this city anymore. Everyone knows where there aren't any traffic jams! Apart from taxi drivers, of course,' he added under his breath.

The passenger didn't say a word, either then or later. He didn't even say goodbye.

MACIEJ BARTOL, an unfledged police commissioner, thought someone had saved his life when he heard his work mobile phone ring. And he was not far from wrong.

For the past fifteen minutes he'd been at his mother's. He had a very close relationship with her generally, but not at this moment. He'd discovered recently that her maiden name, Bogdanowicz, indicated that she might have descended from the Tatars. Now, he was almost certain there was some truth in it.

Things had already gone very badly when he'd told her he was to be a father and not a very happy one at that, but when, regrettably, he'd added that he wasn't sure how it had happened, her large, expressive eyes had begun to narrow into slits like those of a wild animal and her eyelids trembled. Something peculiar had happened to her lips, too. The anticipated attack had followed.

The tirade – along the lines that perhaps she really hadn't talked to him enough about matters concerning men and women when he was an adolescent, that if he wanted to she could, albeit unwillingly, make up the deficit and explain to the thirty-five-year-old fully-grown man where babies come from – was only broken by a silly ringtone. The cabaret tune didn't suit the situation, and not for the first time.

He hoped it was something important; an innocent lie which would enable him to escape was out of the question. He didn't know how, but his mother always knew when he was lying or even when he wasn't telling the whole truth.

Fortunately, the call was from Piotr Lentz. The two men worked together but weren't bound by friendship, so Lentz wouldn't be phoning without good reason.

'Hi, where are you?'

'Ogrody. What's happened?'

'Good, you're not far. Get yourself over here. The prosecutor and SOCO are already on their way. No point in talking. You'll be surprised. 6 Góralska Street.'

'Where's that?'

'Sołacz. Go down Wojska Polskiego Street and you'll see a disco on the right. They're all here.'

He glanced at his mother who was looking at him, listening and, for a moment, looking almost normal.

'I'm sorry, I've got to go. We'll talk later.' He assumed a serious expression.

'Fine, and I'll buy you a couple of textbooks in the meantime. Primary or secondary school level, what do you think?'

'Stop, mum. It's hard for me, too!' he answered, knowing full well he shouldn't have said anything, let alone complained. Too late.

'You're finding it hard!' He almost jumped away; he couldn't remember when she'd last shouted so. 'How far gone is the girl?'

'Two, three months... I think?'

'No, it's impossible, I wouldn't have brought up my real son like that! I'm calling the hospital. I was so sleepy after giving birth and newborns all look alike. After all, mistakes do happen...'

'I'll call you, mum. Bye.' He smiled to himself as he closed the door – he used to be the spitting image of her when he was a child.

The relief was almost physical as he ran downstairs.

He'd put off talking about it to his mother for almost a month. And not long ago he'd been happy not to have to listen to her grumbling so frequently about his having let Malina go. It was so damn painful every time. They'd been together for six years. He'd been the one to mess things up. When, a year ago, they'd both agreed to part, he'd been the only one who'd thought the separation was temporary – it couldn't be otherwise. Then he'd seen her with another guy. And he lost ten kilos.

But now what? He'd have to let his mother know that things would work out somehow. Because somehow he was going to have a baby with a girl he hardly knew, whom she'd never seen and whom even he hadn't seen all that frequently.

Perhaps he was lucky somebody had been murdered right then.

Perhaps it wasn't going to be some plain old chase, all tidied up in the morning when everybody had sobered up. Perhaps he was going to have to work from morning to night and everything, in the meantime, would fall into place of its own accord; that did happen at times.

He almost immediately ruled out a drunken brawl in which somebody had butchered someone and was in no state to mumble why, or doggedly mumbled he had a reason and one which couldn't wait. This wasn't the street for it or the area. But why hadn't Lentz said 'you'll see for yourself'? Why 'you'll be surprised'? He thought about this a little longer but not for too long; he arrived fairly quickly.

He could already see the flashing police lights from the wide dual carriageway. He'd definitely never been to this street. Large houses, which must have fulfilled their purpose of isolating and hiding themselves from both each other and the city even before the war, concealed themselves among enormous trees covered in the first November snow. The narrow street seemed to scream that it couldn't stand any more cars, that it had always been peaceful here. All this looked more like a mountain spa than close to the centre of a city of over half a million inhabitants.

He parked at the end of the pavement. A quick glance at the cars told him who was already there; everyone, it seemed. He didn't even have time to approach the small group of people by the fence before seeing Polek struggling with the zip of his jacket.

Polek was standing closest and was the first to speak.

'Well, hello. How long do we have to wait for you? I'm going to freeze to death.' Without waiting for a reply, he went back to battling with his zip.

'Hi. So why are you standing here?' Bartol asked pointedly.

'Because I want to do this bloody thing up.'

Bartol smiled to himself. He knew that even if Polek succeeded in dealing with the zip initially, it wouldn't move any further. He knew the jacket; it had already been too tight a year ago and today was no more than a reminder of a miracle, the miracle of a diet a couple of years earlier. He had no idea why Polek was trying to squeeze into the jacket now, and could have said something but didn't dare. He had himself recently devoted a fair amount of time to combing and ruffling his hair across the increasingly broad stretches of his forehead – so he would certainly have met with some unwelcome repartee.

They were friends. In spite of everything. Perhaps to spite each other, or simply because of all this.

Bartol, taller by a head, was – apart from his ever more nervous habit of raking his hair from temple to forehead – rather calm in speech and manner. Slender. Angular. As if entirely made up of hinges. His too-long arms dangled from his shoulders, his thin legs were awkwardly connected to the rest of his body, his knees were pointed. He didn't sit and stand but rather folded and unfolded.

Polek was corpulent and full of roundness. Round head, round eyes, round back and belly, everything round, smoothly flowing from one part of the body to another. Even when gesticulating furiously, he would generally trace huge and small circles with his hands – and he liked to reason with himself and others even when he knew he was wrong; sometimes simply for the sake of it. Just as he was quick to fume and rage when angry so he would quickly simmer down, soften and forget what it was all about. He said: 'can do' or 'no way'. Nothing was ever 'can do' for Bartol; his mother, who taught Polish, saw to that.

Recently, however, they hadn't talked to each other as much or as often as before. Nor, for a month, had they gone for a beer. It wasn't really either Polek's fault or his wife's that the pleasant weekend at the Agrotourism farm which they'd visited as a foursome with his wife's nice friend hadn't turned out all that well. Although it would certainly never be forgotten, and would somehow have to be explained to the new human being who had just then decided to exist.

It shouldn't have been like that, perhaps, but something unspoken, something like remorse on the one side and reproach on the other, hung in the air.

Two more cars pulled up.

'Who's the bugle call for?' asked Bartol presently.

'I've no idea,' replied Polek, finally giving up on his jacket. 'Can't suss it out, no way. Have a look for yourself. It's a museum in there with a still life at its centre. I've never seen anything like it,' he added.

Bartol had never heard of Polek ever visiting any museum whatsoever, not even a wax museum. He'd no idea where the comparison had come from. He wanted to ask but decided not to and, unaccosted by anyone else, stepped inside.

Everything here was old and solid. The walls, the doors, the furniture inside. The enormous, oval table, the chairs, the escritoire were not like the antiques in the Stara Rzeźnia market which he visited every other Saturday. They were identical to the ones in the antique shops on Stary Rynek which he visited only rarely, feeling like an intruder and knowing that nobody was going to make him feel otherwise. That's how he felt now.

In every room everything was in perfect order; it looked as though everything had been in the same place for years.

The coloured porcelain parrot on the piano seemed to say: 'I've been living in this place twice as long as you've existed, son.' Bartol stopped himself from picking it up and checking where it had been born; Meissen porcelain figurines from Miśnia could cost thousands. He'd once discussed such figurines with a shopkeeper for a good two hours. He'd never imagined he'd be interested in porcelain birds but he was, very much so.

He smiled, thinking that – fortunately – he couldn't afford such a hobby. He wouldn't have been able to invite the guys around. As it was he had a lot of explaining to do regarding his ballerina; the rare mechanism of the music box wasn't a convincing argument.

He continued to look around. He wasn't in a hurry, knew that the body was in some other room. The SOCO dispersed in a spiral and were still far away, tracing an ever-wider circle further and further from the corpse.

As he slowly made his way towards another room, his attention was riveted by an inconspicuous round table. He'd already seen one like it – in a terrible condition, admittedly, but he'd still stared with disbelief at how smoothly the surface had slid apart and the concealed legs parted in different directions to form a long, exceptionally long table. He couldn't remember what tables like these were called but knew they were extremely rare; the battered one had been too expensive for him.

A glass vase containing long-dried stalks stood on the table. He didn't know much about flowers but once more had the impression that he'd seen such colourful patches on the blue glass of a jug somewhere in a book. A familiar voice tore him from his thoughts.

'Bit of a museum, eh? I've heard it's your hobby, junk like this. I'm taking shots of everything but if you want something for your album, tell me. Have you seen the still life yet?' It was one of the technicians.

'Not yet. What's all this about a still life everyone's going on about?'

'I don't know. That's what somebody called it and it's stuck. It goes well with the client, go and look for yourself,' he suggested and went back to taking photographs.

Bartol knew the technician but couldn't recall his name. He had no memory for names – name days, birthdays and so on.

He decided to come back later. Perhaps he really was taking too long looking around right now; everything simply fascinated and interested him, not in the way it should.

He reached a room which might have been a study. Through the half-opened door he saw an entire wall lined with yellowing or gilded book spines – also old. Everything indicated that this was where the drama had taken place.

After a while, he understood that the word 'drama' was exceptionally apt in describing what he saw. He understood, too, what everyone had had in mind.

On the floor lay the corpse of an elderly man. It was naked; only the hips were girded with something like a narrow towel. The towel wouldn't have been strange had it not been for its red colour, which contrasted dramatically with the grey, wrinkled body. The position in which the man lay was also extremely theatrical.

Bartol had the impression that a curtain would fall presently and the play would come to an end. Nothing like that happened. He continued staring at the naked body and thinking he'd not seen anything like it before.

The right arm lay casually close to the body while the head rested on the left hand; one leg was slightly bent, the other straight. The face was peaceful, sleeping. The faint grimace clashed with the blue groove around the neck, which should have made the face look as though the man were experiencing a nightmare, not an afternoon nap.

'Have you ever seen a client so peaceful while being strangled? 'Cos I haven't!' Polek stood leaning against the door frame, waiting, as if indifferent, for an explanation of what he saw.

'No. He didn't fall asleep like that by himself,' replied Bartol. 'The cord must've been thick, like a piece of rope. Besides, he might have died earlier from a heart attack or something, and was strangled just to make sure he was dead or to make it look like a finale.'

'What finale?' asked Polek, shifting from one foot to the other.

'A spectacular one.' Bartol knew he was watching a performance but didn't know who it was for. One spectator, the perpetrator, just them or the whole world? 'We've received an invitation,' he said, shrugging.

'What invitation are you going on about now?'

'For the performance which has just started. Can't you see?'

Polek didn't know whether he saw or not; either way, he didn't like it.

And he was not the only one.

It was clear that the officers would, more than likely, not leave before morning. The house must have been the smallest on the street but still measured about two hundred cluttered square metres. There was enough to do.

One man and hundreds of objects from his life, his parent's lives and probably the lives of his grandparents. A rarity in a country torn by wars and a workers' party. It aroused respect and perhaps nostalgia for a world which was no more. Everybody was strangely quiet, more focused than usual; perhaps because shootings were rare where there was a museum and order; they were far more frequent where there was a brothel and bedlam.

It was getting late, what was generally agreed to be late – as always in winter. In summer 7pm was almost the middle of the day, but not in January, when it had already been dark for over three hours.

Briefing for the investigative team was set for eight in the morning. Meanwhile, as much information as possible was to be collected about the murdered man and neighbours were to be questioned – they might have seen or heard something, something could have drawn their attention. The usual stuff.

First of all, Bartol had to question the woman who'd called the police. Before asking who she was, he'd imagined an elderly woman who did the cleaning or shopping – that had seemed the norm.

But, not for the first time that day, he was taken by surprise. The police had been called by a female architect with an office a couple of streets further down. And that was where she was waiting to speak to him. She was a bit shaken and there was no cause to take her to the police station, at least not that day.

He had no difficulty finding the office; it really was nearby. Another beautiful villa, also old but in a different way.

The slick, sophisticated office of registered architects, decked out with strangely suitable aluminium components, was going through its second youth, fitting in with new times and assignments. The sign informing that architectural engineer Romana Zalewska worked here could not have been smaller yet caught the eye.

From a distance, he saw a tall, slender woman open the gate and door for him.

'Good evening, I'm Romana Zalewska. You must be from the police. It feels as though I've been waiting forever.'

'Good evening. Maciej Bartol. I'm sorry. I came as soon as I could.'

'So I gather. I should be the one apologising. I'm a bit edgy. I was just looking for some cigarettes, even though I don't smoke. Please come in. Would you like something to drink?'

'Yes, coffee, if possible.'

'Then please wait a moment.'

He sat on something which was neither an armchair nor a chair and found it surprisingly comfortable if a little too low for an official conversation. As usual, he didn't know what to do with his legs. Sliding them under the table, the way he liked, was out of the question – the table was too low. He ran his fingers through his hair; at least his hair remained neatly dishevelled.

He cast his eyes around. Everything was modern, mainly grey and metallic; only one wall resembled a painting, decorated with gold-red patterned wallpaper which seemed as though it had been taken from the upholstery of palatial furniture. Perhaps that was why the interior appeared to him more feminine and friendly than all the other shades of grey and aluminium which he'd recently come to expect in such offices.

The architect fitted in with the place. Straight, narrow, black jeans, a white shirt with a collar cut moderately low, promising fine breasts; dark blonde hair tied back in a ponytail, a short fringe. She could have been forty-five but he wasn't sure; she looked good, very good indeed.

When she'd brought the coffee and gone back for an ashtray – because that must have been the only thing missing on the table – he unwittingly followed her with his eyes to the door of a kitchenette and gazed at the wall opposite. There hung a large group photograph. He scarcely recognised her. It was difficult, at first glance, to spot the resemblance between the shapely, elegant and self-assured woman and the hunched, podgy girl in awful glasses and overstretched brown-grey jumper.

He didn't notice her come back. She, too, looked at the photograph.

'Youth and studying weren't my best time,' she said with singular tolerance in her voice. 'Oh well, the day must have upset me. I don't like talking about myself, let alone going back to the past. I try to make sure I don't have time. Your turn now.' She broke off as quickly as she'd started.

'You phoned the police, although I've been told you weren't professionally connected with Mr Antoniusz Mikulski nor were you part of the family.' He heard himself utter the murdered man's name for the first time.

'I didn't really know him. I called because there was a light on in his study.'

'Yes. I know. I also know you were very effective. It's not every day that a patrol car turns up because there's a light on. Please try to explain calmly everything in as much detail as possible. Do you have time?'

'I do now.'

'So we don't have to hurry. Good. From the beginning, please.'

'More or less thirteen years ago, fortunately after my divorce – because it wouldn't have been so simple otherwise – I managed to sell the piece of land I'd inherited from my parents.'

Bartol put away his ballpoint pen; he hadn't expected quite such a long story. He took a sip of coffee. It was better than he'd expected.

'I got a hefty sum of money quite unexpectedly – they've built a parking lot for a large supermarket on the piece of land. I decided to buy a house. It was completely unlike me to arrive at somebody's house asking them if they'd like to sell. But, I don't know, it was one of those days, one of those moments, maybe someone had egged me on, I can't remember. What I do remember, is ringing the doorbell of the house. Mrs Aurelia Mikulska appeared in the window, quickly opened it and asked: 'How can I help you, child?' You know, she was – how can I put it... the perfect picture of an elderly lady, like those you see in pre-war films, as if from another world. Her voice, attitude, dress, calm and some sort of warmth, her silver curls – everything was perfect.'

Bartol caught himself thinking the same thing about the woman sitting opposite – she had matured with perfection. Looking furtively, he caught sight of a white lace bra-strap and took a snapshot in his mind; the strap lay attractively against the faint tan of her skin. He could almost imagine the rest.

'I drank tea from an old porcelain cup, learned that neither that house nor any other in the street was for sale but enjoyed myself anyway. When it grew late I decided to say goodbye. She then asked me to wait another fifteen minutes, because at precisely seven o'clock her husband would emerge from his study and be curious to know who'd come to visit them. I was surprised because for a good hour I had had no idea that anybody else was there apart from her. It was so quiet. I discovered later that it was always like this. Between six and seven in the evening Mr Mikulski worked in his study, writing or reading, so I gathered. He was a restorer of monuments, buildings, or something like that as far as I remember. It was exactly as she said: at seven o'clock Mr Mikulski emerged, greeted me and went to the kitchen. I was afraid he'd be wanting his supper – at a quarter past seven, for example – so I quickly took my leave. I went there once or twice after that' – she grew pensive – 'but I never saw Mr Mikulski again. Not long afterwards I bought my house. And I've also acquired a certain habit. I always, or almost always, drive down Góralska Street on my way to work and back. It's a bit of a roundabout way but I always have the feeling that something separates me from the city, a private corridor.'

She paused for a moment and lit a cigarette. Very awkwardly.

He let her continue without losing her flow. He realised that the story was a necessary part of the whole, that it was the construction on which rested a rational explanation. He was talking to an architect, after all, and not some gossiping neighbour.

'I always smoke when I'm nervous. I don't even know how to inhale but it does help a bit. A habit acquired during exams. As I was saying, when I pass the house in the evenings I always look up at the window – by force of habit. For thirteen years the ritual repeated itself. On the dot of seven the light went out – sometimes... this might sound silly, but I can' – she shuddered –'sorry, I could stop at three minutes to seven to wait and watch. His desk lamp would be on even in the summer when it was overcast and it, too, would be turned off on the dot.'

Again she paused a while.

'I had a terrible day yesterday. A construction project was turned down for no reason at all. It can still be salvaged because the conditions of construction are vague, as is their interpretation, but still, the time, nerves and so on. I left the office and took the same way home as usual. I was sure it was half past seven. I gathered, when at home – by some programme on TV – that it was well past nine. I had no idea where the hour had gone. It preyed on my mind a bit but I was already quite exhausted and didn't want to think. In the morning, I visited a construction site with a client and took the usual route to the office. I was alone in the office at about four drinking coffee, and have no idea why it occurred to me that the light had been on and that was why the previous evening I'd thought it wasn't even seven. I hadn't realised that, subconsciously, I regulated my daily rhythm according to the window. But that wasn't the worst of it. I realised after a while that something must have happened; I was convinced of it. Mrs Mikulska died some two years ago. Mr Mikulski was completely alone and could have needed help and, above all, could have needed it yesterday. I got to the house as quickly as I could. And had another shock, the light was off but so what? It was a quarter past four. I rang the bell. I hadn't even thought of what I'd say if he'd opened. 'Mr Mikulski, why aren't you working in your study?' But nobody opened anyway. I was sure something wasn't right. I was made to believe I was wrong for too many years, and have grown sensitive. If I'm convinced about something, I fight for it – in both my private and professional life. Which is why I didn't let some duty officer brush me aside. I wasn't worried about making a fool of myself. I'm not scared of looking foolish anymore either. And there it is, the whole story. You know the rest better than I do. Would you like something else to drink?'

'No, thank you.'

'I'm just going to get some water. All these nerves and too many words perhaps. I'm sorry.'

Thoughts ran through Bartol's mind. He knew it would be easy to check whether Antoniusz Mikulski's world really had been ordered in this way, but to find out who had destroyed it would be far harder. It didn't look like a coincidence.

He heard a glass shatter in the kitchen.

'Just one more question. Did you see anything strange in front of the house? Somebody lurking and watching you ring the doorbell?' he immediately began as soon as she returned.

'No, nothing strange apart from the light being on and off.'

'Please try to remember as many details as possible by tomorrow. Maybe you saw something suspicious earlier on, as you drove past. Please don't hurry to answer now. We'll wait until tomorrow.'

'You can be sure that if I saw anything it'll come to me. My whole life is made up of details. That must be my curse. What does anyone want to stare at a window for?'

He wasn't sure whether the two thick wrinkles on her forehead appeared only then as, lost in thought, she pulled back her hair, or had been there all along.

He said goodbye and left.

For a while, he stood by his car. It was already late, exceptionally quiet and somehow uncanny. There were practically no lights on anywhere as though no-one lived here, as though the city were somewhere else.

The enormous trees had grown grimmer. There was no wind, the trees didn't want to talk.

THEY VISIT THE CEMETERY as though it were a café; somebody ought to install a vending machine with cakes and tea, the man in the strange glasses thought with disgust.

The smile was long to disappear from his face, slowly, almost naturally. The old woman had turned away a long time ago.

Impatient people, who had practically mastered the art of smiling and achieved a level of near sincerity, yet didn't have the time or intelligence to round it off with precision, amazed him. He loathed botched work. When he invited a smile to his face, he didn't allow it to leave for a long time. Well practised.

He looked after his cheerful expression like other people look after their teeth – systematically and to the point of boredom. He practised and trained it; he didn't want to give time a free hand – it could have revealed too much, hampered. He neither wanted to nor could trust his genes. So he laughed often and easily. In women's eyes – disarmingly.

His well-exercised facial muscles gave a fine performance, sculpting friendly wrinkles, radiantly turning down the corners of squinting eyes and catching parted lips in funny brackets.

He presented this trained smile as easily and readily as young body-builders their freshly pumped muscles.

He cast his eyes around again. Soon there'd be nobody; it was starting to grow dark. The woman who'd accosted him belonged to the brave anyway; dusk chased old women away.

Now the candles burned only for ghosts.

For a moment longer, he allowed his thoughts to run in disparate directions as he looked around, soaking up the darkness and silence, feasting his eyes on the incongruous scenery.

He gazed at the joyful flicker of votive flames, comically reined into kitschy forms – in memory.

Aesthetics of the living in honour of the dead. All this repulsed him.

Stone and flowers torn from the earth, cut and decorated –
with an aim incomprehensible to them – into shameful shapes.

He looked up. Only the huge trees, swaying in the wind,
lived their own life without looking down. They've got time,
he thought, and one day they'll cover and bury all this. They'll
steal the light from the yews watching over the graves, planted
to dispassionately measure out pain.

The taller the yews, the less the pain.

He didn't intend to wait until time brought relief. He wasn't
going to let it flow smoothly, wasn't going to mute anxiety with
daily life. He'd already tried.

Makeshift solutions – anxiety had to be killed. A fractured
soul couldn't be plastered over with appearances, couldn't be
decorated with frilly accessories like a Christmas tree in order
to make it colourful, make it glitter with shiny lights and hide
it as it slowly dies in a pleasant atmosphere.

Once he'd suffocated, now he breathed freely; once he'd
deceived himself, now he deceived only others. When he needed
them. When he pulled the strings of people seemingly alive
yet as dead as puppets. When, just like a whore or politician,
he told them exactly what they wanted to hear in order for
their wooden souls to come alive momentarily, irrigated by
the illusion of understanding, empathy and other nonsense.

Only weak people allow themselves to be so deceived.

I know how much it hurts; I know what a great loss it must
be; I know how you're feeling; I know what it's like; I know how
awful it is. I'm very sorry. It shouldn't happen, it shouldn't have
happened.

Little ditties.

He looked around a while longer and unintentionally read
the epitaph on the grave nearby: *How can we live without you,
it hurts so much.*

He laughed out loud as he gazed with disgust at the plastic
flowers – practically immortal – hideous things.

And what if one can't live with them in this world? When there's a problem of surplus and not of lack? Someone will understand – as if.

Is somebody going to say: I can imagine what you feel; I'm sorry they're alive; it shouldn't happen; it shouldn't have happened; it's so unfair?

He looked around one more time; he was now entirely alone.

He was slowly calming down, setting his thoughts on the right track.

He pulled a small gold pendant out of his pocket and carefully placed it beneath the lettering on the next vacant place in the queue to the unknown harbour. From another pocket he extracted a rope of triple twine, wrapped it around his clenched fists and started to repeat as if in prayer: *Funiculus Triplex Difficile Rumpit, Funiculus Triplex Difficile Rumpit, Funiculus Triplex...*

MACIEJ BARTOL couldn't wake up, and rose groggy; then he stood staring blankly out of the window for a long time. An old man wound his way between the blocks on Bukowska Street. Bartol had known the man since he was a boy. The old man had always walked with an ugly little yapping mongrel but for the past year had only carried a leash which swayed lifelessly in step; he obviously couldn't walk without it anymore.

The old man disappeared around the corner. Actually, all the old men and women were slowly disappearing, and Bartol didn't intend to get used to the new residents who treated the blocks like stopovers – while studying, before getting a loan, before buying a house. It seemed to him as though he was the only one who didn't have any far-reaching plans; and he wasn't all that sure whether that was a good thing.

In the end, he opened the window to wake up faster. He sensed, straight away, that the frost had eased and saw the snow had melted.

Exactly as he hated. Everything was grey: grey air, grey remnants of snow, grey world. One more time the word 'grey' ran through his head and he woke up for good.

He remembered the end of the past day with distaste; rarely did he think so badly of himself. His head started to ache.

He'd been preparing a report on Antoniusz Mikulski's post-mortem and exchanging, with Olaf Polek, the information they'd gathered when the latter ended by mentioning that the mother of Bartol's future child wasn't feeling well. She worked with Polek's wife. Besides, it had been Polek's wife who'd introduced Bartol to her, seeing as they both seemed lonely.

Now there'd be three lonely people. Was that better than two?

He phoned and drove off to the girl's new apartment in Polanka.

She did, in fact, appear very pale, although he wasn't entirely sure if it wasn't the effect of the background.

The walls were grey, simply grey. Who paints the walls of their apartment grey? Right then he heard the question: 'How do you like the new colour?'

He must have taken his time replying because he then heard:

'You chose it yourself.'

He practically choked on his – instant – coffee.

'Don't you remember, I preferred desert sands or sunbeams.'

He did recall something. A conversation they'd had two weeks earlier. About colours! He hadn't been listening; he'd been thinking about something else, wanting to leave as soon as possible. Repeatedly asked whether he preferred desert sands or some sort of sunbeams, he'd answered that what he liked best was lunar dust. He later decided not to be spiteful; she didn't really want anything from him. Too late.

There was dust – and lunar at that – on the walls. Never, never in a hundred years, would he have imagined it to be the name of a colour – as it was he already felt bad.

He improvised – it would make a wonderful undercoat for colourful wallpaper, it'd look good in the middle, he'd bring the samples himself, he'd help her.

Supporting himself with what he'd seen earlier at the architect's office, he somehow managed to wangle his way out of it but, as it was, he knew he wouldn't tell his mother about it that year, or the next – perhaps one day when things were different.

He stayed a while longer. The mother-to-be was only tired; other than that everything seemed in order. He asked her to rest more, and left.

Before going to bed, he drank a large vodka.

He never had much energy in the mornings, now he had even less.

Nevertheless, he decided to get to work as soon as possible, even early; there the whirl of other people's problems needing to be solved would suck him in.

When, at a quarter to eight, he arrived in the room where they usually gathered, Lentz – first as always – was already there, Polek was just entering and right behind him – their present boss. The only one with whom they were all relatively happy. Over the last years, the bosses had changed in quick succession and some of the men didn't even try to get used to the new one – in no time at all there'd be another election.

The boss wasn't in a good mood. He merely informed them that they were to work on the numismatist and weren't to forget the Byelorussian woman who used to stand on Grzybowa Street but hadn't stood there for a month, unlike their investigation which was at a standstill. This especially annoyed Polek who rebelled saying he'd already learned several languages while questioning that 'wild game'. The boss couldn't care less; he simply asked whether Polek expected a pay rise for this, because if not then he'd be well advised to temper his Polish and not talk about the murdered girl in that way, if only because – apparently - somebody had recently brought Polek's daughter home having found her on Stary Rynek.

The comment hit the mark. Everyone was instantly serious wondering how he knew.

Polek's fourteen-year-old daughter hadn't, in fact, spent the night at her friend's a month ago as she'd so nicely told her parents she would. It was a good thing that someone from the vice department had miraculously recognised her among some drunken teenagers at two in the morning in the Czarna Owca.

Polek didn't say a word. He ground his teeth in rage and only exploded once the boss had left.

Bartol didn't pay much attention to him. The investigation into the case of the girl was almost wound up; all they had to do was wait for the perpetrator to get bored of Byelorussia.

He liked the word 'numismatist' being used to describe Antoniusz Mikulski. They had, indeed, had a serious theft of old coins a couple of years ago, and for a good six months they'd all walked around amazed. They never knew who they were going to question – elegant antique dealer or unwashed trader, in turn, round and round in circles. All the numismatists knew each other and all talked about things nobody could understand. They bought and sold money for large sums of money, conned each other, enjoyed doing so and didn't take too much offence when they were conned themselves. All that counted was who knew most, who was the first to catch on, who was cleverest. And the man whom everyone spoke of with the greatest recognition and who apparently had the largest collection and – what went hand in hand with it – real money, had half of his teeth missing and no intention of having new ones put in. Because, as he explained, sellers couldn't care less whom they were selling to as long as it was for the highest sum possible, and buyers love to buy from someone stupider than themselves – and he was guaranteed to give just such an impression.

The case had never been entirely cleared up, nor was it known if the numismatists hadn't somehow sorted it out between themselves. The aggrieved party had allegedly come to some agreement with the suspect, whom he himself suspected; they'd made some sort of exchange and carried on doing business with each other.

Ever since then, whenever the team was dealing with something totally removed from the reality in which they were immersed on a daily basis, somebody evoked the numismatists and everything became clear, at least where information was concerned.

Now they all put forward what they'd managed to determine the previous day and what had reached them from the lab. Not much.

Antoniusz Mikulski was seventy-eight years old and, according to the doctor, could have still lived for a long time; there was nothing seriously wrong with him, just a slight arrhythmia of the heart was recorded. His death had resulted from strangulation;

he must, however, have fainted beforehand or lost consciousness. The presence of any substance that could have helped him do so was not ascertained. None of the questioned neighbours had heard or seen anything – not quite neighbours because the two villas standing on each side now housed solicitors' offices and the people who worked there rarely looked around, so Maćkowiak stated. That – possibly – left the clients who'd arrived or left at the time; a list was established.

Mikulski, ever since the death of his wife eighteen months ago, had lived and coped alone. He'd also done his own cleaning. They had one son who'd settled somewhere abroad, the States apparently, and wasn't married. Nothing was known about any grandchildren. The list of phone calls he'd made didn't reveal anything either. A call to the doctor's surgery and to an acquaintance, Edmund Wieczorek, from whom they obtained some initial information. Mikulski hadn't used up all his phone credit. He didn't own a computer and the television set probably wasn't working. There was only a small radio in the kitchen. Mikulski had once been an important figure in the administration of regional restoration and, after retiring at the beginning of the nineties, never appeared at his old place of work, nor was he ever invited anywhere – he was not liked. Antoniusz Mikulski himself never belonged to the Party ,whereas he did have an ambitious brother who'd even rubbed shoulders at the Ministry of Culture and was not a liked figure even among his own. The brother had died childless twenty years ago.

They didn't quite know who to inform about Mikulski's death. There was some hope, however, that the son – or eventually some relative – would turn up seeing as there was a large estate to inherit. A solicitor had once held Mikulski's will but Mikulski had visited him in August asking for it to be destroyed. The solicitor couldn't remember whether Mr Mikulski had said why or whether he was going to make out another one.

Slowly, a picture of a totally lonely man was emerging; whether the world had so ordained it or whether it was of his own making remained unclear.

They could find no motive for the murder, nor was there anything they could get their teeth into. There were no traces of a break-in, struggle or robbery. The latter could not be excluded, although there was nobody at present who could have confirmed whether anything was missing or not. There was, admittedly, an empty wooden box on his desk but it could have been used for anything and had no lock.

Since they didn't really know where to start and the technicians hadn't yet returned a report of their findings (at present, they only had one unidentified broken fingernail), they decided to start with the possibility that something may have gone missing.

They took seriously the hypothesis that there'd been something so valuable in the house that it had been worth stealing only that one thing without needlessly running the risk of selling off other antiques. Perhaps not many people knew about the existence of that something. Perhaps nobody other than the murderer and the victim who could no longer say anything. Nobody, therefore, would look for it. Perhaps, as an art restorer, he had recognised something others hadn't seen, and taken it home – times had been different. Perhaps not everybody was as honest as the two female art historians who had recognised an El Greco beneath a dusty painting so that now everybody could look at it in Siedlce museum.

They also had to search for something in the dead man's past. Some old troubles perhaps.

Olaf Polek eased the helpless tension by stubbornly maintaining that the whole thing had to do with coins, that he suspected the numismatists for the whole masquerade with the red cloth; they were capable of anything. One way or another, the police officers decided they'd ask around among various antique dealers and traders. This Polek had to take care of. The dead man's one and only acquaintance, Edmund Wieczorek, eighty years old and in a wheelchair, also had to be paid a visit – there was no point in summoning him to the station. Seeing Lentz cough, Maćkowiak allocated the assignment to himself.

Only Maciej Bartol and Piotr Lentz, wiyh his cold, remained in the room.

Both had time on their hands; one was waiting for the female architect, the other for a lawyer who hadn't been in the previous day.

Lentz really did have a bad cold. For the past three weeks. As usual, he'd initially been very interested in his illness, suspecting cancer of the lungs, larynx or bronchi, if there was such a cancer. He studied and held forth with excitement about the symptoms which, also as usual, were practically all manifest. An X-ray and another test had dispersed his fears. As if to spite himself, he'd then grown sadder and refused to treat what was nothing but a banal cold. It seemed absurd, but after cancer of the prostate and all its symptoms had turned out to be mere sand in the kidneys not worth bothering about, cancer of the bowel simply the effect of beetroots in his diet, and a whole spectrum of other fascinating diseases which had ended up being nothing but minor ailments, nothing surprised anyone anymore. Lentz had never been seriously ill; nobody knew how he'd react if faced with a real problem. They often wondered whether it was Lentz who worked himself up like that or whether his mother – with whom he was still living although he'd turned forty-five – aided him in this; nobody dared ask. He was easily annoyed and stayed annoyed for a long time.

'I once bought a puppy, you know,' he began unexpectedly, wiping his nose with his hand. 'A little white Bolognese.' Bartol hadn't known, nor could he imagine it, but he didn't laugh, didn't comment – besides, he wouldn't have known what to say; he just listened, staring at Lentz with some amazement.

'The dog had some sort of convulsions several times a day,' continued Lentz after a while. 'I did the rounds of several private vets and every vet made a different diagnosis: epilepsy, a dodgy heart and such like. They told me to give the dog back since it was going to die anyway. I couldn't. It was only in a state-run clinic that a wise vet told me the dog's nervous system was being poisoned by worm toxin. The dog had been treated for worms but those particular worms had proved resistant. A banal explanation but he was right: he saved the dog's life. But what I'm thinking about is what he said at the end – a wise doctor, as I say: you always have to start with the simplest diagnosis and only then start to look for something interesting. Interesting cases are tempting but truth is often more banal. I remembered that very well and often recall his words.'

Bartol had an entirely different opinion on this particular point, unless Lentz was thinking exclusively about work. In which case it could, to a certain degree, be true. He remembered how Lentz had once insisted that the wife had been the murderer, because she'd the most to gain by getting rid of her husband yet nearly everybody else had thought it had been the case of an unfortunate accident with a fatal ending. Lentz had been right.

'And you know something? I think nothing's going to be that obvious this time. We have to make sure it wasn't burglary, then find the person who inherits the house. Maybe he or she couldn't wait. But it all looks odd, very odd. Have you studied the photos yet?'

'Cursorily.'

'Then take a good look at these. Precisely these.' He passed him two photographs.

One of them showed the whole of Mikulski's body on the floor, the other was a close-up of the so-called towel around his waist. The tiny letters running down the length of the entire piece of material were clearly visible. They couldn't have been taller than half a centimetre. One sentence repeated over and over: *Dum Spiro Spero*.

'I checked what it means at home yesterday. Which is, more or less: 'as long as – to breathe – to expect'. Don't laugh, I don't know any Latin, I don't even know how I came to have a small medical dictionary at home.' Lentz coughed. 'Anyway, they don't look like words usually found on a towel or whatever you want to call the thing, because it doesn't look like a towel to me, especially on a corpse. There's nothing there about washing but there is about potential loss of breath. We've still got to find some other maxims in that house. I don't like it.'

Bartol didn't like it either. He was surprised, however, that Lentz was only telling him now. Lentz anticipated his question.

'Don't look at me like that. I didn't want to fire away with infinitives. If it sounds like nonsense then let's check out what's most likely before we learn Latin. Mull it over a bit, you're good at that. So long – I'm off to interrogate my parrot. I can already hear her squawking.'

Somebody was, in fact, kicking up a fuss in the corridor saying her time was precious, was being wasted.

Bartol, left alone, began mulling it over. He stared dispassionately at the photographs. Out of plain curiosity. He wondered why he didn't feel anything.

Perhaps because everything seemed so unreal, inauthentic; as a rule, these things looked all too real, too true. As a rule they looked very human, including what dwelt within the human being – and was not necessarily dormant.

But here… Even without the Latin on the piece of red cloth, this was beyond the norm.

Fortunately, he didn't have to think long about where to start. There was a call from downstairs. The female architect was already waiting for him.

He went down to fetch her. Noted that she appeared different from the previous day. She probably hadn't slept; there were shadows under her eyes. He caught sight of her before she saw him. She was dressed in black from head to toe. The black polo-neck, as if made for two necks, almost reached her mouth; her long fingers barely poked out of the sleeves. Her black jeans were partially concealed in a pair of high boots.

She couldn't have wrapped herself up more tightly. Overalls or armour? She looked quite sexy but he immediately associated her outfit with the large, grey-brown jumper on her photograph. Room to hide there, too.

She looked shorter. He studied her for a while before she noticed him.

'Good morning, let's go upstairs.'

'Good morning. Maybe it is, but you don't look so good either.'

He was taken aback. Her directness took him a little by surprise; people were usually tense before being interrogated.

'I see you haven't slept well either. Isn't it a daily occurrence in your profession – corpses, bad, evil people?' she continued once she'd sat down.

'A daily occurrence, no. Day-to-day business is the same as yours, different people, various pieces of paper. Thankfully, not everyone murders other people as often as they'd like. Something to drink?'

'Some coffee, please. Instant will be fine, lots of milk.'

She'd forestalled him again.

'I'm sorry we don't have a proper espresso machine. Can't see us getting one either. You visit this station often?' He smiled.

'No, but I can guess by the handle on a door what I'm going to be treated to. Part of the job.'

A long time elapsed before they'd noted down and set the previous evening's statements in order.

The second chapter of questioning started with a second coffee.

'I know you weren't in touch with Mr Mikulski but maybe you can remember something, something specific...'

He didn't have time to finish.

'I don't want to but unfortunately I have to suspect something. It's the windows again.'

He didn't say anything but his face must have taken on a peculiar expression.

'Washing the windows this time,' she added. 'I didn't immediately remember about Mrs Krystyna,' she continued. 'Mrs Krystyna used to clean my office for a couple of years, and a few other local offices too, as far as I know. I had mixed feelings about her. Not her, perhaps, but the situation, to be exact. She was a good worker. You hardly saw her but could immediately see when she hadn't been. My best employee, all in all, except that she often asked to be paid in advance. She later admitted, she needed the money to pay lawyers for her sons who were always where they shouldn't be, not from any fault of their own, of course – they were good lads, it wasn't their fault and so on. I felt sorry for her. They are her children, after all, but, on the other hand, the computers were mine. Not that she was going to steal them, you understand, it's not that, but she might have moaned about the cleaning, how hard it was with all those cables, all that equipment, or something like that. The problem resolved itself a year ago. The place was undergoing lengthy refurbishment and Mrs Krystyna wasn't needed. I was to phone her when it was finished but didn't – nor did she phone me. I hire through a cleaning agency now and don't ask about children anymore.' She paused for a moment. 'I'm telling you all this so you don't jump in with accusations. She's a good woman and I've never suspected her of anything. But I do know that Mrs Krystyna washed Mr Mikulski's windows and that she has the sons she has.'

'Did she wash the windows when Mrs Mikulska was still alive?'

'Yes. Probably for about a year before she died. I remember her telling me that poor Mrs Mikulska had broken her leg washing those windows and it wasn't healing. It turned out that it wasn't ever going to heal because she had some sort of cancer. She grumbled something about the same thing being in store for her because she'd almost fallen off a ladder, but better that she fell than the old man because who would look after him – that's the way it is when you don't have children.' She broke off for a moment. 'We even talked about the Mikulskis a little. I won't say I didn't think about those antiques and those children which it's good to have, the same as I'd thought about my computers, but I didn't say anything at the time.' Again she paused briefly. 'Tell me, please, was it a burglary?'

'We really can't say or exclude anything at the moment, although there aren't any traces of a typical murder involving burglary or assault.'

'Thank God,' she sighed with relief.

'Why do you say that?'

'I saw one of Mrs Krystyna's sons once, standing with his mother. I only glimpsed him from the car window, but it was enough for me to assess him as being capable – in the worst scenario – of something typical and maybe also some sort of primitive rape.'

'We have to check it out anyway. Do you remember her surname?'

'Yes, Bończak. She lived in Rybaki. Please don't say you learned this from me. It's unfair on Mrs Krystyna. She was a hard worker and I've no reason to suspect her. I'm contradicting myself but...'

He didn't allow her to finish.

'I don't think there'll be any such need. Would you like to add anything?' He very much wanted her to add something; he was in no hurry to take the next step which awaited him.

'No, I can't recall anything else at the moment.'

'Did you know Mr and Mrs Mikulski's son?'

'I saw him a couple of times.' Bartol had the impression the question embarrassed her. He decided to continue along this path.

'And when was the last time?'

'About ten years ago.'

'Was he at his mother's funeral?'

'I don't think so.'

'How do you know?'

'I didn't say I know but I think.' Two thick furrows cut her forehead. 'Mrs Bończyk was.'

He watched her stiffen and tense, preparing for an attack. He saw he'd played it wrong and decided not to ask any more questions.

'I'll see you down, if that's all.'

She got up.

'There's no need. The building isn't very complicated.'

'But I have to accompany you.'

'Well, if that's the case.' Here she smiled, unexpectedly and broadly; in an instant her face softened.

Well, that's goodbye to fine perfumes, he thought, watching her leave. Beautiful Rybaki, nothing but small fry – every other one with a record since nursery. His men had even mentioned one such fish recently who, born in prison, had waited eighteen years to find himself in there again, was knifed in a fight and died. A career like that, a street like that.

Bartol phoned the local police. Twenty minutes later he already had information concerning both Mrs Bończak and her sons. The sons were doing time like good boys, and Mrs Bończak, surprisingly, was at home.

She'd broken her leg.

Edmund Wieczorek, hiding behind the kitchen window curtain, gazed long and calmly at Matejko Street. There was still time, he thought, about ten, fifteen minutes.

He had the ideal observation point; the four-window bay protruding far beyond the façade of the building practically hung over the pavement. It sufficed for him to wait, and he knew perfectly well how to wait; that's all he'd done for the past ten years. He'd grown used to it, even liked it.

No force could have torn him away from the window. He knew it was good to know one's opponent and be properly prepared. Much could be read from the gait and bearing of a man, and he wouldn't have such an opportunity if he didn't set eyes on the man until he was at the front door.

Years of observation had turned Wieczorek into a master; that's how he thought of himself. Many people would, no doubt, have shared this view if they'd only had the chance, but now no more than a few were at all interested in his existence. Such was the curse of the elderly.

Mr Edmund was practically shaking with excitement; only a couple of minutes to go.

'Just play it right, just play it right,' he repeated in his head.

Nobody had appeared as yet, nobody who might have been the policeman who'd called.

'Aha, a car's just parked, that could be it, no, it's a woman,' he was now talking to himself. 'Ah, there he is, that must be him, fat, heavy. Good, a slow thinker. If he's out of breath before he gets to the first floor, I've got him.' He laughed scornfully. 'I'm in for a good time. What a surprise, and so soon. Who'd have thought that old Mikulski... such a bore. Oh, he hadn't been all that nice lately, hadn't listened, hadn't picked up my calls, serves him right. I don't know much but I'll think of something. Aha, there's the bell, great, it's him.'

He walked up to the door, pressed the intercom, opened the door, adjusted the cushion one more time and sat down in his wheelchair.

'He's taking his time. Panting.' Wieczorek listened to the sounds coming from the loudly creaking, enormous staircase. 'Good on us, Edmund, just play it right, just play it right,' he whispered to himself.

Maćkowiak walked very slowly; his knees had been giving him pain recently, both knees. He grimaced first at the tenement, then at the sight of the high stairs.

'I hope it's not the top floor, otherwise I'll go mad. Why is it always me who gets the stairs?' he complained to himself. 'I'll switch to the corruption squad and get high-speed lifts.' He smiled; he'd prefer to climb even to the very loft.

He didn't complain to anyone because he didn't like complaining. As it was, he knew that everyone would say the same thing his glib orthopaedist had said: 'Lose at least fifteen kilos, then we'll start to treat your joints or they'll improve of their own accord.' He recalled the words as he slowly mounted the high, wooden steps.

'As it is I'm only eating half of what I want. It's as if I was on a diet,' – he praised himself and once more smiled the smile of good-natured people – 'while being overweight.'

Generally speaking, he was the least stressed policeman in the entire station. They'd only once seen him annoyed at work and that was when the sweet buns, which he'd brought himself, had disappeared from the table. All ten of them.

Ah, the first floor thankfully, he thought, seeing the number on the door.

The door opened slowly to reveal a small, elderly man in a wheelchair, wearing a tie.

'Good morning, how punctual,' Mr Edmund greeted him amicably.

'Good morning,' Maćkowiak replied.

I'm in for a wheelchair like that, he thought, but the frame's going to have to be stronger.

The apartment was large; too large again, it seemed, for one man. Even the clutter of furniture – this time from the Gierek era – didn't diminish the impression of space. The furniture was decidedly too low.

'You live alone?'

'Ever since mummy died nine years ago,' said Mr Edmund pulling a forlorn face.

Maćkowiak didn't feel all that sorry for him as he studied the box-like furniture. The same as in his own apartment, but with one difference; he constantly had to squeeze between the furniture at home, while here he didn't even rub against it even though it stood on both sides of the hallway. For a brief moment, he envied the old man. He himself lived in three rooms with his wife, daughter, granddaughter and fat dachshund, Sunia. A vet had told him that both he and the dog had to lose at least half their weight. He never visited the vet again.

'You already know why I'm here,' said Maćkowiak, and Mr Edmund hung his head. 'I'm very sorry your friend has passed away but we need to talk...' He broke off suddenly. 'Are you feeling all right?' he asked, seeing Mr Edmund's head still hanging. It only now occurred to him that he was dealing with an old man. He became scared of potential complications, the wheelchair, the first floor and everything else.

'There aren't many of us left, you know, and it's hard for those of us who are still around, but what can one do, what can one do...' Mr Edmund nodded sadly. 'One has more friends up there than here... But I'm not going anywhere yet, my turn will come, too. Please don't worry, it's only my legs that don't work, my heart you might envy.'

What a spiteful old man, thought Maćkowiak. He heard me panting on the stairs, he must have heard. Okay, we're not going to beat around the bush.

'Mr Antoniusz Mikulski was murdered two days ago. Please tell me when you saw him last, what you talked about. As far as you remember.'

'We can talk about cholesterol, too!' riposted Mr Edmund, frowning none too sternly.

'Sorry if I formulated that badly,' said Maćkowiak, now a little amused.

'I spoke to him about two weeks ago, but you must know that already. We talked about German armaments in Africa during the Second World War. We argued. I believe that the "Desert Fox"'... But that probably doesn't interest you. Anyway, I didn't want to argue over the phone, it costs money, so we arranged to see each other the following week. I went to see him. He was a bit strange. I asked what the matter was but he didn't say anything. Then, after that young man arrived with whom he had a long discussion about something in the kitchen, he was absolutely good for nothing. I said goodbye and went home. I was even a little offended. I never saw him again. No doubt I should have questioned him more about what was on his mind. I'm not nosy – usually that's a virtue – but this time, obviously...' He paused then, shaking his head, added: 'Who'd have thought, who'd have thought.'

Slowly but surely, we're getting somewhere, thought Maćkowiak, and asked: 'Would you recognise the young man?'

'This might disappoint you, but yes. I had a good look at him... I can help draw up an identikit of the man.'

'Excellent, but you'll have to get yourself to the police station. We'll help you, of course.'

'Please don't worry yourself. I'll get myself down the stairs, well, perhaps with a little help. It's just that I can't walk for too long.'

Wieczorek had already rejected the option of being carried downstairs yesterday; it could have discouraged them too soon.

'Then perhaps you could accompany me straight away? That would be best. Your statements could prove very important.'

'How shall I put it? The pleasure's entirely mine? Give me ten minutes, please.' He turned his wheelchair and propelled himself to another room.

'It's worked, it's worked! Good for us, Edmund, good for us,' he whispered to himself with satisfaction.

Maciej Bartol had been stuck in traffic for twenty minutes and not moved twenty metres. And it wasn't even rush hour. He was livid, like everyone else. He wondered whether anybody worked in this city or only drove to the centre and back. What were all these people doing? Eleven o'clock, shouldn't they have been in their offices or at home? He preferred not to think what it was going to be like at three.

He picked up his phone and glanced at his mirrors to make sure there wasn't a police car nearby. He hated using the speaker mode and hearing the echo at the other end. He didn't even want to think about some stupid earphones. The prospect of being stopped for driving and talking over the phone didn't appeal to him either. What driving? – he thought, seeing only three cars manage to jump across the crossroads.

Only two days earlier he had slipped onto the roadside, having been flagged down by a regular patrol car. He'd even heard the boy say: 'Don't you know you're a danger?' before he'd pulled out his identification and merely nodded his approbation of the authority's vigilance. The older cop had smiled understandingly and shrugged. Bartol had thought that that was it, but no. The younger one had added, in all seriousness: 'You ought to be setting an example.' Maciej had been astounded. He thanked the boy for his advice, predicted a career for him, closed the door, drove away and called back.

Finally, he was across the intersection.

He called the police station. The news was good, if not excellent. Maćkowiak was bringing in a granddad who could recognise someone whom Mikulski had argued with a week before his death. At last, human reactions in this still life.

He tapped out his mother's number, hoping she might remember some Latin dicta. When, after a long while – no doubt she was searching in her handbag for the phone –

she replied, he asked: 'Do you know what *Dum spiro spero* might mean?'

'Come over and I'll tell you.'

He might have predicted this would happen, but he hadn't.

'This is serious, mum, take it seriously.'

'I treat your life very seriously indeed, as well as the life you've brought into being. You had a responsible father, your child evidently hasn't had the same luck, but it's not its fault. You aren't twenty anymore for me to feel sorry for you. Your child should be going to school already and have long eyelaashes, just like you-know who.'.'

He regretted having phoned.

'Are the girl's parents in Poznań?'

'Mum, this is not the time!'

'It was the ideal time to prolong the species so time must be found for the consequences – yes or no? I'm asking you again!'

'No, she lives alone, her parents live somewhere near Kielce.'

'Have you thought whether she's got anybody to call if anything should go wrong? Any friends, because she hasn't got any family! She's carrying a second heart within her yet hasn't a soul to speak to! Which phone number did you give her? The private one you hardly ever use? Don't even answer that, I know the answer. Please arrange for the three of us to meet this week and no later! It wasn't supposed to be like this but it is, so welcome to the grown-up world.'

There was a silence but he didn't dare end the conversation.

'And apart from that,' she now said in a gentler tone, obviously deciding enough was enough, "Dum spiro spero means" as long as there's life, there's hope'. It's from Seneca, it sounds like him, but I'm not sure, it could be something from the Bible. Phone me this evening and you'll find out more. I hope I'll find something out from you, too. Just tell me, what's the context of those words, if it's no secret?'

'They were found on a murder victim.'

'I might have guessed. It appears not everybody's hopeful, so to speak. In his case, somebody's destroyed the hope, think about that.'

'Thanks, mum, I will.' He wanted to end the conversation as quickly as possible, and not just because he'd already arrived at his destination.

'Remember, as your mother I'm still keeping them intact for you – faith, hope and charity – don't abuse that. I'll wait for your call or, even better, come over. Bye.'

He parked exactly where he'd wanted to; a rare occurrence of late. He stared at the shabby-looking tenement and couldn't get out of his car for a long while. It's all got to fall into place – it's got to, otherwise I'll go mad.

The staircase, as nearly always, looked even worse than expected. From the ground to the top floor – on which Mrs Krystyna Bończak lived – it was adorned with messages for the owner or administrator. The authors had taken care over the assortment of coloured sprays, less over the words which were frequently repeated.

The door on which he knocked was less shabby. He heard the clicking of crutches on the other side.

'Good morning, you can't even leave a sick woman in peace,' Mrs Bończak said as soon as she opened the door. He had no idea how, but she knew she was talking to the police.

'Good morning, Mrs Bończak,' – he tried to be as polite as possible.

'Might as well come in, seeing as you're here.' She turned, leaving the door open. She could have not let him in, could have kicked up a row, yelled, but she didn't. Her voice was dispassionate, resigned to everything. He felt sorry for the women, mothers; they all looked practically the same – scared, although the eyes were sometimes aggressive, and the hands tired, always tired.

This woman looked a little better, he thought. Maybe the husband who generally drank and beat her, had died soon enough, and she'd sorted things out a little. She'd dispensed with another farce, and all she had left were her beloved children and the hope that they too would sort things out for themselves.

That, at least, is what he thought as he looked around the flat. It was very small, barely two tiny rooms with a blind kitchen. Everything appeared more than modest. The TV set could have been the pride of its manufacturer who wouldn't have believed it would work for so long, but it did, as the preview of the thousandth episode of some serial demonstrated. The only thing which made the flat different from numerous identical ones was that it couldn't have been cleaner. It was clinically clean. It smelled of corrosive cleaning agents, rather than cheap vodka, cheap cigarettes and dirty linen.

'How do you manage to keep it all so tidy with that leg?' he asked out of pure curiosity, as his eyes rested on the plaster-cast which reached almost to her thigh.

'I just take all day doing something that would usually take me an hour. But I haven't got anything to do anyway so I don't complain.' She suddenly broke off, as if she'd remembered this wasn't some pleasant chat, and squinted at him. 'You know that there's nobody here to make a mess, so what are you really looking for?'

'I'm here because you knew Mr Antoniusz Mikulski. Unfortunately, he's been murdered. We're checking on everybody who might have been in touch with him and, as you know, there weren't many.'

He thought she turned pale, but wasn't sure. She wasn't upset but frowned deeply and, for a while, didn't say anything.

'That it could happen here is normal, but there, in that other world? I suppose I ought to be pleased the boys have been in prison for the past six months, shouldn't I? It could've been worse.' She uttered the last sentence to herself; then a moment later roused herself. 'Would you like a cup of tea? It's cold today.'

He hadn't expected her to say that. He followed her into the kitchen to help. Once, in a flat like this, he'd been offered some juice in a glass from which he could have lifted all sorts of fingerprints; he hadn't even wanted to think whose. Since then, he hadn't usually wanted to take the risk, but now he had no such qualms, even sensed that a familiar experience from years gone-by awaited him. He wasn't wrong. The tea appeared in a glass with a saucer, and was brewed from leaves. He couldn't remember when he'd last drunk tea like this, but the memory was a good one. When they sat down, he asked: 'When were you at Mr Mikulski's last?'

'I'm probably out of the picture, too. I broke my leg a month ago, in front of the block, and haven't gone out since. The last time I washed his windows was before All Saints. I don't clean any more, but what would the old man have done? I thought every six months wouldn't do me any harm. He coped better than any other man I know and only said he couldn't manage the windows. And I thought – how many times was it still going to be, two, six?'

'What do you live off now?'

'I work a clothes stall in Wilga. Don't have to travel. They've even insured me and apparently don't sack people. We'll wait and see. The work's better now so I'm not so worried. The boys won't be out for another two years. And since my husband's dead I don't have to kill anyone; besides, he helped me out with that himself.'

'What happened?'

'What could've happened? He drank himself to death. Blue in the face, even in his coffin.' She smiled, no regrets.

'Did you talk to anyone about Mr Mikulski? Perhaps someone asked you for details?' Not a good question. Even as he asked, he knew he'd blown it.

'Do you have any children?'

'Not really...'

'What's that supposed to mean? You really do or you really don't?'

'I've got one... on the way...' He didn't have to answer but he did.

'Well, then you'll find out for yourself. I've got good sons but I'm no fool. They lost their way, but how could they have done otherwise, I ask you, with all those shoes costing a week of my wages flashing around all the time, and no work for them? I can't understand this world. Stary Rynek to the left, Stary Browar to the right and, all in all, I'm the only one who's old and poor, and they, mere youngsters, saw all this, all those luxuries as if at arm's length and were supposed to understand they weren't for them. They were good boys when they were little. The younger one was good at drawing.' She tried to reach into a drawer – probably to show him some drawings – didn't manage and waved it aside. 'Doesn't matter. Then as soon as girls came along, it all started. Their friends weren't as bad as the girls. Have you heard the way girls talk? I can't believe it. They boss, goad, tempt, tease. It's all their fault. Have you read my younger boy's file?'

'No, not yet.'

'Then read it, see where the mugging came from. How can you scream, how can a girl scream down the whole street that his is so tiny you need glasses to see it? They're young lads.'

'Everybody's got their own problems but solve them in different ways, you do realise?'

'I realise perfectly well!' She nearly got up from the table but quickly sat down again, as if she'd suddenly remembered about the plaster-cast, that she had a guest and couldn't start scrubbing the floor right away to stop herself from thinking. 'You know how easily influenced they are? Remember they've been brought up without a father.' He'd heard enough on the subject of children; besides, he was afraid she'd start crying. Fortunately, she calmed down. 'That's exactly why anyone you ask will tell you I cleaned in the Nowy Teatr. I knew that neither my boys nor those girls would go there. What was I supposed to say, that I was practically alone in some office where there was nothing but cables and computers? To work from morning till night to pay for lawyers? I'm no fool. Maybe my boys will come to their senses one day. You'll see what it's like.'

He didn't want to see anything or even think about it.

'Can you tell me anything else about the Mikulskis? What they were like? Did they have any visitors, family perhaps?'

'They were different to the people here or on Wspólna Street. As if unreal, from another world. And they also talked to each other in a strange way. They didn't even talk about the son who'd left. They probably didn't have any grandchildren.'

'How do you know?'

'I know old people. If they've got grandchildren they go on and on about them until you've had it up to here. Your mother's lucky.'

Slowly, this was becoming unbearable.

'Would you be able to state whether anything's gone missing from the apartment?'

'No, I don't think so, I only washed the windows, you know. When I do things I do them quick. I don't have coffee, smoke cigarettes, take breaks. And there were a lot of things there. If would be different if I'd done the cleaning. But see if there are any traces on the carpets. If somebody took anything you'd see. The same as on the walls. That much I can tell you. Nobody ever moved anything there. Apart from the furniture, books and junk, there was only an old television set, probably like mine. I remember Mrs Mikulska saying she'd gone to the post office to change the radio and television licence to a radio one, saying she didn't intend to watch television anymore. We laughed because the clerk had said it was impossible, if she had a television she had to pay because she could watch it. To which Mrs Mikulska replied that she was the one who'd bought the television set and it was hers, but she hadn't bought television so it wasn't hers, and she wasn't going to pay or watch anymore but she might look at the television set from time to time. I don't know whether the clerk believed her, but I noticed afterwards that she'd covered the television set with a tablecloth which she never removed. Nor did Mr Mikulski. That's the sort of people they were, you see. Here, people steal electricity because it's there. It's a different world. Nobody's probably even heard of a radio and television licence.'

'Did they have any visitors? Can you remember anyone?' he asked, wondering at the same time whether by paying for cable television he was actually paying for the licence or not.

'The postman, maybe. I don't think they liked guests. I think Mr Mikulski did the cleaning himself – not because he liked it, but to avoid anyone bustling around in his apartment as long as he possibly could. Except for the windows. He was getting a bit weird but he coped, I'll give him that.'

'How long do you still have to be in plaster?'

'Two weeks, they say.'

'We might visit you again,' he said, rising.

'Should I be pleased, or not?'

'You don't have to give it any thought. It doesn't mean anything. We have to talk to everyone.' He passed the crutches to Mrs Bończak and made towards the front door. Once there, he retreated and asked: 'What did you have in mind when you said he was getting a bit weird?'

'Nothing much, but when I wanted to throw some old flowers away – they were withered and didn't really fit in with the otherwise clean apartment – he shouted at me to leave them alone. He'd never even raised his voice before. I was a bit annoyed. All I'd wanted to do was throw some rubbish away even though I didn't have to. But once I'd gone it occurred to me that the flowers could've been important, maybe someone had remembered about him, or thanked him for something. Maybe I'll hold on to dried flowers one day if my grandchildren give them to me, who knows.'

He quickly went down to his car. One thing he knew for certain – he had to find himself in the house in Sołacz as quickly as possible; it wouldn't give him any peace. First he came to a standstill by Kupiec Poznański, the office and shopping centre, and almost entirely forgot about the word 'quickly' a few yards further down on Podgórna Street. Here, the cars didn't seem to be driving, only pushing each other along as they sluggishly climbed the hill.

He had a long time to think it all over.

As far as Mrs Bończak's sons were concerned, what he heard was more or less what he'd expected. He liked the ruse about her working in the theatre. He'd ask the local police to check whether that was what everybody really thought, but was almost sure it was true. If she'd told her sons the truth, there'd have been evidence of it already. Offices like that had everything those good boys stole – expensive mobile phones, laptops, cameras, and Mikulski's apartment was furnished with antiques. Everything could be taken and would bring quick money without venturing too far from home. One of the lads would have stalked her over the two years, and under some pretext or other paid her a visit. From what he'd heard about them he guessed this was only the beginning of their careers and – once Mrs Bończak told him there wasn't any work for them – he was convinced of it. He wasn't entirely sure whether she realised they weren't looking for work, certainly not such as wasn't mentioned in the penal code.

He remembered the local cop's words: 'Maybe not this time, but you'll meet them before long, that's for sure.' Of the mother, he had a good opinion.

He also decided to call an antique dealer he knew. He exchanged some needless information with him then asked:

'One question – tell me, what do they call those unobtrusive, round tables which pull out to seat ten or twelve people?'

'Have you got one? Buy it, or sell it – to me.'

'No, I haven't, I only wanted to know what they're called.'

'Is that so?'

'Let it be. 'Bye.'

'Just tell me, where'd you find it?'

'In a museum.'

'Is that so? Drop by with it. Bye.' He hung up.

Up until that morning, Bartol had thought he kept seeing the table simply because he couldn't remember what it was called. He'd phoned the dealer to get it off his mind but knew that wasn't what was bothering him. Those unlikely dried stalks just didn't fit in. They didn't fit in with the apartment, didn't fit in according to him and they didn't fit in according to Mrs Bończak, yet they were important to Mikulski. Perhaps there was a simple explanation as to why the elderly man had been so sentimental.

He phoned the police station. They were still compiling the portrait of the man Edmund Wieczorek had seen. And it wasn't easy, according to Maćkowiak. Bartol heard that a technician was still milling around on Góralska Street, therefore nothing stopped him from going there. At four, they were all to meet at the station.

He covered the last couple of kilometres in an unexpectedly short time. He was surprised; he hadn't taken a particularly better route – there were simply no understandable rules.

The street looked different from the previous day, gloomy and depressing. There was no snow on the enormous branches or pavement. Mush and greyness, as everywhere. All that remained was a sense of peace, of not being in the city.

The apartment also looked different – also grey.

The previous day, in the strong light of photographic lamps, the well-preserved French polish on the antique furniture had experienced its second youth, gleaming, sparkling and reflecting – as in a crooked mirror – the porcelain figures, silver sugar bowls and everything else on it.

Now all this had turned dull; the feeble bulbs shone too sparingly and the thick curtains didn't allow any daylight in, which – as it was – wasn't very bright.

He greeted the two technicians. They were tired and didn't feel like talking: blending in with the ground, they were finishing with the carpet on the ground floor.

He didn't immediately make his way to the dried flowers, but studied the walls and floor. There were no traces of furniture having been moved. To make sure, he moved one of the paintings on the wall and was certain – the place hadn't been painted for a long time.

Nothing else drew his attention.

Relatively calm, he approached the table with the flowers, or whatever they were called. He didn't know much about flowers, especially when they looked like this.

They'd survived, leaning against the curtain. The decorative tissue pressing into the vase might once have been yellow; now it had more or less faded.

The huge bow had faded, too.

Carefully, he pulled the flowers out of the vase. His intuition hadn't misled him; there was a note attached to the ribbon.

Did they come from the association of dead poets or retired cultural administrators?

He asked one of the technicians to snip the note off and search for fingerprints.

There weren't any. The technician believed the note might have got wet many times over before someone had decided to dry the whole lot. He also said they'd be able to say what the flowers were and how long they'd been drying, if it was important.

Bartol opened the note and saw some Latin words with the postscript 'For Aurelia'.

It was important.

The technician secured the flowers, carefully wrapping them in foil.

The police officer went back to his car. He didn't notice the people walking past scrutinising him.

'Just look at that, some people have all the time in the world to stare at tiny little notes. Could be a bill of exchange before the war, but now? Must be a love letter. Hasn't he got a phone or something?' one of them said to the other, loudly enough.

Bartol didn't hear or notice them as they passed.

He stood still, hundreds of thoughts racing through his mind.

Was it a lucky coincidence or sheer chance that he'd found this Latin twaddle? Maybe he was supposed to have found it? Or maybe it was all the same to whoever had left it?

He stood there a good ten minutes before climbing into his car. The frost was setting in again; puddles of slushy snow were starting to freeze over.

He found the number he'd recently called.

'Hello, mum.'

'You're generous today. I haven't been home yet, haven't had time to check for you.'

'Can you talk; not driving, are you?'

'No, I'm still in the parking lot. Why?'

'Do you have a pen? Can you jot something down?'

'Uhm, go on.'

'*Expecto Donec Veniat.*'

'I've no idea what that means but I've noted it down and will have a look. Or no, listen, I'll give you Magda's number, she'll...'

'No, I don't want the number of some Magda. Have a look if you can, if not, we'll get someone to do it.'

'As you wish. Were those words found on the corpse, too?'

'No, on some sunflowers, I think they're sunflowers.'

'A large circle with little yellow petals all the way round?'

'Yes.'

'Then they must be sunflowers. You know as much about flowers as about women.'

'You can't let it go, not even for five minutes.'

'Forgive me. I don't react well to sudden changes in status. Are you surprised? It's not even twenty-four hours since I heard I'm going to be a grandmother. Don't worry, I'll simmer down,' she said, calmly now. 'Drop round this evening.'

'If I can. Drive carefully, look what's happening on the roads. A farce for the traffic police and the whole mess will end up in A & E.'

'Listen, son, do I have to remind you that I've had my driving licence some twenty years longer than you? I can tell you what winters used to be like if you want, and don't tell me there weren't so many cars around because the roads are like they used to be. Goodbye, see you this evening.'

On the radio, too, there were warnings about driving conditions. They're allowed to, he thought enviously. They talk into thin air and nobody answers back. He listened to the latest on traffic jams. Not good news; a fury of helplessness overcame him. The worst combination.

On top of all this, through the rear-view mirror he saw someone blatantly trying to join the traffic, first choosing the fast lane to turn left then playing the fool as if he didn't know he had made a mistake – anything to outsmart.

The news ran on as though an accompaniment to the situation on the roads. The ready-made lessons in respect, co-operation, parliamentary babble repeated day after day worked miracles – the wily feather-brain had numerous imitators.

He switched over to a music station and, half an hour later, arrived at headquarters.

He met Maćkowiak in the doorway.

'Well, did you get anywhere with Wieczorek? Do we know who Mikulski argued with?'

'Not so fast. I've just driven him home. He said he'd had enough for the day, so it's enough, although I don't know who was more tired – him or the man working with him. The granddad's stubborn and keeps saying that's not it. It's not easy to outtalk him, I know something about it.'

'Maybe he can't remember?'

'Don't even say that to him or he'll send you off to be examined. He's healthy even though he's well over eighty. At that age, my mother used to ask me where my brothers were and I've only got sisters – four of them. Maybe he just needs time.'

'Maybe. We'll see what happens tomorrow. Anything else?'

'Nothing interesting as far as I know. Polek's not back yet. But, talk of the devil,' he added as Polek appeared at the door with Lentz.

'Nothing as far as I'm concerned. Can somebody make some tea or coffee? The heating's gone in my car – like the air-conditioning in summer – and they say I was born with a silver spoon in my mouth. Tea might be better.'

'Raspberry syrup or just lemon?'

'I know you're doing your best, Maćkowiak, and I thank you for it. Carry on working. Ok, who wants coffee or whatever? I'm making it. I've just done some classes in politeness. What have you got?'

'Not much. Ah, here's the new prosecutor.' Maćkowiak nodded towards the man searching for the phone ringing in his pocket. He searched long enough for everyone to hear the annoying buzz of a fly terminated by the loud slap of a fly swatter – three times.

'I didn't see him yesterday. Who is he?' asked Bartol.

'Jan Pilski. He was here yesterday with prosecutor Maczek but was in a hurry to get back to his fiancée. He's getting married and has moved here for her sake, or so he boasted to somebody, as if it was worth boasting about. We're going to have to get used to him. Maczek had an attack of the pancreas last night and is in intensive care,' replied Polek.

'Well, well. The pancreas, just like that.' Lentz clearly came to life.

'No, he liked his tipple, in relative moderation though, compared to the norm around here. Could happen to anyone.' He looked at Bartol and Maćkowiak, then at Lentz and regretted his last sentence. Lentz started to massage his stomach with interest.

Pilski finally took the call. They couldn't help hearing what he was saying because he started to walk in the same direction as them, a metre ahead.

'Hello, darling. I can't talk long, I'm at work... Briefly, it's important... all right. Choose it yourself... yes, yes, I know we're supposed to decide together... I know, I think pale pink will look good on the invitations... Yes, especially with dark pink lettering... I'm not just saying 'yes'... Who had some like that... what film was he in... Fine, we'll go to the printers this afternoon. Yes, love you, bye.' He moaned as he slipped the phone back into his pocket and loosened his tie as though wanting to believe that was what was stifling him.

The men looked at each other and smiled in sympathy. The squashed fly suited the situation perfectly.

Pilski walked on to the chief's office while the rest of them entered the briefing room.

'Olaf, did you hear the happily engaged man?' Maćkowiak laughed with his entire body.

'I heard. He's still got six months to go – if he makes it, cos it's going to hurt. If I've got the name right, he's fallen in love with the daughter of a used car dealer. She's a token employee of her father's company while her mother is a living symbol of the history of sheet-metal work. Now both women have something to do from morning to night. They're probably testing whether he'll bear up to it. The wedding, apparently, is in June. I know her father, he's a good guy. Assembles model airplanes after work. This one here's going to be assembling, too.' They all laughed. 'He made the choice, he gets the deserts.'

Only Bartol stopped laughing and looked at Polek. The latter quickly changed the subject; the issue of conscious choices was not so self-evident of late.

'I must have questioned all the traders I know and one numismatist. Nobody's heard of Mikulski. He didn't sell or buy anything, nor did he exchange coins. Someone remembered him from his days as a restorer but apparently he was quiet. He had a brother high up in the Party so nobody really spoke to him much in case he informed on them. I'm not surprised. The man who remembered him thought he'd died long ago. And you, have you got anything? What about that piece of fingernail?' he asked Polek.

'It needs to be checked out but I think I know the woman it belongs to,' answered Bartol.

'How do you know it's a woman's? Is technology so advanced it can tell that fast?' asked Polek.

'Traditional circumstantial evidence. There were traces of pink nail varnish on the fingernail, as far as I know,' Pilski replied, smiling broadly as he stood in the doorway. The door to which he had made his way earlier must have been closed.

The expression on Polek's face seemed to say he'd just decided they weren't ever going to like each other.

The fly started buzzing again. Pilski muted the ring-tone but his move was unsure, as if he was scared of what he was doing. A moment later, he changed his mind; turning towards the wall he took the call and justified himself quietly. Polek wanted to comment but Bartol forestalled him.

'Before we check, we can take it that it belongs to Krystyna Bończak. She's the woman who cleaned the windows,' he said, recalling her broken and badly painted fingernails.

'That would fit. It lay near the curtain,' said Polek, looking pointedly away from the prosecutor.

'Could it have anything to do with the case?'

'We have to take a close look. She's got talented sons. Got a boarding scholarship to Rawicz jail, but personally I don't think so. I spoke to her an hour ago.'

Perhaps he would still have added something but refrained, seeing that the new prosecutor, having finished his conversation, was trying to make his presence known and cover up the indelible impression he'd made.

'I'm new here and haven't met everyone so let me introduce myself. Jan Pilski, prosecutor. I've been assigned to the case in Prosecutor Maczek's absence.' Slowly his voice began to assume acquired gravitas. 'An absence which, as you know, may be considerably prolonged. I've already acquainted myself with the post-mortem and preliminary technical reports. Please forgive me if the non-legal questions I ask seem banal but – was really nothing found at the scene of crime, no traces apart from the fingernail?'

For a while nobody answered; they looked at him dumbfounded. He differed from them, not only by his pink tie and hair gel. It occurred to Bartol that life wasn't easy for these cultured types either and he didn't intend to make it any harder, so he was quick to answer first – not to give Polek, who was already getting ready, a chance.

'The question isn't banal. In ninety percent of cases there's always something – a fingerprint, hair, skin, even vestigial traces – which we can multiply and send off for analysis but this time, apparently, there wasn't and that's what's so strange about this already strange case. To sum up: we have two women fairly loosely connected with the event but we're going to look into it. One important lead is the man described by Edmund Wieczorek. We're making up an identikit. Apparently he visited the deceased a week before his death and they had an argument. As for now, he's our chief suspect. Apart from that we're examining the material in which the dead man was partially wrapped. It's quite interesting, as Lentz remarked. I've sent it off for analysis, which he knows, along with the flowers, which he doesn't yet know.'

Lentz was a little surprised but didn't say anything, nor did the others. All just listened, while Pilski pretended to listen even while tapping something out on his phone.

Bartol had taken a long time, certainly longer than usual, trying to explain his suspicions, yet Polek still asked: 'Come on. Do you seriously think those Latin words mean anything? If he wanted to tell us something, he'd have written it in large print.'

'Perhaps the show's not for us, perhaps it's a coincidence, I don't know and have no idea how to check. So, for the time being, let's be conventional and concentrate on the argumentative man. If all goes well, we'll have the identikit ready by tomorrow.'

All didn't go well. Edmund Wieczorek paid headquarters several visits even though drawing up an identikit only takes a few hours at the most. Sometimes he didn't feel well, sometimes his eyes caused him trouble, sometimes he changed something he'd already changed before. He infinitely taxed everybody's patience, which already seemed taxed to the limits. Nobody, however, could do anything about it – he was elderly and clearly taking advantage of it. Meanwhile, despite numerous interrogations, he was the one and only person who could add anything to the case. The fact that everybody had grown to like him a little wasn't without significance either. As soon as he arrived someone would make him tea with four teaspoons of sugar, the way he liked it, without even asking. They also liked to repeat the cutting retorts he made left, right and centre, which sounded especially amusing coming from an old man. The prosecutor let himself in for it with his ringtone, infallibly associated with his future wife and dreams of eventually doing away with her. The unsuccessful and poorly thought-out replacement in the form of birdsong, which Wieczorek also had the opportunity to hear – Pilski's phone rang frequently – didn't help. He acknowledged it with one sentence: the man shouldn't have any illusions, there wouldn't be any birdsong after the wedding, at most only croaking.

All this allowed him to be tolerated for longer. There were also many indications that in spite of his age he had a very good memory.

After many obstacles – the greatest of which was not that the age of the young man in question turned out to be about forty, which seemed natural only to Edmund Wieczorek and amused half of headquarters – they had more than a good identikit portrait of the suspect.

It seemed only a matter of time before they found the 'young man' although no-one suspected it would happen so fast.

Maćkowiak almost choked on his biscuit when, for what could potentially have been a boring interrogation, the last to turn up was one of the lawyer's clients who'd left the office on Góralska Street precisely at the time in which they were interested; he'd been abroad previously.

It was a matter of routine questions but Maćkowiak didn't have time to ask them. He recognised the face of the man being interviewed as that of the suspect. The identikit portrait lay on his desk; he always kept these portraits so as to ram the image into his head and remember it when needed – he had no memory for faces. Yet never before had he recognised anyone so quickly. Now a man sat in front of him who differed from the one depicted on paper only by his strange suntan – an angrily red nose and white rings around his eyes; the desired effect, it later turned out, of a skiing trip. Maćkowiak obtained a detention warrant in record time; it was a question of murder, too many facts spoke against the identified individual, Przemysław

Górniak. Not only did he clearly answer to the identikit but had been at the scene of crime at the time corresponding to the event.

The man was completely outraged and horrified by the allegations. He insisted he'd never been to Mikulski's house, that he didn't know who Mikulski was and that he didn't even know the man existed. Nor could he remember whether he'd gone straight home after visiting Przewalski's office or not. He shouted and broke down in turn: that it was all some sort of farce, that he was going to turn forty in two days and that they were finally to reveal those hidden cameras; and if it was all a silly joke he'd even take his own wife to court.

He stubbornly maintained that he had nothing to do with the case. All that remained was to confront him with Edmund Wieczorek. Polek and Lentz went to collect the old man, having first phoned to congratulate him on his successful identikit. The first thing to surprise them was that he wasn't at home even though, on previous occasions, he'd opened the door before anyone even had time to ring the bell, as though he'd nothing better to do than wait for them.

They returned to their car and drove away, parked on a neighbouring street and twenty minutes later arrived at Wieczorek's door again. This time they didn't ring, only patiently listened. After a while it became clear that the old man was at home, only didn't want to open the door; after ten minutes of persuasion he was in the car on the way to headquarters. He didn't utter a word and didn't want to say why he hadn't opened.

Nobody had expected such a turn of events. Some of the information they'd gathered and which started to form a whole – surprising even the most experienced police officers – came from the suspect Przemysław Górniak with whom, as it turned out, it had all begun and, for the time being, ended. The rest Edmund Wieczorek unwillingly confirmed himself and thus became a legend. The story was repeated many times on various occasions and at numerous police training sessions, just as before it had been repeated at estate agents' training sessions.

Przemysław Górniak's presence in the vicinity of the murder could have been considered a complete coincidence, something which could not be said of the previous address of his office as financial advisor. Nine years earlier his office had been right next to Edmund Wieczorek's apartment. Górniak had inherited the apartment from his grandmother and that's where he started working. Just as the location had suited him perfectly, especially in those days, so quite soon it proved to be too small. He'd decided, therefore, to start chatting up his neighbour, asking whether he wasn't planning to sell his place in exchange for something smaller and cheaper. Perhaps it hadn't been too polite a move but Górniak had needed to make a decision and breaking through to the neighbouring apartment had seemed the best solution. Edmund had been a little offended initially but after a couple of days paid him a visit, saying that perhaps it was a good idea; however, he wouldn't move until he'd found the right place, and for this he needed help, obviously.

And that's how the whole dance had started. For Przemysław Górniak it lasted nearly six months. The apartment was too important for him and maybe that was why it took him so long to admit that perhaps Edmund had no intention, and probably never had had the intention, of selling his apartment; he was simply enjoying himself, looking – at least once a week – at apartments to which he was driven, all the while holding pleasant and interesting conversations, seasoned with his own reminiscences.

Górniak hadn't concluded the matter very politely, so he admitted. He'd finally sold his own apartment and bought another which, to this day, served as his headquarters; and had no regrets. He recounted the story many times later on; he once even got talking to somebody he knew whose wife worked in property. He'd been very amused to hear that Mr Wieczorek had really got going. It wasn't only apartments he was looking at now; he was also interested in houses out of town, and when you look at a house, you might get lucky and be offered tea and cake. The journey, too, took longer with more time for reminiscing.

Estate agents hadn't worked so closely with each other at the time, and Wieczorek's property was very attractive in those days and easy to sell as an office, which pulled the wool over everybody's eyes. All he needed to do, after all, was find another place. Many agents were taken in and it took a long while before news spread through the grapevine about a pleasant, elderly gentleman on Matejko Street who was having a good time in a most original way. As far as Górniak knew, Edmund had, quiet recently, been agreeably driven around by a newcomer on the market. Edmund Wieczorek more or less confirmed all this, absolutely denying, however, that he'd never planned to exchange his apartment. On the other hand, he did admit to not knowing Mikulski very well, and knowing him only because he'd once been a postman in Mikulski's neighbourhood. He remembered their son when he was still little; the boy hadn't been to his mother's funeral; and Wieczorek later learned from Mikulski that he'd died abroad. Wieczorek had read about Mrs Mikulska's funeral in a newspaper and had gone in the hope of meeting someone he knew, but hadn't met anyone. He'd phoned Mikulski a couple of times, counting on his wanting some company. Mikulski hadn't wanted any.

He passed on his information totally offended, like a child. Only the threat of being punished for making false statements put him into an excellent mood; perhaps it was the very thought of being taken to court – where he'd never been – or that of new friends in prison where, as they all realised, he'd no chance of going.

The only thing that worked was constantly reminding him of the importance of his statements. All he didn't want to say was why he'd picked on precisely Górniak; but he did say that next time he would chose somebody who was dead so that they wouldn't turn up so quickly.

The situation could have been considered comical although it wasn't in the least. The sole natural suspect had evaporated in a most original manner.

There were more employees from the funeral parlour at Antoniusz Mikulski's funeral than people who'd come for the ceremony. Neither did any potential beneficiary appear.

The search for Mr and Mrs Mikulski's son also brought poor results from an investigative point of view. They established with some difficulty that he had, indeed, been to the United States and, surprisingly, had realised the American dream: he'd started working in a small computer company which had expanded enormously and brought fabulous profits for shareholders and, consequently, for him.

This set half of the underpaid workers of Poznań's police involved in the investigation, dreaming. The remainder joined in when they heard the reason for the son's quitting work: apparently he'd set off on an expedition around the world in search of something or other.

Only a little more exotic, and somehow maliciously just, was the unconfirmed information that he'd disappeared somewhere in Burma or Laos. They couldn't establish why Antoniusz Mikulski had been convinced his son was dead, whether simply because he hadn't given any signs of life or because someone had brought Mikulski the news. The solicitor who, as a neighbourly favour, had drawn out the deceased's will couldn't remember exactly but was quite sure that the estate was to become the property of some society which looked after monuments and works of art. Nor had he been greatly surprised when Mikulski had decided to destroy the will. Old people, apparently, were easily offended and sometimes successfully managed to exploit their possessions. Mikulski hadn't made out another will.

Analysis of the flowers and the cloth wrapped around Mikulski didn't bring anything special either, apart from the fact that the flowers were, indeed, sunflowers, a new but popular variety produced in Holland, which meant absolutely nothing since they could have just as easily been bought anywhere in Europe. They might have been standing there from four to nine months.

Likewise with the cloth analysis. The material could have come from China. It contained many dyes prohibited in Europe but that didn't mean there'd been any particular obstacles in importing large quantities. The embroidery was not factory-made but had been made to order using an embroidery machine made in Italy, equally popular in Poland as in Asia. Most of the workshops dealing with publicity embroidery were called but nobody remembered this particular commission.

There was only a momentary stir when, during the police officer's visit to the antique market on Stara Rzeźnia on Saturday, a trader showed Maciej Bartol some cleverly concealed hiding places in the old escritoire. The latter wasn't greatly surprised to find similar drawers in Mikulski's desk. In one there'd been pictures of naked women painstakingly cut out of old German and French newspapers; they looked like goods smuggled in during socialism, in the '50s or '60s perhaps, and carefully concealed from the authorities or from the authorities and the wife. The police looked through the photographs longer than any other documents; someone smiled; someone sighed; someone concluded sentimentally – so harmless and bland.

Some photographs of the son were also found. He wore sunglasses in all of them as if he never visited shady places. The photographs didn't appear very recent.

Only one drawer contained a latter day piece of paper: a new business card belonging to a licensed estate agent called Ksawery Rudzik.

Maciej Bartol sensed it could be important because Mikulski had remembered the hiding place after many years. Unfortunately, this too proved a dead end; nobody answered the phone. The owner of the estate agency where Rudzik worked wasn't very talkative. He simply informed the officers that Rudzik had overdone it in life as in work; he'd been too quick to jump from a Fiat 500 into a Jaguar – figuratively speaking and literally – because a couple of months ago he'd crashed into a tree. When asked whether Mr Mikulski had ever been their client or whether the villa on Sołacz had ever been the object of a transaction, he grew very annoyed, denied it and added that Rudzik might have been doing something behind his back, it was typical of him – or rather would have been.

The female employees of the office turned out to have more to say and to a certain degree explained their boss's dislike of their former colleague. Although the women were more considerate, their attempts not to speak badly of the deceased – as was the custom – weren't very successful. They soon presented Bartol with a dubious picture of an avaricious man in an avaricious reality. The Jaguar, which he'd driven of late, belonged to a very wealthy woman who owned a great deal of property, looked as though she were going to own even more and was one of their best clients; she bought a lot and bought it quickly. Rudzik had become her own personal advisor in real estate– and not only that, no doubt. He'd left his girlfriend – who apparently was very nice – and the agency. With a licence he could act as a free agent. Thanks to his ties with the woman he also took a couple of good clients with him: hence the boss's extreme dislike.

Then had come the avalanche: they did away with exams, any old bungler who'd done a course could do what he'd worked so hard to do; dreams of an élite, closed circle had gone up in smoke. Apparently, Rudzik had taken it very badly. The girl poisoned herself. They saved her but didn't manage to save his mother who suffered a massive brain haemorrhage, maybe because she had high blood pressure, had no medication, was ashamed and had pined away. One of the agents knew somebody in the village next to the one where she lived. Apparently, when Rudzik had arrived there, a couple of women had stifled their own conscience by shouting that he'd killed his mother; somebody had even spat at his feet. Apparently, he'd climbed into his car drunk and hadn't even covered ten kilometres. Nobody saw what happened, there were no witnesses; it's possible that he drove into the tree on purpose – so some people say. The girls didn't believe it though; they didn't think it was like him, whereas it certainly was typical of him to visit old people in their home or press his business card on everyone whether they wanted it or not. Apparently, he was terribly ambitious.

The meaning of the Latin sentences given the situation was elusive although naturally the words made everyone think, each man in his own way. The ancient saying *Dum spiro spero* found on the piece of cloth – 'while there's life there's hope' – seemingly wise, in another context – was uplifting. *Expecto donec veniat* which was found on the card with the flowers was a complaint made by Job who had argued with God like an aggrieved party in court and, when translated, literally meant: 'I'd wait until such a moment arrives', and when elaborated upon was supposed to mean: when I can understand that all this makes sense, that something else exists, that I'll get to live – with the latent accusation: the Lord is not really making it any easier for me which isn't nice when a mere sign, a hope, would suffice. All in all, not very original, considering that everyone wants the same.

Keys without a door.

The symbol of sunflowers apparently gave no interesting indication, beyond the canon of European art; family tradition could neither be excluded nor confirmed; nor had any circle of friends or lovers or anyone whosoever thanked Mikulski for anything.

Christmas came and went, and the progress of the investigation grew slower by the day.

II

HARPSICHORD, a country mongrel, didn't bark at the postman doing his afternoon round as it normally did. It didn't even poke its nose out, as if it wasn't there. It lay curled up in the corner of the old shed, licked its paws and nervously wagged its tail from time to time. It was waiting for its master. He was the only one it trusted.

***

Olaf Polek, a husband of many years' standing, ate his dinner. He mashed his potatoes in with the sauce, the way he liked them. He didn't tear his eyes away from his plate. He was trying to be exceptionally agreeable ever since morning and the more he tried to be agreeable, the more disagreeable his wife became. He didn't know what was wrong with her.

***

Franciszek Konopka, a young farmer, pretended not to hear his mother call. He wasn't in a hurry; he was eating the same soup for the third day running. For two days it had pretended to be broth, today it was tomato soup. He was watching his new fighter cockerel.

***

Magdalena Walichnowska, translator, had eaten her fill and fallen asleep. The felt-tip pen, clasped ambitiously in her hand with the intention of still noting something on the sheets of paper which had fallen on the floor, was now performing the task of its own accord, scribbling asymmetrical patterns on the orange pillow.

**

Daniela Bartol, future grandmother, had already managed to freeze some of the *gołąbki*, the stuffed cabbage leaves. One never knew when they might come in useful. She'd made them with her son in mind. It was always the same: don't worry, things will turn out fine. Just like his father. She smiled to herself every now and again.

**

The girl, four months pregnant, stared at her belly anxiously. The creams weren't helping; the thin marks appearing on her stretched skin were getting further and further apart. She wanted to cry, and not only for that reason. Possibly.

**

Małgorzata Barszcz lay totally motionless; she wasn't getting up at all that day. Only her open eyes and the infrequent blinking of her eyelids showed she wasn't asleep. Nor was this an entirely conscious decision on her part. Her body was slowly ceasing to listen to her. It was heavy, unwilling and practically unable to move. It was happy this way, nobody was telling it what to do anymore, wasn't giving it unquestioning commands; it simply existed, concentrating only on distributing oxygen and other nutrients to every cell individually – more slowly than usual, no need to hurry. Only the clenched muscles of her jaws had been forgotten and had not received the order 'at ease'; the rest were on a well-earned holiday for which they had waited so long.

Forty years of concentration, tension, vigilance, subordination. Of hard work over every word, every move, without a moment's respite, without rest, because that's how it should be, because that's what her head had come up with as though it were in an aquarium, separated from all the rest. Once so proud of her consistent politics to conceal feelings, favour muscles and skin, she hadn't expected a rebellion.

After all, the plan had been clear.

Balance: key word, motto, religion.

Not equilibrium but balance, to be precise: at every moment, in every situation, without a break.

In all its guises: to be balanced, to behave in a balanced way, a balanced style of dressing.

Anything to be unlike her mother, to be normal, like everybody else.

Not some sort of coloured bird, some sort of artistic soul.

All her life she'd had an aversion to anything that was different, whether naturally or ostentatiously. Tolerance could dwell somewhere on the side, but not with her, not in her house.

She'd spent her entire childhood hidden behind glasses, behind a plait and in navy-blue clothes, locking herself up in her room as far away as possible from her mother and all those people who were forever there.

Walking down the street she could always tell who was going to end up in their house. She knew immediately: the hair was much longer or much shorter than anybody else's; glasses covered either half the face or only the irises; stripes where others wore checks; everything was exaggerated, more modern than modern.

That stupid laughter and silly conversations from morning to night about life, art, the possibility of expressing oneself – as though one could do it better. The constantly unpaid bills, strange food, strange music.

'It's wonderful, Margaret. What do you want, Margaret? You've got freedom, Margaret, like I never had. Look at the funky jacket I bought myself, Margaret, you can borrow it. Margaret, you're as boring as your father. Maybe you'll grow out of it, Margaret.'

She grew out of it to such an extent that on the day she turned eighteen she legally changed her name to Małgorzata. Her mother never forgave her, and insisted on introducing herself as Halika; somebody had lost the 'n' from the name Halinka – 'and it sounded so cool'. They were never friends. She didn't want a grown-up friend; she wanted a normal, boring mother, red-haired if she really wanted, but not bright red hair – 'although she looked so passionately fiery'.

She finished studying medicine: something concrete, prestige, stabilisation.

She avoided parties, dances and all surreptitious squeezing of her breasts. She'd seen it hundreds of times.

Living with her mother, she didn't invite anyone home; the few chance visits always ended the same way.

'What a cool mother you've got. Super. Not like mine. I've got to go or she'll moan that she's got to warm my dinner up again, that I'm drifting around.'

She tried drifting once and didn't come home for the night, slept at a friend's.

She counted on her mother shouting at her.

She was met in the morning with full understanding, a conciliatory look and warm words that she might have told her, that it was normal at her age, that she had a modern mother, that maybe she'd go straight to using a coil because who remembers to take the pill, that she wasn't going to poke her nose into anything else, the girl was, after all, seventeen, and that now they could talk about boys.

She left home.

She moved into her boring father's apartment; he was now

getting bored in Canada and there were no signs of his missing the soulful mother or mundane daughter. He hadn't had time to get used to either one.

Nor did she miss anybody or anything.

She led a balanced life.

She became an optician, wore a late-autumn or early spring-coloured skirt suit, went on organised excursions on which it was possible to see so much, brought back souvenirs, invited girl friends to dinner where they could quietly talk about work, savour the food and beautiful porcelain. Nothing makeshift, no odds and ends, no coloured mugs.

No matchmaking.

One day she mentioned that she'd once got burnt and that had been enough. She never commented on sighs and reminiscences that that's what love is, that's men for you.

She loathed the memory of it but it nevertheless came back at times.

The memory of loud music, laughter subsiding, her sleepy room and that enormous tongue which tried to fit into her mouth and spread the disgusting taste of stale wine. She'd managed to scream.

So what if nothing else happened, so what if he'd never come back, so what if we won't talk about it anymore, it's better that way?

The man never came back; she never spoke about it to her friends.

All in all, nothing had happened; she'd never drunk wine, never been kissed, so it wasn't much of a loss.

When did someone or something upset the construction, as elaborate and stable as a house of cards? When did someone disturb such an established foundation?

Was it at the reception during the training course to which she didn't want to go? When, as usual, she didn't have a way out, everybody was going so she also went, although nobody knew how much she despised this other, required aspect of professional trips. The group madness when the calm, balanced, daytime listeners at various symposia mutated into night-time cowboys and tavern tarts, forever playing games fit for schoolchildren. Everyone was prettier, better and free on that intoxicating night, far from home: because it was all so wonderful, life was so short.

Was it when that man had sat next to her, the one who was younger than her and wore strange glasses and a gold cross around his neck; she'd almost suffocated, would have run away immediately had she not been sitting by the wall. Seven people would have had to get up and, on top of that, it was still too early, too rude, not the done thing.

She was worried he'd start flaunting his feathers like a peacock, that it would take a while before he turned to easier prey.

That's not what had happened. She'd been greatly mistaken. From the very beginning when he'd suggested they sit quietly for a while and talk, at least that way they'd be left in peace, wouldn't have to get acquainted and shift from foot to foot, and he wasn't planning to fall in and out of love between drinks because that was so irresponsible.

That he had watched her that day, had immediately noticed she was so well-balanced, so different from all the others, different from her friends who were too heavily made-up and grateful for dim lighting.

That this should be appreciated in today's world when everything was for show, had no principles; that it was important to be well organised in both one's professional and personal life; that it wasn't worth living on credit, literally and figuratively. That living for the moment was overrated.

She'd started to melt. For a good couple of hours, she'd talked like she'd never done to any man before. Not that she had ever given anyone the opportunity. From time to time she caught the eye of one of her friends who smiled knowingly; she knew these smiles but that evening she didn't care.

He'd talked a lot, so had she – like never before.

She'd even told him about her former name, about how silly it was. He understood her perfectly well, adding that in a country of Kasias and Asias it must have been difficult and didn't suit everyone, certainly not somebody who, at any cost, didn't want to be different, that he didn't like loud women, preferred stability, peace, seriousness.

They didn't arrange to meet again, didn't exchange numbers; that, after all, hadn't been the assumption. She was the one who'd suggested she'd take the glasses to one of the night shelters in Poznań; she happened to come from Poznań and she'd certainly take those special spectacles with the Latin writing to the place he'd asked.

He'd kissed her hand in gratitude. She loathed it, hadn't reacted on time. Hadn't regretted it.

He hadn't tried to injure her shoulder by yanking her hand up to his forehead and squashing his dribbling lips on it as usually was the case.

She recalled those five seconds hundreds of times. He'd taken her hand so lightly, held it, bowed his entire body and looked at her – with gratitude, pleadingly, disarmingly? She'd just felt his warm breath and dry lips which perhaps had touched her hand or not – it was all the same; her whole body had become unhinged in a split second, a shudder, sweat, a pleasant spasm below her navel.

At the beginning, before everything waned, when she'd just set all the details in order, she could recall that transitory feeling, that spasm of some sort of plexus of muscles and nerves about which she knew very little. Sometimes she had timidly imagined different endings, her hands unknowingly running over her body more boldly than usual. Then what?

Shame, fear, the door slightly ajar, an unknown direction, and then what?

Her suit, balanced in shape and colour, clung too closely

to her body which, on top of it all, was covered in sweat. Shaking inside, she'd finished her drink, gone back to her room, then home.

Both there and here she couldn't sleep.

The old method of tiring out her brain and body with work and sport didn't work.

She went to that night shelter; she'd always been helpful – within norms, without exaggeration. This time, too, she had promised.

This time she even examined the eyesight of people she always avoided at a distance. But she couldn't awaken any empathy in herself. She already knew them all; they, too, wanted to live differently, had not adapted, were dirtily colourful – street artists proud of themselves, in love with maxims and cheap wine. It's not by chance that she'd chosen ophthalmology; at least people like these rarely visited her. They didn't care whether their vision was clear or not.

The man who worked there, the man for whom she'd brought those special frames with the Latin writing, was also strange, some sort of fanatical do-gooder. Overly pleasant at first, he didn't even thank her. He stared like an idiot and disappeared somewhere, probably used to getting what he wanted. She'd formed an opinion about people like him and this had only confirmed it. She wasn't going to be a do-gooder, unless it was by correspondence as usual; some Marysia or Mateuszek falls ill, one text message and that's it.

She tore her Achilles tendon playing squash, a common injury, especially if one plays to win against oneself.

Two jobs at opposite ends of the city had to find a replacement. For a long time.

In the end, she had to get off the train which never stopped. At a station in an open field.

A month at home, with only herself, with her thoughts. For the first time in ages – she couldn't remember how long – she began to write prescriptions for herself.

At first, there wasn't any sense in styling her hair, then shaving her legs, then getting out of bed.

IT LOOKED as though April had decided not to fool around that year by offering both summer and winter; nor, as if to spite its place in the calendar, did it intend to blossom. There was neither sun nor snow; it was neither hot nor cold; nevertheless, everyone grumbled as usual – because it rained and the wind blew. Because there was no heatwave, because there was no frost, because it was nondescript and that wasn't good either.

'It can't go on like this. It's got to come to an end at some stage,' Maciej Bartol repeated on his way to his mother's house, a little unwittingly and a little senselessly yet over and over again. As if such talk could help. Besides, he was constantly saying and doing senseless things of late. He was sure of it, and not only because that was what his own mother maintained.

Four months ago, he'd informed her that she was going to be a grandmother. He even remembered it had all gone pretty smoothly. He'd deluded himself that it was going to be the same as always, like when he was at school; she'd whinge a little then hug him like a son, like her child.

He'd deluded himself.

Not at all slowly, not at all smoothly, not at all so he could grow accustomed to it, he started to play second fiddle.

He felt like a sad circus clown who has to appear in the interlude because such were the rules of the show, because he acted as background to the real *artistes*; and sad, well, that was just the make-up he wore, the part he was playing; deep down inside, after all, he was very happy – the show was so beautiful, such wonderful things were happening in that pregnant belly.

He couldn't understand it all. Once, she'd always – but always – been on his side, even up against the whole world. Once they'd been able to talk until the early hours of the morning like friends, about almost everything. And now?

Right from the start, from their first meeting as a threesome, it was as though she'd ceased to understand him, as though she stood against him, had gone over to the side of the enemy.

When he argued, for example, that he hadn't expected she'd be such a wonderful mother-in-law, she responded with the avalanche that unfortunately she didn't have the chance to experience being a mother-in-law – which was a great pity – but fortunately she'd see what it was like to be a grandmother. And these were two different matters, as if he didn't know.

To his timid statement that perhaps the child hadn't been an accident, perhaps this was a way to get some sympathy, after all she so loathed manipulation – always spoke to the point, face to face – she said there was nothing to talk about, what had happened had happened, maybe there weren't any accidents and, as it was, he ought to be pleased someone wanted to replicate his genes although if truth be told, if she were the girl she'd think twice about those genes, of course.

And so on and so on.

He couldn't understand this convoluted logic. It was as though women's logic was founded on an entirely different premise, on a theory of chaos unknown to him where only women could find their way, instinctively, without difficulty, with a mutual understanding of the twisted rules.

The culminating point came when both women pressed the ultrasound photograph on him.

Black and white dots on a slip of paper with the question: isn't it beautiful? Isn't it touching?

Absolutely wonderful, absolutely beautiful, he almost saw its teeth. He was a step away from disaster, from exploding. Luckily, this ended with nothing more than an idiotic expression on his face. Besides, they weren't looking at him; he'd understand it all later, apparently.

All he understood was that a month was not 'later'. Another miracle: black and white dots on film, similar in content, except that it was easier for him to assume an idiotic expression; it was slowly growing on him.

Now another outrage which couldn't be delayed lay in wait – after which he'd no doubt suffer again. And right from the morning at that, when he'd wake up thirsty and hungover, his head abused with the drunken search for an answer to the question – when was this finally going to end?

Very slowly he walked up the stairs, cast his eyes around, noticed that the neighbour had changed his front door, studied it for a while but still arrived at his destination. He rang and opened the door; he had a key. At the threshold, he decided to take a defensive stance in the face of... in the face of he knew not what, nor did he expect anything good, not these days.

'Hello mum. I got soaked. I'm sure I'll catch a cold,' he said, coughing and sniffling. As he pulled off his damp jacket he recalled a time when something like this had always done the trick, had set the kettle boiling for hot tea, a blanket ready, and a warm word.

'All right, I'll make you some tea but first sit down. We've got to talk seriously.'

The tone of her voice indicated that those times had come to an end.

'All right, but I'm in a hurry.' He thought that maybe this would work.

'Then pretend you're not. I've come to the conclusion that I have to talk to you. She doesn't want to ask you but I think you ought to be at the delivery, no two ways about it!' she said in a determined, raised voice.

'If there are no two ways about it then why are you talking to me?' Bartol thought he was either really coming down with the flu or just shaking all over as if he'd never stop. He'd never even taken anything like this into consideration. 'Come on, I thought that watching the 3D ultrasound scan was the worst of it but no, you've got more goodies up your sleeve. How on earth do you imagine it all?'

'How do I imagine it? I imagine it quite naturally. You've no problem examining corpses ripped apart with their guts hanging out but you're scared of birth?'

'Mum, it's not a question of being scared!'

'Then what is it a question of? An allergy to life? Is it so hard for you to welcome your son into the world?' she said in an offended tone, knowing she'd now pinned him down.

'What? You already know it's a boy?' Bartol asked, collapsing into a chair, utterly stunned. It wasn't even the fact that it was a boy; this something was slowly losing its impersonality. First, it had started to move and now it had decided to have a gender. It was too much information in one go; hard to evaluate.

'We went to the doctor's today, who said he thought he saw something dangling there so it's probably going to be a boy. I'm pleased – I've obviously not had much success with you, so now I'll really apply myself. I'd no idea you were such an emotionally neglected child.'

'Mum, I'm pleased, too, and I had no idea either, but say what's on your mind - clearly, so that somebody like your failure of a son can easily understand.'

'I want you to be present at the birth. Which part of what I'm saying don't you understand?'

'Why is it so important to you?'

'Because I know it is for her, too. Because I remember how frightened I was, how much I wanted your father to be with me. But times were different then. They weren't that willing to let fathers into the hospital. So I'd prefer you to be with her, just in case something happens, or simply to be there. It's always a bit easier when one's not alone at difficult moments like these. She's terribly frightened. Is it so hard for you to imagine?' She ended her reasoning in a completely different tone of voice, calm, muted, a little sad, as if she no longer expected an answer.

'All right, I'll be there if you like.' There was no point in fighting.

'Good, that's good. But I want you to be the one who wants to be there.'

He decided he would never, but absolutely never, try to understand women, including Our Lady. It wasn't enough that he'd agreed; he now had to believe that he'd thought of it himself – as usual.

'Couldn't you have said this normally right from the start, and not begun almost screaming and all that?'

'I could, but why should I when this tactic proves so extremely effective? To be honest, I thought it would be harder. I'll keep some of the arguments I didn't use for later. Besides, I've already told her that of course you'll be there. Because I think you've been well brought up, although sometimes there's room for doubt. I've got a delicious cheesecake. Get changed, you're completely soaked. Some of your old clothes are still there in the wardrobe.'

She said this on her way to the kitchen so he didn't see her face, but even her gait indicated she was laughing, triumphantly. He almost heard it.

He decided to eat something proper as well, seeing as he was there. He knew she wasn't going to harass him anymore; it looked as though she'd won everything she'd wanted that day. Luckily, she wasn't in the habit of returning to something once it had been dealt with.

'Have you got something more substantial, mum? I'm a bit hungry.'

'Of course, I do. I've made some *gołąbki* for you, just like you like them – buckwheat and lots of cabbage. I'll just heat them up.'

Everything had been prepared, with a number of variations. If that hadn't worked - then calmly and gently, and appetizingly. Was it possible to stand up against this? So what if it would have taken longer, if he'd resisted longer, explained his reasons, only to fall in uneven battle crushed by the force of arguments all leading to the same conclusion – that he was merely a man, unable to understand higher matters?

It crossed his mind that there should be more women in the police force, special units which could pacify in various ways. He couldn't remember whether there was any vodka left in his apartment but decided not to take the risk and drop into the night shop. He was sure it was going to hurt; he was going to get drunk alone – yet again. He didn't look or wait for anyone who could understand him. Things would, after all, work out somehow; after all, he was going to have a son – admittedly with no tree and no house. But he'd started somewhere.

He'd almost begun to feel sorry for himself when his work mobile resounded with the cabaret ringtone he thought suitable for the occasion, as though it, too, were mocking him.

It was Lentz. Bartol couldn't help but feel that something was being repeated, and a moment later knew why.

'Hi, where are you?'

'Ogrody. Has something happened?'

'I heard you're getting ready for some leave. Don't, if you can help it. We've had a murder in Mościnno, twenty-five kilometres from Poznań. You take a left somewhere halfway to Buk, so the local police tell me. They said it's all very strange. A quiet, single man, strangled. No signs of a break-in or burglary, he's just – peacefully dead. You know what it reminds me of?'

'I can guess. No point deliberating. I'll be there in about forty minutes all going well. Are the rest there?'

'They're just being notified, I think you're the first. I'll see you then, bye.'

'Bye.'

This time he wasn't very happy with the timing; five minutes later and he'd have eaten in peace. The familiar aroma of *gołąbki* was wafting through the air. A couple of years ago, he wouldn't have waited but now he thought pragmatically – a moment wouldn't change anything. He had to eat anyway.

'I'm in a terrible hurry, mum, so if you could...'

'I didn't expect otherwise. You can come now,' she called from the kitchen.

'I'll eat and run. I've got to go.'

'But of course!'

'Mum...'

'It's all right now. I wasn't intending to persuade you to do anything else today anyway, although there are still a couple of things we need to talk about.'

'This time I didn't expect otherwise. Can't you tell me everything in one go or write it down on a piece of paper so I've got time to prepare myself, get everything in order?'

'What on earth? Do you think I bought you in a shop or something? With ready instructions? Like a washing-machine – if I read them I'll know straight away that if the machine doesn't work it means it's not plugged in. I heard you're in a hurry, so eat or it'll get cold.'

He said no more and started to eat. Despite his hurry he tried to cut and separate the food carefully so that every morsel was perfect – the cabbage separate, the stuffing separate. She watched him. She'd stopped fighting long ago. Obviously that's how it had to be: she'd take an hour wrapping everything only for him to unwrap it all on his plate. Like a little boy.

The *gołąbki* were the same as ever; they carried the unique taste of security and well-being and despite the irregular circumstances, despite the constant squabbles recently, tasted the same – of peace, constancy, home and something else which couldn't be put into words.

He ate and stopped being angry at his mother as he watched her sulk, worry and wash the dishes. He shuddered as a thought occurred from nowhere: one day it might no longer be like this; along with her would disappear this one and only, unrepeatable, best combination in the world – cabbage, meat, buckwheat, spices and conversation, arguments – which, after every bite, after every word, spread certainty through his entire body that she was the only one who accepted everything he brought her, who loved him whatever happened although sometimes in her own way; who was always there for him. The very essence of being present.

There must have been an odd expression on his face because she was gazing at him with a faintly indulgent smile and said, as though to a slightly thick but conscientious pupil: 'Don't look so worried, it's not that terrible.'

'What are you talking about, mum?' he asked, a little edgy now.

'I thought you were worrying about the birth, but what's on your mind?'

'I've got to fly.' He walked up to her, kissed her on the cheek and added: 'I love you so much.'

Now she was the one with an odd expression.

'What's happened to you?'

'Nothing, I just wanted you to know. I'll call tomorrow, bye.'

He swiftly slipped on his jacket and ran out of the apartment leaving his mother with a slightly worried look on her face. One might have thought she was analysing an opponent's move in chess, wondering whether the latter had, indeed, done something peculiar or whether the strategy was premeditated.

She'd been playing this game for the past thirty-odd years.

It wasn't easy to get to Mościnno. The village was behind another village which itself was out-of-the-way and separated from the main road by a forest. Strange it should even have a name, consisting as it did of barely a couple of scattered houses. Yet even here one could feel everything was about to change. It was dangerously close to the city, which had already sent its first scouts to divide up the land and change it forever. Or so announced the foundations of an immodestly huge future house which would forever shame the couple of dilapidated peasant buildings, once so proud of their enterprising owners who'd miraculously managed to mix their sweat in with the cement they'd procured in order to build identical blocks, unable and unwilling as they were to differ from others.

Seeing several parked police cars, Maciej Bartol drove up to one of the houses.

He showed his ID to some officers he didn't know – probably from the local station – and learned that 'the ones from Poznań' were already inside. Slowly, he approached the outer staircase, a practical answer to an impractical ground floor half-sunken into the ground with the aim of deceiving administrators of the past era into believing it was a large cellar with windows, because who needed a bigger house? After all, everybody was supposed to be equal. He remembered his mother explaining many such peculiarities of the former system which it was difficult at times to imagine. He remembered a fair amount but not enough not to wonder how it was possible to live in a country of such absurdities. His mother didn't miss the old days either, unlike many retired teachers of her age, even though she frequently said present-day reality was also absurd but at least offered a more attractive wrapping.

This particular reality hadn't managed to find an attractive wrapping, he thought as he climbed stairs eaten away by salt and age. He still had time to run his eyes over the farmyard where a small, spotted mongrel – probably not there by chance – stole between the shrubs, its tail between its legs. It seemed to Bartol as though the dog lay low waiting for all those people to leave so that it could return to its post and bark like crazy scaring away postmen, neighbours and other colleagues – as its vocation dictated.

He was just going to go in when he heard a car arrive. Polek and Maćkowiak.

'Hi, here already?' shouted Polek from afar.

'As you can see. And what happened to you – lost your way?' Bartol replied with a question.

'Guessed right. Bad signposts. I was just the driver. It's Polek kept getting the directions wrong like a little miss,' added Maćkowiak, his belly shaking with laughter.

'Let it go. I only got it wrong once. Big deal. And don't say "little miss" because my daughter never gets it wrong and I hope she's reconciled with her gender – although I'm not so sure. Nail extensions yesterday, paintballing today,' Polek complained as he mounted the stairs.

'Any of us here already?' asked Maćkowiak.

'Since you've only just arrived it can only be Lentz inside,' answered Bartol.

'What's happened?' asked Polek.

'I know as much as you. Haven't been in yet.'

'And what, you're just standing on the stairs admiring the view?'

'Don't play the wise guy and let's have a look for Lentz,' decided Bartol.

Lentz appeared of his own accord and informed them from the threshold: 'We've got to wait a bit. The prosecutor's upstairs and there's not much room. It's hard not to trample over each other. They've marked out a very narrow access path for the time being. Want to safeguard as much as possible.'

As he said this he rummaged in all the pockets of his jacket in search of cigarettes. Bartol smiled to himself as he watched him struggle. Lentz hadn't smoked much in the past but recently, having diagnosed problems with his circulation, he'd started to chain smoke.

'The body's sitting at a desk. We've got another loner, strangled successfully for no apparent reason – at least I can't find one, or my cigarettes for that matter,' Lentz added to himself.

'What do you mean, sitting at a desk?' asked Polek in disbelief.

'Literally!' he retorted, now clearly annoyed.

'Who found it?' asked Bartol coming to terms with the fact that there probably wasn't going to be a better description.

'The old woman next door.' Lentz calmed down and, with a gesture, scrounged a cigarette off a passing technician. 'She couldn't stand the dog howling. Maybe she meant that doggie over there.' He pointed to the mongrel lurking in the bushes; everybody turned. The dog also turned as though it knew they were talking about it, and hid deeper in the undergrowth. 'I don't know if we'll manage to talk to her today. The emergency operator couldn't get any sense out of her. Every other word was a plea for God's help and now she's moved on to Our Lady. They've given her a sedative so maybe she'll finally leave Our Lady in peace, too. Besides, somebody's sent for her son, maybe he knows something.'

'I'll go there later,' decided Bartol.

'Is there anything more on the deceased?' asked Polek.

'Not much. His name's Mirosław Trzaska. He moved in a couple of years ago, bought all this for a pittance. There weren't many buyers. There was nobody left on the farm. Someone had been quick to get rid of it. Mirosław Trzaska – from what they've managed to ascertain – worked in Poznań in a night shelter and a couple of other places, too. He was some sort of community worker with a very good reputation. All those who talked to him last and whom we called, spoke of him this way. We've got quite a bit of questioning to do. The address book on his mobile is endless.'

'Unlike Mikulski's,' said Maćkowiak.

'We've no reason to connect the two murders yet.' Hearing Maćkowiak's last comment, prosecutor Pilski, who'd just appeared in the doorway, joined in the conversation. In his long coat and bizarrely tied colourful scarf with its Oriental pattern, and hair smooth with gel, he didn't fit in again.

'Nobody intends to connect them,' said Polek, throwing him, or rather his scarf, a look of disgust.

'Of course, one could draw vague connections...' Pilski backed out awkwardly.

'Well then, we're drawing them and that's it,' Polek snapped back.

He'd been in conflict with Pilski for a long time without any obvious reason. This was how he described it: 'I hate pink ties because I feel as though I'm talking to someone who's just got away from a garden party and since I don't have a garden, only a balcony, we're worlds apart.'

The rest of them, on the whole, kept Pilski at a friendly distance.

'I'm going inside. It's freezing,' said Bartol after a while.

'I'll take a look around, too.' Maćkowiak joined in. Polek turned without a word and walked ahead.

'I'll do the rounds of the neighbours. There aren't that many. Then I'll phone around. When are we meeting back in the office?' asked Lentz, tossing a cigarette butt practically under Pilski's feet.

'Seven, I think,' replied Bartol.

Although they were now talking between themselves, both glanced at Pilski out of the corner of their eye.

The latter stood there for a while, then crushed the still glowing cigarette butt with his shoe and left. It was hard to know what was going on in his mind.

When Pilski was no longer there, Lentz passed on some more information he'd acquired and went to question the neighbours.

They formed a tight team.

If one of them allocated themselves a task which was essential anyway, nobody opposed. Besides, they knew that Lentz and

Maćkowiak were better at talking to people and gathering all sorts of generally available information, while Polek was in his element searching for shady sources whose shadiness nobody even intended to look into and which he sometimes didn't want to disclose. Bartol proved best at bringing it all together – although recently he couldn't boast about spectacular success. They'd come to a halt with Mikulski's case despite the fact that never before had they called for so many expert opinions.

They'd not committed any apparent procedural mistakes; nobody blamed them. Nobody but himself.

He was afraid the same was going to happen here.

Like the time before, he slowly made his way into the depths of the house and looked around. The area across which they were allowed to move wasn't large, as was the case with the whole house. The corridors were too narrow, the rooms too narrow, everything was somehow too small, cramped. Even if he hadn't known there was a dead body sitting at a desk, all this would have been strange enough.

Like a stage set again.

There had been too many things in Mikulski's house – a lovingly stored and dusted collection of his entire life. Here there was absolutely nothing. As though someone had stepped onto a train with a good luck charm then suddenly decided to end his journey.

From initial information it appeared that Trzaska had bought the old farm along with the dilapidated house. There must have been a huge amount of objects, both necessary and unnecessary. The walls must have borne the weight of many successive layers of wallpaper. Renovation would have been understandable but what Bartol saw couldn't qualify as renovation. It looked rather as though someone had begun by lighting an enormous fire and the memory of the previous owners had gone up in smoke. Then, where it had clung hard to the walls, he had clumsily torn the wallpaper down along with the plaster, and painted everything white, not caring about uneven surfaces. Then brought in astoundingly little furniture.

Bartol stared at the extent to which one's needs could be cut. He loved objects and their beauty. Never would he have thought that somebody could, of their own volition, find them totally unnecessary, that somebody could reduce their role and number solely down to their essential function. He'd heard about contemplative religious orders but here and now this seemed absurd.

In no way, however, could he deny what he saw: one bed, one stool by the bed. In the kitchen: one table, one chair, one wall-shelf – small but still too spacious for one shallow plate, one bowl, one pot, one glass, one set of cutlery. He couldn't see any fridge or television set. Walking through successive rooms, almost as empty and equally whitewashed, he reached a small room furnished with a small table and no chair. He couldn't believe what he saw. On the table stood a computer. Real in this practically unreal reality. An ordinary, modern object which existed in these old-fashioned surroundings. Nor were there any of what one could have considered necessary accessories, no CDs, printers, pads, mouse. It stood there alone and appeared terrifying, as though someone had locked the whole ordinary, familiar world into some extraordinary, familiar form.

He didn't know what to make of it all. He was even pleased to see Gawroński, the chief technician. A rare occurrence since they weren't exactly fond of each other.

'What do you make of it all?' he asked simply as if he simply expected a reply and not a taunt – although that was how it usually ended when someone accosted 'Gawron', 'the Rook', at work.

'I've no idea. I've probably got too much junk at home. The boys are pleased. They'll be done quicker.' He lost himself in thought; the contemplative atmosphere seemed to affect everyone. 'Maybe a life like this is better, who knows?' Gawroński asked after a while. 'Have you seen him yet?'

'No. Is it okay to enter now?'

'Yes, you'll see him from the hallway, through the open door. It's a small room. It's already well secured and photographed. There's no need for you to rummage around. A chair, a small cross and him.'

'What sort of cross?' asked Bartol.

'Ordinary. Free-standing, for praying probably? Oh, and there's a Bible – I think. He's got his hand on something like that. Spick and span apart from that.'

He waited a moment longer for more comments but none came. Both looked at the walls blankly.

'I think I'll go upstairs now,' Bartol spoke first.

'Go on. And how's it going with Mikulski, anything becoming clear, my friend?'

Maciej merely muttered that he was working on it, and started to climb the stairs. He knew perfectly well the question was spiteful, which didn't surprise him in the least. He hadn't expected Gawroński to be all that serene.

He passed a few people; most of them perfunctorily acknowledged his presence and returned to their monotonous brushing, shining of lamps, dusting with powders, most of which were unknown to him.

He approached the door to the room where the murder had taken place and couldn't say anything other than that the man was sitting at his desk. Almost naturally, as though dozing and about to wake up at any moment. Gawroński was right; his entire hand rested on a Bible. Bartol saw the typical gold lettering on the thick cardboard of a cover which enclosed hundreds of thin, evenly cut pages. The Bible was closed but he noticed coloured ribbons, bookmarks perhaps, inserted between specific pages. This wasn't the time to open them; there was still work for the technicians to do.

He stared at the scene for a long time, one thought racing through his mind: were two chairs excessive? He had seven, and hundreds of objects which seemed to have a more interesting life than his own. He adored them without ever really using them. In fact he was asking himself the same thing Gawroński had asked a moment ago: did he have too much junk at home, or was it a good thing he had it, otherwise he'd go mad?

What did he actually see? A man who was neither praying nor reading, simply sitting at his desk as though painted in 3D. Again he had the same impression as in Mikulski's case: that a curtain would shortly be drawn, that this wasn't the real world. He walked up closer. A blue mark around the man's neck, a slightly contorted but on the whole unremarkable expression on his face. Glasses perched on his nose. There wouldn't have been anything odd in this – he could have been about sixty and, theoretically, could have been reading – were it not that someone must have put the spectacles on his nose after his death. Bartol was wondering why when his attention was riveted by the long metal plate on the frame. He was used to larger and smaller logos but this one was certainly a little too long, the frame wasn't all that modern. He strained his eyes and slowly began to read: *Speculator adstad de sui.*

He went downstairs calmly but his voice was no longer calm when he spoke to Gawroński.

'I want to know everything about the glasses on the man's nose. Literally everything. Where they're from, what they're made of and where the metal plate with the writing or whatever you call it could have been manufactured, and anything else you can deduce from them.' He spoke quickly and decisively, thus offending Gawroński who was himself in the process of giving instructions and didn't like being interrupted.

'And what, the rest isn't important?' he asked, annoyed.

'Everything's important and I know you're seeing to it. And keep an eye out for any other maxims. There were two in

Mikulski's house, there ought to be at least as many here. You didn't let sleeping dogs lie. Your intuition was spot on when you asked about Mikulski today. Well done. I'm off to do some work. We'll see each other tomorrow.'

Bartol quickly reached the front steps leaving Gawroński – who didn't know how to react to the surprise registered on the faces of the few technicians who'd have to add the gift of prophecy to their boss's many talents – slightly stunned.

He went outside and, for a moment, stopped halfway down the steps. He breathed in air which, with the tiniest bit of good-will, could have been called fresh.

He couldn't say that he was entirely surprised, that it hadn't already occurred to either him or anyone else, but vague connections, as Pilski described them, were one thing and the certainty that they were dealing with the same man, the same murderer, with something they'd never dealt with before, was quite another.

He'd already come across a double murder in the past, a double suicide at that, but the murders had been committed at the same time and without a stage setting.

Polek, standing on the stairs, tore him from his semi-stupor.

'I've heard the news. Are you sure it's the same guy who did Mikulski in?' he asked without beating about the bush.

'Yes, I'm sure,' replied Bartol.

'Well then go and tell that prosecutor. He's by the ambulance.'

'Let him be, Olaf. I'm going to question the old woman, then go to the station. You check whether we haven't ever pow-wowed with this Trzaska or got any mutual acquaintances. And when you talk to people, ask them where he got the glasses from. Maybe somebody'll know something.'

'I'm to ask about his specs?' Polek asked as if his reputation would suffer.

'Yes, the ones on his nose to be precise. They're also adorned with a Latin maxim. Do your best. And get Maćkowiak to go to that night shelter. See you.'

It wasn't far but he drove to the neighbouring house. He didn't intend going back to that place, not that day anyway; it was too crowded and his thoughts were too scattered.

He got into his car and almost automatically called his mother. It was the quickest way to find out what the words could mean.

'Hi, mum. I've got a favour to ask.'

'What, more Latin?' she was quick to enquire.

'How do you know?' He couldn't hide his surprise.

'You rarely miss me so much as to call so soon after we've just seen each other. Besides, this reminds me of something, I'm still on the ball. Watch and learn, I'm not going to be around forever. Appreciate it as it comes.'

'I do. Mum, do you know what "*Speculator adstad de sui*"' might mean?'

'I've no idea, but wait, I'm on the internet. Spell it.'

Bartol spelled the words and waited as instructed.

'I can't find anything here, unfortunately. Phone the expert you called before.'

'The problem there is that he wrote very nicely but said there wasn't any connection between the two dicta.'

'Some expert. He could at least have said that he couldn't find any but to immediately go and say that there wasn't one – since there must be some sort of link.'

'You've put that very nicely, thank you.'

'Listen,' she began after a while. 'You remember me telling you about the girl Magda who spoke so beautifully about medieval symbolism? I told you to get in touch with her then. Besides, I wanted to get you to meet her before you'd any responsibilities... Never mind, water under the bridge,' she added more quietly, as if to herself.

And that was why he hadn't phoned her at the time. He remembered how, before he'd told her about the pregnancy, she'd suddenly been interested in some Christian iconography so as to tell him about the fine young woman she'd met. What beat it all was her asking him to go and return a dictionary she'd borrowed from the girl. He hadn't gone; he'd been sure she'd taken the dictionary especially so that he could get to know the young woman, like kids in a nursery. He'd had it up to his ears with this match-making. He hadn't wanted any new acquaintances, neither then nor later; although things turned out otherwise. His intuition must have been good. And he wasn't in the mood to meet anyone now either, but felt there was no way out. He would have had to get another translation from the man who'd tried to be agreeable but whose whole body communicated just how much he couldn't abide ignoramuses like him.

'Do you still have her phone number?'

'I do, and what of it? It's nothing to me whether you meet her now or not.'

'Don't bicker, mum. This is serious.'

'All right, all right, I was only looking for the number. I'll send you her card. Her name's Magdalena Walichnowska. I've jotted somewhere here to call before twelve or after eight in the evening.'

'Magdalena Walichnowska, that's nice. To call after 8pm? Is she pretty at least?'

'Now stop being silly and stop complicating matters. I've had enough for this year.'

'Oh, come on! I was only joking. Just send me the number, okay?'

'You know what? Go buy yourself another sense of humour because the one you've got must be some sort of reject, price reduced several times. Bye!'

A moment later a message arrived with the number. He called immediately even though it was outside the stated hours. After five rings, the answer machine replied: 'I must be doing something more interesting than taking calls. Record your message!'

He didn't intend to leave a message, decided he'd phone later.

He put the phone aside, drove off and turned. He didn't even manage to shift into third gear before he had to slow down. A large four-wheel drive appeared from behind the bend and came towards him at great speed, turned left and stopped before the freshly laid foundations of the future house. It must have braked like that only to make mud splatter as high as the roof, proof that it had been driven in the country.

'Fine,' he said to himself out loud. 'They've come of their own accord. That's one thing less to think about.'

He thought he'd ask the new arrivals some preliminary questions about whether they'd seen anything or not. Before he saw them he heard a booming guffaw and a squeaky giggle.

He looked at the couple climbing out of the car. The man must have been coming up to fifty, was quite fit and quite wrinkled; the woman was too young and wearing loud colours.

No doubt, when buying the trousers which were too tight and the polo shirt a tiny bit too small, he hadn't been able to resist admiring himself and had pulled his stomach in as much as he could; not more than a metre away from any mirror, however, he'd already forgotten to do so. She, less than twenty, bravely copied him and wore clothes which were too small.

He was in something like an unfastened, coloured, leather jacket, she in a loose jacket, the top of which was two sizes smaller than the jumper beneath it, a jumper which didn't cover her belly anyway.

As he got out of the car, Bartol decided to fasten his own jacket. He found it cold so was all the more amused by the couple in love, who clearly couldn't care less about the weather.

As Bartol started to approach them, the man turned towards him with determination, stopped, drew himself up straight, assumed an offensive stance and attacked: 'What do you want?'

Bartol pulled out his ID, recited the usual formula and introduced himself. The offensive stance became defensive but not devoid of aggression.

'Come about that cement I had stolen two days ago, have you?'

'No, no I haven't,' Bartol replied calmly.

'Of course not. As if the police cared!'

'I think they do. Please report it to the local station, I'm from another department. Most probably between 4.00 and 6.00pm yesterday afternoon your neighbour, Mirosław Trzaska, in that house next to yours, was murdered. Perhaps you saw something?'

The girl stopped smiling, the man, too, grew very serious but a moment later regained his vigour.

'We were at a show yesterday and, anyway, we still live in Poznań, don't we Niunia?'

Niunia nodded and clung harder to the man's arm. She was so tiny she could easily have been his younger daughter.

'That can be proved, can it?' Bartol asked just in case.

'Of course it can. We weren't alone. Wacek took some photographs. Remember, Niunia?'

Niunia remembered.

'Did you know Mirosław Trzaska?'

'I don't hang out with this rabble. Well, just look around.'

Bartol didn't intend to look around; he was finding the man more and more irritating.

'All this is just spoiling my view.' The man indicated his not-yet-existent windows.

'They've all lived here a long time and you're new, as it happens.' Bartol started to enter into an unnecessary discussion.

'So what? I've bought ten hectares here, and one for Niunia because she wants to plant some flowers, and I'm going to buy some more, and for Niunia, too. That bit with the forest next to it because she wants her own mushrooms. So there!'

He glanced at Niunia, who pulled a sweet face as if she'd

just been given a lollipop, and stuck out a bust which could not go unnoticed.

'Well, I didn't want to tell you. It was supposed to be a present from the Easter bunny,' the man gushed. After a moment, he continued: 'I don't intend to get to know anybody here for the time being. I'll wait. Admin says there's no problem with building permission because the land's poor and the farmers a load of crap. What do they have, you tell me? Five hectares. And they're going to build a dual carriageway to Buk nearby. Down a bit and we're here. I'm going to fence all this in and turn it into a private compound. You should buy something here yourself. They're dumb peasants, selling for a pittance.' His good mood was returning as he looked at Niunia's beaming face.

'I don't intend to buy anything!' replied Bartol, quite angry now, but not wanting to enter into any kind of conversation. 'Please report to police headquarters in Poznań tomorrow between eleven and twelve o'clock.'

'What for?'

'In order to make a statement.'

'Niunia, too?'

'Niunia, too.' He tried not to raise his voice. 'Here is my card.'

He gave one first to the man – he was standing closest – and as the latter slipped it into his wallet, he gave one to the girl. Unwittingly, for a split second, his eyes rested on the breasts popping out of the girl's low-cut top. Niunia seized the moment and stuck her breasts out even further, tilting her head to one side. Her expression indicated that the money wasn't being wasted.

Bartol, a little disconcerted at being caught sneaking a look, swiftly asked: 'May I note down your details?'

'But of course!'

The man pulled out his driving licence, the girl her ID.

'I told you to get yourself that licence,' said the man to Niunia. He didn't need to say this but probably did so just to hear the answer.

'Why? You're such a good driver and I'm scared of driving by myself anyway,' she replied, gluing herself to his arm again.

Bartol returned to his car. He finished noting down the couple's details and once more glanced at the four-wheel drive. The man was phoning somebody; Niunia was gazing out at her new allotment by the forest. It seemed to Maciej as though she'd grown in stature; she was not sticking her breasts out so much but had raised her chin. He thought that, if Niunia waited a little, she'd grow into quite a loaded young lady. He glanced at her again. She was still staring at her future land; he was sure she was even licking her lips. She's not as stupid as she makes out, he thought. She'll wait.

He said goodbye and decided to let Maćkowiak question the couple the second time around; he had no wish to see them again.

He crossed the road to the house where the woman who'd reported the murder, lived. The gate wasn't pulled-to and probably couldn't be. Last year's stalks beneath the windows didn't resemble any garden plants. A path trodden across the grass and mud led to the front door which, in an old-fashioned, uninviting way, gave on to the yard.

Then, in the yard, Bartol saw something which he wouldn't have expected. Dozens of nearly new cages, large and small and all in perfectly good condition, served as aviaries for an enormous number of colourful birds. He'd have called them hens and roosters except that none of them resembled what he'd describe as poultry. Some of the hens had the appearance of small sheep, while the roosters looked like proud and stately eagles with nearly twenty-centimetre long feathers on their enormous talons.

There were all sorts, colourful and beautiful. Bartol stared, fascinated by the madness parading in front of him. These follies which he was looking on could have served some ordinary purpose, but surely only by chance. What they manifested was the artistic flair of nature and man, who also liked to tamper.

He fixed his eyes on a small, proud cockerel with an enormous, multi-coloured, glistening tail, which didn't walk but strode like a Tyrannosaurus Rex and closely observed him. The bird wasn't peacefully inclined, that was for sure. Bartol wasn't scared of animals on the whole but he'd never open that particular cage.

He'd have stood there staring for longer had he not heard a squeak and the loud grating of the bedecked front door against the ground.

'And where did you spring from?!' First he heard the croaky voice, then saw a head appear from behind the door-frame.

'Police. Mrs Regina Konopka?' he asked, standing below. He didn't even attempt to walk in her direction.

'Then show me those, you know, those papers.'

'Here you are.' He pulled the ID from his pocket. He might just as well have pulled out a road sign, she wouldn't have been able to see it in that light or at that distance, but it sufficed.

'You'd better come in then.' She opened the door wider.

He climbed steps as dilapidated as the ones he'd climbed before. From that point Mrs Konopka marked the way forward. Meandering, she led him to a room downstairs. It couldn't have been further from the front door but must have been the most presentable. In the meantime, he took a good look at her. The wrinkles etched into her face spoke a great deal; for example, that the last time she'd smiled whole-heartedly must have been during the '60s or '70s when a neighbour had broken her leg or some such incident.

The house, too, was in character with its owner, who clearly didn't like cleaning but did like to cover everything with colourful, poorly ironed tablecloths. The room in which they sat resembled all the others except in two things: in the place of honour stood an enormous television set also on a flowery tablecloth, and in the armchair – covered with a larger tablecloth - slept a young man.

'He's asleep. He'll probably sleep for a long time because I gave him the pills those doctors of yours gave me. He's upset about this Trzaska man,' Regina declared with concern in her voice.

'What on earth do you mean?' Bartol was aghast. Taken aback at first, he quickly concluded that if the pills weren't supposed to harm an elderly woman they certainly wouldn't harm a young lad.

'God never bestowed me with good health, I'm ill with blood pressure, don't feel well,' she said, putting on an ailing face.

'Have you told a doctor? Shall I go and get you something? One of the medics might still be around. And what is your blood pressure, high or low?'

'I'm ill with blood pressure!' she informed in a tone which brooked no argument. 'I don't need any of their medicine,' she added.

'Fine.' He'd no intention of arguing with her. Her blood pressure was clearly so awful it couldn't be measured. 'Let's talk about how you found Mr Mirosław Trzaska and what was your relationship.'

'What do you mean by that?' she started yelling.

It suddenly dawned on him that their conversation was beginning to sound like some cheap joke – and because of him.

'Nothing. I'm only asking whether you knew him well.'

'What do you mean, well? Normally! He was new. Bought the house from the Ławeckis. Always greeted me but didn't go to church.' She emphasised the last words plainly and firmly. 'That's people for you nowadays, no fear of God in them, like those opposite. Have you seen those tramps? When I think how I sold him that land by the road... My son didn't want to,' she admitted honestly, 'but I promised him those hens. Bought myself that television and did right. Why should I watch the world in some tiny box? I went on pilgrimages, too. Prayed for my boy not to bring anything like her home, you saw, didn't you?'

Looking at her face he didn't know whether she'd been to the sanctuary at Licheń or Łysa Góra, the supposed site of a witches' coven, unless it was one of those combined pilgrimages, two in one for the balance.

'So how did you guess that something had happened to Mr Trzaska?'

'That mongrel howled all day and all night. Howled before, too, because why keep it indoors? But a bit too long this time. I went over, knocked and – nothing. So I brought the ladder which was leaning against the wall up against the window. A bit scared I was but...'

'Couldn't you have asked your son?'

'Why should I? Besides, I didn't like him going there. The man said all sorts of nonsense to him. Maybe he was some sort of pervert? How could I know what I was going to see through that window?' she added reasonably.

'Right, and what did you see through the window?' He must have been finding everybody tiresome that day.

'He was just sitting there, without moving. I ran home and phoned. It's a good thing the phone was plugged in because that one there' – she pointed to her son – 'unplugs it at times. It didn't bother him when there were those quiz shows where he knew the answers and we couldn't phone, but now I know the answers and phone sometimes, he yells at me. No good he is, just like his father!'

Bartol looked at the sleeping son and thought that even if the lad had wanted to smother his mother with a pillow he wouldn't have succeeded: she was the kind who'd suck oxygen in through the feathers.

But he had to ask even though he didn't want to talk to her.

'Can you tell me where you and your son were yesterday between four and six in the afternoon?'

'Why?' she asked, taking offence.

'Please don't upset yourself. It's just procedure.'

'Procedure! What procedure?!' she started to shout.

It didn't surprise him; he'd expected her to shout.

'Please answer me,' he asked as calmly as he could.

'It was Hela's turn yesterday,' she said as though there were no need to explain anything.

'Hela's turn for what?' he asked calmly again.

'We meet every week at a different friend's house.'

'That was from when to when, and where was your son in the meantime?'

'Where was he supposed to be? With me. We meet at four. He takes us there then brings us back. It must have lasted until eight yesterday or I might have got home even later. After that TV serial, you know, where all these people have got problems, the one...'

'That means what time?' He wasn't interested in what problems people had.

'The neighbour will know better because she wears a watch. I don't like wearing one,' she replied, offended by his lack of understanding for the misfortunes in episode 518.

'Please tell your son to report to police headquarters between eleven and one tomorrow. I'll leave you my business card. He can call if it doesn't suit.'

'And why's that?'

'Procedure. Haven't you seen that in this television over there?'

'I have, too.'

'Well, there you are. Please pass it on to him. And one more thing. Was anyone lurking around here recently? Any unknown cars drive past?'

'Those punters are always hanging around, but apart from that I haven't seen anything.'

It took him a long time before he realised, in a roundabout way, that she didn't mean punters but hunters.

He glanced in sympathy at the lad again and said goodbye to Mrs Konopka. He really did feel tired. Her eyes followed him as she stood at the door. He didn't stop by the birds; he didn't want to provoke another discussion. She clearly did.

He climbed into his car, pulled away and after two hundred metres, just beyond the bend, drove off to the side and halted. He pushed his seat and leaned back. Lay down and tried to collect his thoughts. He couldn't collect them.

Nor did he manage to do so later, at home. Tired, he couldn't fall asleep.

Mikulski with his baroque splendour, Trzaska with his monastic rendition.

The performance was on, he had no doubts about it, but so what if all he saw was the stage and didn't even know where the wings were?

Act II had just come to an end.

Would there be a third? Would he be on time?

The solution wasn't simple, but it was there somewhere! Lurking. Waiting...

HIDDEN IN A CONFESSIONAL, curled up, invisible.

Nobody's going to guess he's there. It won't enter anybody's head to check the chapel partially obscured by scaffolding. To open the little door, pull back the curtain, and see, in place of a confessor, the grown man curled up like a child, arms wrapped around his legs, head pressed to his knees.

He'd picked the place well. He'd prepared himself well.

He'd wait another hour, perhaps two – as many as was needed.

It didn't trouble him that his legs, arms and neck were slowly growing numb.

He'd long grown to accept the stupefying pain which came and went according to a rhythm known only onto itself. It was better not to move. The smallest twitch, even of his little toe, passed on an impulse which dug red hot needles right into the middle of his head. He then knew he had to wait until the body stopped demanding action. Endure, calm down.

Dig his eyes even deeper into the protruding bones of his knees so as to make fiery images once more appear beneath eyelids raging with pain.

He exhaled slowly, inhaled even more slowly, not giving his lungs as much oxygen as they'd like; it was better this way.

He heard his heart beating, almost like that other time.

The same music. Three beats – boom boom... boom, and again boom boom... boom, like a song, like a dance.

A divine rhythm insulted by the sound of his guts.

The primitive gurgling of his stomach and intestines which dispassionately changed everything entering them into one and the same shit.

Transferred, propelled, packed tight.

He waited a long time until he was sure it was dark night, that nobody would come in, that he was alone. Very slowly he opened his body.

First, the head.

First, he gently raised it a little then began to rotate. Very, very slowly.

The numb muscles of his neck didn't allow it to move faster ,as though surprised they'd once borne such a weight; they couldn't get used to it.

Then the neck.

Then the fingers of one hand, then the other.

Finally the entire rebellious rest, as though out of spite for having had to wait, now didn't want to move. Had to be forced.

Consistently, until he was erect, his posture proud.

Last of all the eyelids; as it was his aching eyes wouldn't see anything for the time being. They, too, needed time to get accustomed to themselves and the darkness.

The squeaking of the confessional door as it opened contorted his face painfully. Another unfitting, hideous sound severing the silence.

He conquered the obstacles of the scaffolding which leaned against the entrance to the chapel, pulled out an antiquated torch and noiselessly crossed towards the gate leading to his place of worship. Was it a coincidence that it was right opposite the altar, dripping with gold, intended for common folk?

On the way, he turned the torchlight on the closed eyes of the bishop slumbering on a tomb. He always looked in that direction when walking on this side. The fatso, content with life, had managed to make himself comfortable after death, too, napping on his side not far from the altar. Always in an excellent mood after life as after lunch.

A while later, the man stopped again and turned the tiny light onto the eyes of a skull beautifully sculpted on a tombstone. At this, too, he liked to look – amusingly terrible as it hung in warning, which was probably why the skull had lost its lower jaw.

He didn't look around anymore; childhood foibles he could allow himself, but he didn't want to become any more distracted.

He arrived. Opened the heavy door and grating; knew it wasn't locked.

And once again he was in his sanctuary, his temple of ideas, just as in the past. Just as when he'd got lost, as when he hadn't wanted to be found.

Again he was the little boy who'd strayed from a father whom he'd so feared that he didn't even shout.

He hadn't shouted when he'd seen the closed door, nor had he shouted later when he couldn't open it for hours, eons.

He'd just sat there in the chapel, staring and shivering. He shivered from the cold and from both fear that his father would find him and that he wouldn't find him. He hadn't known which he'd feared more.

And he'd shone that torch of his to tame his loneliness.

And they'd been with him, not looking at him, but they'd been there: the mighty ones and the less important.

He knew them, knew what they meant and asked them, each one individually, each in its own way, each one for something different; and they'd listened. In the dim light of the torch and even when he'd turned it off.

Although he didn't like them as they were now, restored, refreshed, beautified anew. But it was them. Without the patina, without time on them, but them. He forgave them.

He also knew that those in the window glyphs had disappeared forever. Earlier scribblings had needed to be revealed. He hadn't been able to come to terms with it for a long time. He didn't look in their direction, could recall them any time he wanted to anyway.

The narrow passage in which he'd got lost had also been walled over. He didn't care.

Once again he cast his eyes around. With disgust he thought about the rubbish heap they were making of the place – an enormous candlestick, a baptismal font, an old pew serving no purpose, pennants awaiting a procession. Why right here?

He turned the torchlight on one of the intruders. He might have expected it: an embroidered Our Lady and a huge eagle. Both wearing crowns of heart-shaped glass beads. As if either needed them. Stupid people. He gazed into the eyes of the Black Madonna. The garish beads didn't suit Her; She knew it and it made Her sad. An eagle wearing a crown wouldn't soar high either.

After a while he stopped taking notice of them, just as the two enormous paintings stuck to the walls didn't interest him.

He looked only at the ceiling. At what was engraved on the walls and in his soul, which he'd never abandon again.

He lay down on the stone floor, like the time when he'd no longer cared.

Again he felt the cold penetrate his every cell.

Again he was a child. Again he shone the light. Again he observed the only boy in the group; his name was Fortitude. And he, too, was looking back at him, dragging his burden, inviting him to climb the mountain.

To achieve what he wanted to achieve. To pay homage to those who were most important, and to himself.

To kill those who'd killed it in him.

He'd lie like this until the morning then go out as he'd done then. And nobody would say anything to him.

And he'd finish what wasn't finished.

And then all he'd hear would be boom boom... boom, boom boom... boom, boom... boom...

RAIN, INSEPARABLE FRIEND of traffic jams, fell over the city. The journey Bartol made from home to work, day in day out, seemed three times longer. It hadn't grown light yet; it looked as though someone had forgotten to switch the daylight on.

He'd just left the house and was already feeling the need for a coffee - instantly. He was afraid he'd fall asleep. He'd already downed one but it must have been too instant. He drove into a petrol station. Drank another two espressos. It took him another five minutes to join the traffic; not many drivers were willing to show kindness to those slipping in from the minor road. The police officer didn't know what to put this down to – a general stupor, poor visibility or a morning aversion to life on such a charming day?

Everyone was moving a little more slowly, sluggishly, lifelessly. The drivers' delayed reactions were, minute by minute, growing increasingly delayed.

He'd done well to slip off. The coffee was starting to work, his eyelids had stopped drooping, his blood, quickened by the caffeine, had started to circulate faster.

It had been on just a day like this that he'd had the stupidest of accidents. That day, too, his thinking had been slower. To his misfortune the reaction of the driver in front of him had been even slower. He thought he'd seen the other man move away, had just looked left, accelerated and halted with the noise of dented metal. He'd been in the car with his mother who'd stared at him in her unique way.

The first time he'd seen her stare at him like that was when he was in Year One at primary school and had faked her signature on a note – using her first name. He hadn't written the surname, hadn't known how to write 'r'. Only much later did he learn the meaning of the word pity.

Bartol glanced at his watch. Half past seven; not really the right time, but he tried to call the Magda girl anyway.

Surprisingly – after three rings – the same voice he'd heard on the machine five times the day before, replied.

'Hello, I see a new number's been trying to get through to me. How can I help you?'

'Good morning. My name's Maciej Bartol. I got your number from...' He didn't have time to finish.

'Ah! Daniela! I take it I'm talking to her son. You've got a great mother. Good, if it's about a translation I've got a lot of work on at the moment but I'll come up with something. Danish and Swedish willingly; as for English, you could do better than me but I'll help if needs be.' Her cheerful voice didn't in the least suit the general atmospheric conditions.

'I'm not calling about a translation, or rather I am, in fact, but it's more like an explanation or...' He was getting lost; hadn't thought he'd be justifying himself right from the start.

'Sorry, I shouldn't have pre-empted you. I'll listen quietly. I'm too full of beans. Woke up to such a beautiful day, could be why.'

He was getting annoyed. Didn't know how to react to her words, couldn't comment on the day because he'd hardly seen any of it through the rain pounding on his windscreen.

'You're interested in symbolism, I'm not expressing myself very well but... but I've got a couple of items... and a couple of Latin maxims... There's a connection between them, there's certainly a connection but I'm not sure what it is... And if you had a moment... well, perhaps not a moment... But if I could show you or tell you...'

'Then tell me, I've got a bit of time now... And I'm in the right mood,' she added brightly.

'They're probably quotations from the Bible.' He was already regretting he'd phoned. 'I'd like you to tell me what they mean or might signify...' He heard himself stammer. He was furious, he had had no intention whatsoever of discussing it over the phone. Fortunately, this time she promptly interrupted.

'All right, we'd better meet. And remember the same thing

applies to the Bible as to people – you torture it long enough and it'll tell you what you want to know. The context is important, the situation, place, time and so on. Drop in and see me at my place tomorrow and we'll discuss what you've got in peace.'

'Can't we make it today? I'll fit in with your schedule if...'

'Sure, you can fit in with my schedule. I'm at Stary Rynek until three, then catching the train from Kraków to Poznań, so if you anticipate any difficulties I suggest we meet tomorrow. I can make it first thing in the morning if it's that urgent.'

'Good, nine o'clock okay?' he asked, sounding totally resigned.

'That certainly is first thing. But maybe that's good, I wanted to get up early anyway. I'll text you my address.'

'Thank you.' He didn't have the courage to tell her she could drop in to see them. 'Is it sunny in Kraków?' he asked out of interest. Although her state of mind interested him more than the weather.

'It certainly is. Not a single tiny ornamental cloud in the sky. See you tomorrow. Maybe I'll bring the sunshine to Poznań with me. By the by, I'm pleased we're going to meet. I'm curious to see what you look like. And please send my regards to your mother.'

'I will. See you.' He was still holding the receiver to his ear when he heard the click as she hung up. For some unknown reason, the only thought he focused on was that he'd have to iron the trousers which had been drying on the radiator for the past three days. As with his mother – one sentence and he'd have to get up half an hour earlier simply to satisfy somebody's curiosity. He instinctively ruffled the hair over his forehead and glanced in the mirror. Now he knew why the two women liked each other.

'Let's hope it's worth it!' he consoled himself.

Presently a text arrived with the address. A street in Wilga. He wondered what he'd find: an apartment left by granny in a low-rise communist block, a modern apartment bought on credit or a loft sniffed out in a tenement? In the end, he bet on the loft. He loathed stairs.

It rained harder and harder, the cars moved even more slowly, people – huddled and drenched – ran from tram to tram. As he arrived at headquarters the rain died down a little.

He parked almost at the same moment as Lentz.

'And what's with you? Over-zealousness not pay? I was sure you'd arrived an hour ago to annoy everybody,' Bartol said, climbing out of the car and stepping in a puddle.

'Nah, I went to the doctor's for a referral. My liver's playing up, or pancreas, I don't know.' He broke off; his grimace indicated he'd just suffered an attack of one of the above-mentioned organs. A moment later he concluded: 'He examined me and wrote out a referral in three months time... Can you imagine?'

'I can indeed. Don't worry, your wait may yet be rewarded,' he replied with amusement.

'Rewarded with what? Death? I went privately, had an ultrasound done of the entire abdominal cavity.'

'And how is the cavity?' Bartol tried to remain as serious as possible.

'And what! Apparently it's fine but who knows,' he snapped.

'Then go again in three months. It's always best to check. Internal control of the health service won't hurt.'

'You're right. Who knows what sort of equipment they had and what sort of a quack he was? Some medical student who's going to use my pancreas to learn which mistakes to avoid.' Lentz had started to regain his good mood.

Bartol waved it aside and didn't dare add that all Lentz had left to be examined was his head. He didn't want Lentz to go on leave right then. He decided to change the subject.

'I spoke to that granny who knew Mirosław Trzaska, but I didn't get to have a word with the son. She'd fed him some sedatives. The poor guy was asleep, might even still be asleep. Either way, if he wakes up he's to come here. He knew the murder victim, used to meet up with him, but was at a young people's rosary circle at the time.'

'That would even fit. Or they're all providing an alibi for each other. The rest of the neighbours, if you mean youngsters, also said they'd gone through a few Hail Marys and about three episodes of a TV programme in the neighbouring village. I went to check, it seems to tally. I also thought that the boy might have given a lift to one of them and been alone for a while but that appears impossible, they all went together. That's all,' he concluded in a normal, matter-of-fact tone, no longer pained, as if he'd forgotten about his recent ailments.

'I don't think it's anybody from there,' said Bartol after a while. 'No doubt we'll learn some Latin like you complain. There was a maxim on the glasses, too. I don't know what it means yet, but I'll find out.'

'I'm not sure it isn't all too much for me. Ordinary human foibles, love, jealousy, alcohol and – to top them all – money, that I understand but this?'

'You're not the only one. When you're done moaning, I'll begin. Let's hope this time it's going to be different.'

'Why? Because two corpses are better than one?'

'Maybe so, maybe so,' Bartol was unrelenting. 'Lentz, we're missing something, overlooking something. It's happened once which doesn't mean it's going to happen again.' He spoke as though trying to convince himself. 'He's leaving his signature. We can't read it yet but it's only a matter of time,' he said as they approached the entrance. 'We've got loads of work this time, masses of people to interrogate. I can't believe we won't find a thread to pull.'

'You trying to fill me with optimism or yourself?' asked Lentz, halting.

'The both of us,' assured Bartol with less conviction.

Lentz's expression hardly changed; he hadn't expected an answer.

'Then keep repeating it to me all day. Even mechanical work sometimes needs encouragement and there's a tedious search ahead of us. Like digging for whatever it is in a frigging haystack or whatever, and I don't feel all that good. What are you doing tomorrow?'

'I've lined up some interviews starting in the morning... ' Bartol didn't have time to finish.

'I'm talking about the evening, if nothing happens, which is unlikely, but one never knows...' Lentz added hesitantly.

Bartol was completely disoriented, and not only because of the sudden change of subject. He couldn't remember when they'd last met privately, if at all.

'I've nothing planned, or didn't anyway. If nothing happens, I'm open, why?'

'It's my birthday, my mother's in hospital and I feel like going out for a drink. I'm extending an invitation to you, no commitment, of course. We'll see how it goes tomorrow.'

'We'll see, but thanks, maybe it'll work out,' Bartol replied although he didn't quite know what to think of it. Did Lentz simply want to go out, or was it the start of a concentrated assault on his internal organs so that they'd be at least slightly abused before his next examination and wouldn't bring him shame by their good health?

Luckily, he didn't have time to give it any more thought. Maćkowiak was already waiting for them. As soon as they entered Maćkowiak stopped dialling and replaced the receiver.

'Hi. I've no energy left to make any more calls. It's the same over and over again. My God, he was such a good man, but nobody knows anything about any family.'

'Yet again. But that's almost impossible.' Bartol was surprised.

'Those who worked with him have no idea. He spent Christmas and Easter at work, organised various Christmas

Eve activities at Kaponier Roundabout and things like that...
I'll snoop around some more tomorrow but it's all so strange.
Is it still fallout from the war or are towns full of lonely people?
I've no idea. I was at a wedding recently – I've got distant family
in the east – and they had a small reception for a hundred and
eighty people. The closest family apparently... And you should
have seen the sausages and other home-cured meats.' He lost
himself in daydreams.

'You're joking,' said Lentz in astonishment.

'No, I'm not. I got some to take home with me. And was
scared of saying anything to anyone at the wedding because
when I called someone 'Mr' a couple of time all I heard was
– "Mr, Mr, I'm your uncle." And here? Is there an epidemic or
something?'

'I can't believe it either. Maybe in Mikulski's case. They were
pretty old and Mrs Mikulska, as far as I recall, was orphaned
before the war, but this Trzaska guy, I don't think so. How old
was he, in fact?' asked Bartol.

'Sixty-four. You're right, we've got to look. Maybe I'll start
with...' He didn't finish; Polek had burst into the room.

'It's peculiar, all this. A Poznań wino until he's fifty and after
fifty – the guardian angel of winos. A miracle.'

'What miracle?'

'What are you going on about?' All were equally surprised.

Looking at Polek, it was hard not to be amazed. And not
only because he was so excited and waving his arms around;
he looked somehow different, too. Bartol thought he'd treated
his hair to some hair gel or something equally sticky which
seemed absurd, bearing in mind how he'd made fun of Pilski
lately. All in all, he looked peculiar.

'This Trzaska...' Polek carried on breathlessly. 'Over half a
century of tiny offences then suddenly that's it. Besides, I'd have
thought that knocking it back for so long, his brain would have
been totally pickled but this guy here sobers up and sends out

emails. You tell me if that isn't a miracle? I even paid a visit to his girlfriend from the wino days.'

If it were possible to look any more surprised, they did so now. Bartol didn't ask when Polek had managed to do all this but simply stammered out:

'And?'

'And! I'm scared I'm going to have nightmares about her. She's still living on Staszic Street and has got a boyfriend now. They'd make a perfect pair of generators if you could draw energy from alcohol.' Polek glanced at his audience and added with a smile: 'She was surprised, too. Mirosław, whom everyone called Lalek and whom, in a tide of affection, she'd briefly registered at her place, had been dead for some time in her books. At least that's what she thought. Love had blossomed when he'd started working as a gravedigger but withered when he lost that job, too, because of his drinking. Which isn't easy considering drink used to be a way into that line of business. You know what it's like, you get sad, cold. Anyway, that was some fifteen years ago, she said. She had to throw him out because he drank without sharing when he had the job and she doesn't like that, not nice. She later heard that he was living at a station, first in Poznań then Warszawa. Some friend working on the railways had apparently seen him and apparently he'd become a real out-and-out drunkard. It's all in that vein. So if that's not a miracle, what is? Eight years of training, eight hectolitres of moonshine, the life of a vagabond and then a little house in the country and a successful steward? Idyllic, don't you think?'

'Olaf, are we talking about the same person?' Bartol finally asked.

'I wasn't the one who wrote out the domicile registration. There's a photograph – must be thirty years old – in his old ID and a current one in his new ID, personal details are the same. That hideous creature on Staszic Street must have held on to that apartment since just after the war, or so it seems. She remembered Lalek; his age and height tally. His appearance, judging by the way she looks, must have revived a bit but we can summon her, get her to identify him if she can.'

'She'll have to be summoned. I don't like it. Did you talk to anyone else who might have known him earlier?' asked Maćkowiak.

'No, she didn't know much about the guy she admitted to have registered – as an exception – but then it's open house at her place, for drinks. As it is, it's a good thing she remembers him at all. All her days seem to merge into one.' Then he added: 'There must have been something about him.'

Nobody said a word. Polek, as though making the most of the opportunity, quickly stood up.

'There's no point in what-ifs. We've got to check the wino link. I'll take care of it.' Saying this, he looked at himself in the window, pulled in his stomach and stuck out his pectoral muscles which, with a little kindness, could be called muscles. 'Maybe I'll find out some more. And keep an eye on that Pilski. I don't like characters in pink tie uniform. Did I tell you what I heard yesterday?'

'No.'

'I know something about people. I was walking past the boss's room, the door was ajar, and I heard him talking with Pilski. What a character. That dandy...'

'Olaf, were you eavesdropping at his door?' Bartol laughed.

'I wasn't eavesdropping, I was just passing by, very slowly passing by,' replied Polek, smoothing down his already smooth hair. 'That dandy must have been trying to facilitate something but our dear boss's deep bass fortunately rang out that, if there were any suspicions that it could be the same murderer, then all the more reason for him not to change anything. The choir's not wasted on him.'

'What choir and change what?' asked Lentz.

'The police choir, didn't you know we had one? And I don't know what the anything he's not going to change is. I was only passing by.' With an offended, haughty expression he looked at Bartol.

'We'll know sooner or later,' riposted Bartol.

'We'll know it's not without reason I've got such strong feelings about the shit. Bye.'

'Bye,' they replied simultaneously, their eyes turned towards Polek as he left. He didn't honour them with a glance.

'No point in what-ifs: for the time being we'll organise what we've got.'

Lentz and Maćkowiak nodded with vigour worthy of the weather outside.

The day brought nothing. Nothing but mud from an enormous puddle which Bartol brought into the house on his shoes. He'd parked in mud because that was the only space available. The alternative was fifty metres further down and he didn't opt for it. He felt tired, very tired, as usual after a load of paperwork and numerous talks with various people. Talks, all of which progressed in a similar fashion, like the drops of rain at the window which he watched as he reiterated the same questions.

He poured himself a glass of vodka, added water since that was all he had to hand. Tasted it. It was sufficiently strong and didn't taste too bad. He had enough vodka and only a little water but that didn't worry him too much. He could always leave a glass outdoors and it would fill up. He sat in the armchair and put his feet up on the coffee table. Started persuading himself that he'd only cover himself with a blanket for ten minutes then go to bed.

He was soon persuaded and slept there until morning.

The glass was nearly full.

'Did you see that man? When did he manage to slip in, it's only morning? The cathedral's just opened. Maybe he's a thief or something.'

'Nonsense. You shouldn't watch so much television. A thief with a huge camera around his neck! He's some kind of tourist.'

'Tourist? At this time of day? Look at him, he's a bit odd, as if there's something wrong with him.'

'I can't sleep recently either. He's a tourist, I tell you. Besides, how can you tell with his face hidden by that camera? He's taking a photograph of that toothless skull, like all the others. Go and ask him if you like, maybe he'll answer in some other language. You can have a chat.'

The man they were discussing tore his eyes away from his camera and smiled kind-heartedly at the nice ladies.

They briskly turned their heads away; they obviously didn't believe they were nice.

'I told you he's a tourist. They laugh at any old thing.'

'Aha.'

He arrived late after all. At Wilga Street, Magda's address. No more than twenty minutes, but still.

Not because he'd overslept, not because he'd spilt coffee on his newly pressed trousers. None of these things. Of a thousand stupid reasons he chose what must have been the stupidest. For a moment he thought he'd seen Malina in one of the overtaking cars. He hadn't seen her for a good eighteen months. He missed her, perhaps not like before, perhaps a little less, but enough to change lanes and follow the car. Why? In order to catch a glimpse of her, see what she looked like, whether she was happy. Perhaps she wasn't; perhaps, like him, she regretted things had turned out the way they had, that there was no going back. Perhaps just so, out of curiosity.

Despite the mist and the slippery road he finally caught up with the car. It hadn't been her; it hadn't even looked like her. It had cost him a good half hour. For half of Głogowska Street he couldn't do anything, couldn't accelerate because the entire right lane was kept for delivery vans unloading all sorts of goods, couldn't turn because turning was forbidden; he could do nothing but rage, and rage he did, first at everything, only then at himself.

At a standstill in the traffic jam on Dworcowy Bridge – which he could have avoided before – he called Maćkowiak. He was counting on his having found something out about the spectacles; last night, he was supposed to have visited the shelter where Trzaska had worked. Sad to say, Maćkowiak hadn't discovered much. As he might maliciously have expected, nobody remembered where those unfortunate glasses had come from. That is, some people did recall a woman optician bringing the glasses as a gift from an unidentified optical company, but she'd been so nondescript that nobody remembered her well. She'd even made out two prescriptions, but one of the men had lost his and the other had lost himself. He'd fallen in love, apparently, and been drinking out of love for a week; since he was in love from morning until night he drank from morning until night and since he loved to the point of oblivion, the chances of finding the prescription were poor.

The day had started badly.

To confirm this Bartol drove up to the tenement on Wilga Street. He'd got it right. It was almost the tallest in the street; furthermore, he was convinced the apartment was going to be on the top floor. It was. Even higher than the top floor, he thought, when he saw narrow stairs leading to what wasn't even a loft but a simple attic.

When the door opened, he was struck dumb.

He'd formed some sort of opinion of what he'd come up against. Since his own mother had hatched plans for them to meet – and not only once if he remembered correctly – the girl most likely had to be single. As for that, his mother knew how to conduct inquiries. The girl had also to be more or less his age. But here, in front of him, loomed a twentysomething young man, taller than Bartol by a head, in jeans and with a naked torso which could have belonged to a swimmer representing Poland.

'Hi, it's a good thing you're late.' The boy winked knowingly. 'Please, come in,' he added and pulled himself up even straighter.

Bartol still hadn't seen Magda but already knew any theory about a brother could be ruled out.

The day had started badly.

A moment later, from behind the boy's massive back appeared a small woman. He didn't see her face; she had dishevelled, wet hair, an odd shirt and an angry expression.

'Good morning,' she said over the young man's shoulder and, craning her head, addressed him: 'Didn't I by any chance say you weren't supposed to be here by now? I'm sorry, I think the alarm clock didn't go off,' she said to Bartol gently, then turned to the boy again: 'But let's not worry about that, it could still go off, couldn't it?!'

As she uttered the last sentence, Bartol had the impression she grew ten centimetres taller while the boy shrunk twenty.

'I only opened the door.'

'The point is you were supposed to have closed it a long time ago, from the outside. Who let you turn off the alarm? Get dressed and good bye.'

'I thought I'd wait and we'd have breakfast together.'

'You can have it with mummy, off you go, because...' She didn't have to finish; the boy was already in another room. 'I apologise once again. Please, do come in. Sit down and give me a minute.'

'Good morning' was all Bartol managed to say.

Taking off his jacket, he not only regretted having phoned, he regretted having come at all. In a blue sweater, after a long time scrutinising himself in the mirror. He may not have ironed the whole shirt but certainly the collar. And here? A naked athlete and a girl with wet hair. He was still in the hallway when the nearly two-metre boy made ready to leave. The boy tried to dally a little longer but the young woman stood in front of him; he didn't try too hard.

'All right, al lright, so now we can say goodbye,' she said opening the front door wide.

'I'll call?' he neither asked nor stated, in a low voice.

'Call,' she replied, a little more gently.

'It was super today and...' he added out loud. Bartol had no illusions; this, he was supposed to hear.

'I've changed my mind, don't call.' She didn't give the lad a chance to finish and slammed the door.

That's just the reaction Bartol could have foreseen. He knew the young man shouldn't have answered back but he had; now he wouldn't have it easy. He knew because of his own experience even though, observing from the side, he was a bit taken aback by the whole event.

'I'm sorry about the scene.' She apologised but didn't look in the least embarrassed. 'As Aristotle said: all animals tend to be sad after intercourse but a rooster crows.'

'He's young,' Bartol said very bewildered. He didn't know whether he was stating a fact or trying to be spiteful.

'I know, I know,' she answered quite naturally. 'Still too much sex in sex. I promised myself in the New Year: nobody under thirty, and what do we have?' she broke off, looking at Bartol. Bartol didn't know what they had. 'April!' she added. 'Manual-steering and being an all-knowing authority is all well and good, but for how long?' Bartol had no idea for how long. 'For a moment,' again she didn't fail to let him know.

'Looks like he's counting on more than a moment.' He didn't know why he was joining in the discussion or defending the youngster. Male solidarity?

'Oh, I know, he's probably still got the watch from his first Holy Communion, so time doesn't fly by for him in the same way, but what can you talk about in the long run with a horny student?'

Bartol didn't know how to answer and didn't want to know what they talked about in the short run. He didn't say anything. He merely wondered whether or not to tell his mother all this; he'd like to have seen her face.

'I'm sorry, this conversation's totally unnecessary. Please sit down. What can I get you to drink?'

'Some water.' He surprised himself. Usually, nearly always, regardless of the time of day, he asked for coffee. He probably wanted to compose himself; besides, he didn't intend to stay long. She handed him a large green glass full of water, excused herself for a moment and went to the bathroom.

He was left waiting much longer than a moment, so began to look around. To his amazement, he had to admit the climb would be worth it, even on a daily basis.

Simple shapes, simple colours. Height and airiness.

Thick ceiling beams and wooden columns naturally delineated the open space without the appearance of doing so. He studied and admired them a long time. They managed to support the roof and give the entire apartment a friendly atmosphere, as if in gratitude that someone had appreciated and smoothed them down.

He gazed at all this with a touch of envy. Next to this, his own apartment looked like a crammed matchbox which little people had stuffed with tiny pieces of junk they'd found here and there.

Here everything was different. Everything was modern, angular, spacious and still too small to dominate the space.

Well planned out.

Some tiny treasures collected during her life or from her travels, but without unnecessary ornaments except, perhaps, a little mole – from a Czech fairy tale – against a background of urban chimneys. Bartol wasn't well up on contemporary art but liked the painting. He didn't know why.

It would probably have been too peaceful here if it weren't

for the enormous triangular alcove stretching across an entire wall and filled with books. Tightly filled, up to the last centimetre. Books standing, lying, at a diagonal. Faded spines of old fascinations interspersed with loud covers of new ones, without rule or regulation.

His eyes fixed on the balcony door. He hadn't expected a balcony in this attic but there was one, and a large one at that – not even a balcony, a terrace.

The view, too, was amazing and this at the beginning of April, on a rainy day. Roofs of the surrounding tenements, little balconies and the tower of the church of Mary the Queen with its enormous clock. Now, in the faint mist, all this looked wondrous, even without it being summer or night.

Beautiful, quite large trees grew in huge flowerpots.

'They're going to flower. Cherry trees.' He'd been staring and hadn't noticed her standing behind him. 'Only another month and they'll be covered in pink flowers. I can't wait. Perhaps I'll wizen up by then, who knows?'

He turned. He could forget his first impression.

Her still-wet hair didn't bother him anymore; she'd pinned it back on the top of her head in some intricate way which, combined with her upturned nose as though from a Japanese anime, looked rather amusing. She was slim, shapely and in a pretty cool outfit. A few minutes ago he almost hadn't known what that hunk had been doing here; now he didn't want to know.

'All right, go on.' She was the first to speak. 'But please remember what I said yesterday: as many details as possible. You're either not going to squeeze anything out of the text itself, or you'll squeeze out whatever you want. And surely that's not what this is all about. We need a background to the crime.'

'How do you know a crime's involved?'

'Your mother told me her son was a detective. Not one from films but a real one, an ordinary one.'

He didn't want to ask what that was supposed to mean. Why not 'one of those'?

'So we've got the preliminaries out of the way,' he said without enthusiasm.

'Indeed we have. I'm all ears.'

They sat on the sofa. He took a while gathering his thoughts without taking his eyes off some small orange cups, as though they might help him. He didn't want to look at her. For the second time he caught himself trying to read the writing on the t-shirt she'd slipped on. He couldn't decipher it; maybe because she wasn't wearing a bra or maybe because the lettering was too small?

'A man was murdered in January.' He tried to concentrate but without success. 'Next to him were... well, maybe not next to him... but anyway, there were some Latin maxims, maybe it was a coincidence... but I don't think so, apart from that we have to check...' He heard himself getting muddled but, fortunately, she didn't interrupt him and listened carefully. 'One was on a red piece of cloth which was partially covering him. It had *Dum spiro spero* embroidered on it – meaning, as long as there's life, there's hope.'

'I know what it means. Do you have a photo of the man?'

'No, I don't.' It hadn't occurred to him, nor had he thought it necessary.

'I told you: details. What would you say if you saw the familiar sign: a cigarette with a line through it?'

He didn't feel like guessing games or playing at being a smart arse, but answered: 'No smoking.'

'Good, and, for example, on a poster at a doctor's surgery with a picture of a pair of lungs above it?'

'Smoking's hazardous to health.'

'To all intents and purposes the same, yet communicating something different. In one case a forbidding order, in the other a warning. I couldn't put it any more clearly. Was he naked? Was he lying, sitting?'

'Naked and supine, covered only with the red cloth.'

'Covered up, covered over or maybe only his privates were covered: which was it?' she asked expectantly and calmly, although with a slightly know-it-all expression.

'The material was draped over him at the hips,' he started answering like a schoolboy in class or at one of his mother's hearings.

'Like in paintings, those found in churches?'

'You could say that.' They were probably misjudging each other.

'And where was the writing?' she asked a fraction more gently.

'The lettering was half a centimetre tall, ran the length of the cloth and, at first glance, was almost imperceptible.' He decided to anticipate her questions.

'Like for the initiated. This is getting more and more interesting. I'd best start noting it down.' She got up, walked over to the shelf and picked up a notebook and pen. 'Not everything can be explained straight away, without material. Please bring a photo next time unless it's strictly confidential.'

He hadn't thought about a 'next time' even though she knew what she was talking about, knew what to ask, knew her stuff, no doubt, quite apart from her conceited tone. He needed someone like that. She was even pretty, average but pretty. Especially when the auburn strands of drying hair, which she kept brushing off her forehead, slipped out of the hair-clasp.

'It's not as confidential as all that,' he said after a while. 'I won't be able to leave the photographs with you but I can certainly show you.'

'No problem. I'm not going to put them up on my shelf. I'll only sketch a copy.' She smiled. 'I understand that, for some reason, you're looking for some symbolic connections. A dead body also holds many meanings, especially when it's naked. Let's say that's the point and the cloth isn't important, it's only there to cover what's unworthy and indecent.' She glanced at Bartol. 'Just don't be offended,' she added, laughing and squinting comically. 'That's not entirely my private opinion although I do agree that Nature could have come up with something a bit different, but never mind.'

'Don't worry, I'm not offended. I like my unworthy parts, I've grown used to them.' He smiled for the first time that day; she was laughing, too. She sat down on the sofa cross-legged and picked up her cup of coffee.

The atmosphere grew more relaxed.

'Maybe it'll be easier if we call each other by our first names. I know your mother – we're on first name terms – but you and I are more or less the same age...'

'Maciej.' He smiled, extending his hand. He, too, had been finding it hard even though he didn't generally like cutting the distance. This time, however, it had seemed a little forced.

'I felt awkward suggesting it. After all, you are a detective, ordinary or not. Anyway, I'm Magda.' She extended her hand. 'Shame it's under such circumstances but I'm pleased we've met. I was supposed to have dropped something off to you from Daniela at one point but didn't have the time or something, I can't remember anymore... But back to the point, seriously now. I promise. Nakedness, especially in a dead body, is associated with man returning to God the way he came, without any sign of having lived on this earth, the way he was born. It might not mean anything but it might, especially alongside a maxim like that. And as for the writing, it's an ancient saying – no-one knows quite whose.'

'Seneca's, apparently,' he broke in.

'Apparently. It would be in character. Reflections like that can also be found in the Bible. It follows the principle I mentioned previously – that if we look we'll find everything there. I've just remembered the Book of Ecclesiastes: "Anyone who is among the living has hope" and then there's something like: "Whatever your hand finds to do, do it with all your might, for in the grave, where you are going, there is neither working nor planning nor knowledge nor wisdom" – I can't remember exactly but I'll get it ready. Anyway, it's vaguely something to do with hope. They were often found together, a corpse and words like that, or more simply such an inscription on a tombstone. Sometimes as a warning or admonition to the living, something like: anything might happen when the head's full of dreams – that was the girls' version – or the men's, while the cards are being played.'

'Thank you, you've explained it clearly. A bunch of dried sunflowers was found in the same house with a note attached to it: *Expecto donec veniat.* '

She said nothing for a long while.

'Maybe you want some coffee? Because I'd like some more. You've presented me with some interesting puzzles. That's good because I thought I was going to get rusty.'

'I'll have some, too, now.'

She made her way towards the kitchen and again set the espresso machine into motion. His eyes didn't leave her. He liked the way she moved.

'Can you dry sunflowers?' she said after a while.

'Yes, like everything else, I suppose, but they don't look very nice after six months. That's one of the reasons we think they might have some sort of significance, seeing as somebody kept them for so long, especially with the note. Although they're not very symbolic, apparently.'

'I see you've already done some homework. Well done. But they do appear in various images, generally associated with the rising sun, hope and so on. At a push they'd suit the words, I'll check in a minute. I don't know where I know it from but I think it's Job who did the moaning.'

'Yes, it's from the Book of Job. Chapter 14, verse 14.'

'Oh, thank you.' She put her cup of coffee aside and started jotting.

'Does it bring anything to mind?' he asked.

'No, or not very quickly. There are a lot of possibilities. One could concoct rebuses, puzzles, stick things together in various ways. I have to think all this over quietly. I need more facts.'

'Okay, I'll bring the photographs and more information about the circumstances in which all this took place. But that's not all. There was another murder yesterday.'

Her eyebrows shot up, eyes opened wide; she froze with that expression for a long while. Then nervously brushed aside her hair, got up from the sofa and started circling the room.

It seemed to Bartol she was behaving just like him but double-quick. First, surprise then, a nervous about turn.

'This isn't funny,' she said after a while. 'In fact, it wasn't funny from the start, but I approached it like a puzzle not bearing in mind what had actually happened. I'm never going to grow up, never going to get any wiser, there's nothing but nonsense in my head! Isn't there a shred of empathy in me? These aren't drawings on a wall! A man has died!' She was talking to herself, her voice growing louder and louder. 'And now another one, and more dicta. There has to be, that's why you're here. What were they?'

'*Speculator adstad de sui,* on the frame of a pair of glasses.'

'I'm not going to make up what it means, I don't know right now. A literal translation's not going to give us anything. It could be an abbreviation of something. I need time. I'll put all my work aside today and look up everything I can. The yogurts can wait.'

'I didn't want to spoil your day too much. I'm sorry.'

'Rubbish. Besides, it's my hobby. I search for information about various products in a number of foreign language newspapers for money. Open source intelligence, nothing interesting, it can wait. What am I saying, not it can wait, it has to wait. You know why? You know what I think? I don't know whether I've seen too many films or it's your expression, but two's not enough.'

'What are you thinking?' He was afraid of her answer.

'The numeral two also means something of course – development, for example, equilibrium, man and woman or, more ominously, light and shadow, irreconcilable opposites and so on. But it isn't a divine number; the divine number's three. The most beautiful of the primaries. Three is greatness, light, holiness. The beginning, middle, end for the Pythagoreans; the Trinity for Christians. In other words, for everybody it signifies perfection. I could talk about it for hours. I might be oversensitive but I can't stop thinking otherwise.'

'It's a bit unprofessional, but I couldn't help thinking I was witnessing some sort of drama either.'

'Exactly, a play in three acts. To put it grandiloquently, these are ominous premonitions. You know what, there's no time. This somebody has it all planned out to the last detail and is following a script. He's written it himself and, unlike us, knows how it goes. With premeditation, as I think you put it. How much time elapsed between the first murder and the second?'

'Three months, more or less.'

'So maybe we've got a bit of time still.'

She approached the wall of books, gazed at it for a long time then said: 'That's probably not enough. I'll have to go out today, after all. Let's meet tonight. Please bring the photographs.'

'All right,' he answered, totally compliant as he got up. 'What time can I call?' he added, now a little more spitefully.

'Whenever you like. If the worst comes to the worst you can always leave a message. After all, I could be in the loo. I don't know and don't want to know how other people resolve the problem, but I don't go around carrying the phone around my neck. I promise I'll call back.'

He made towards the hallway. As he pulled on his jacket, he glanced at Magda. Perhaps she was even pretty, perhaps even more than averagely so. Opening the door, he was the first to speak: 'Good, I'll see you soon. I wish you success.'

'Thank you. Not very romantic circumstances but it's nice meeting you.'

'You too.'

She leaned towards him but stopped mid-way.

'We don't know each other all that well, sorry.' She extended her hand.

'Not at all.' He squeezed her hand, a little too hard; she was very slender.

He walked down the stairs slowly but still had to halt on the half-landing. As always, when angry with himself. He started staring at the floor.

Who'd put lino on old, wooden stairs instead of restoring them? When were people in this country going to start respecting what there was left? Why didn't anyone think about it?

Why did it always have to be like this? Why did it always turn out that she had to be right, that sooner or later it turned out that he should have listened to her? Why did even her convoluted grumbling always make sense? After all, he could have dropped in on the girl and talked to her earlier, perhaps he'd have got further, known more? Where did he get this narrow mentality from? Who was he trying to spite?

But maybe that's not what it was about; maybe he could have returned that damned dictionary and everything would have turned out differently?

Now what? He wasn't going to compete with that boy and besides, he was going to be a father soon.

For a change, he ran down the rest of the stairs two at a time. He no longer cared about the way they looked. He wanted to run away without really knowing from what.

He nearly knocked over an old woman who passed him in the doorway.

The mist had started to lift. You could almost see it rising and dispersing as it tried to reach clouds which hung obligingly low as they consented to hide the city from the sun. The weather was still inclement. It was best not to expose oneself to it. Bleak thoughts, making the most of the darkness and damp, clung to each other more readily than usual. Cars moved along even more sluggishly as though, apart from eternally red lights, they increasingly felt the resistance of the air, heavy with grey dampness.

Halfway between Wierzbięcice in Wilga and the station, Bartol stopped thinking about anything whatsoever. His head began to ache pitilessly: because of the wavering air pressure, diagnosed the radio cheerfully. He agreed with the diagnosis and found some painkillers in his glove compartment. Luckily, he arrived at headquarters relatively quickly or as quickly as it took for the pain to ease off. He didn't know what to put it down to – the pill, which he rarely took, or the building which always acted as a remedy for his own problems.

There, he heard that a certain Franciszek Konopka was already waiting for him. For a moment, he couldn't recall any Franciszek. Until Mrs Regina Konopka suddenly appeared in front of his eyes and, of course, Franciszek. Bartol wondered how long he'd been waiting. He ran up the stairs, jostling somebody again; he didn't know whom he apologised to.

'Good morning. Maciej Bartol.' Out of breath, he greeted the boy already seated in the interview room. 'Sorry I'm late but I'm glad to see you're awake,' he added in a friendly tone as he removed his jacket.

'Good morning,' the boy merely muttered back, and lowered his head again.

Bartol wondered when Franciszek had developed this reaction of turning in on himself. Was it before the huge pimples had appeared on his face, followed by the scars which served as a reminder of badly treated acne?

He thought about himself, about his skin. What would have happened if he hadn't spent many humiliating hours at the beautician's? He remembered how he'd tried to flee the first time; he hadn't got very far. His mother had been in the waiting room. At the time, he'd thought she was spying on him; he hadn't borne in mind the fact that she knew him very well, since he was born.

He hung up his jacket and started questioning the boy.

'You know what's happened. Can you tell me any more about Mirosław Trzaska? Apparently you were friends?'

'I wanted to be but my mother wouldn't let me.'

'Why not?' He wasn't surprised.

'I don't know,' he mumbled.

'It's not going to be easy,' he thought. Franciszek was young, with complexes; he probably hadn't dared bring 'one of those' home, or any other. That's probably why he went to bed with the hens. He decided to start with that.

'I was looking at your hens yesterday. It's the first time I've seen anything like it. They're beautiful. I especially couldn't tear my eyes away from the small cockerel. He looked aggressive.'

'Did he?' Franciszek suddenly came to life. 'It's a Japanese fighting breed. He was hard to get hold of. It was entirely by chance. The rest are crested and green-legged hens. It was Mirek's favourite, too, that cockerel. Valour and beauty rolled into one!'

'True. There was something of the Uhlan about him. What else did he say?' Bartol already knew he'd knocked one wall down, not to say the henhouse.

'He justified my mother saying that, in her own way, she was worried. I was a late child, you know, my older brother died on a motorbike when I was little. But he also said I ought to do something with my life, become more independent, get out of the house a bit, that I ought to go to school again. I was good at technical college but my mother got ill after my father died. I only had a year left but somehow didn't finish.'

Bartol felt sure she'd fallen ill with blood pressure.

'He nearly convinced me once,' Franciszek continued of his own accord, 'and I told my mother. She fell into such a rage we had to call an ambulance. She screamed saying I wanted to leave her, send her to her grave just like my father did. Although, you know, he'd died earlier. She didn't let me visit him later, kicked up terrible rows, screamed he must be some sort of a pervert, that they were everywhere. I preferred not to listen so I let it go. Besides, he hadn't been quite himself recently, since his dog went missing. Harpsichord was found three days later but Mirek seemed out of sorts.'

'The dog was called Harpsichord?' laughed Bartol.

'Good, isn't it? He'd found it when it was a puppy. It had whined so much which is why he called it that, so he told me. He adored the dog.'

'When did you last see Mr Trzaska?' Bartol asked as a formality.

'Three days ago. I met him in a shop. We even had a pretty long conversation. He said he'd thought of a strategy.' He started smiling to himself. 'I was to tell my mother the European Union pays more per hectare if you pass your final school exams. She'd have believed it too, because she thinks people from the Union are stupid enough for that sort of thing, and since they're handing out money anyway they might hand out some more. It wouldn't have been a complete lie because I might have learned something else and got something out of it. She's now ready to sell all the land.' He grew pensive. 'And then? We agreed I'd get all the papers ready and he'd sort it out because I don't really know where to go. I've lost the knack of town.'

'Do you have any idea who might have done it? Did Mr Trzaska have any enemies?'

'Mirek! Sorry, Mr Trzaska. He said he hated any titles to his name. He told me to call him that himself.' He reflected. 'Enemies, no. Nor burglars – because he didn't have anything.'

Something seemed wrong to Bartol. Konopka was confirming everything Trzaska's colleagues at work and a platoon of homeless people had said about him. But it wasn't in character with the Trzaska of fifteen years ago and with what Polek had discovered.

'Did Mr Mirosław have any family?'

'Everybody's got some sort of family.' Franciszek pondered and after a while added: 'But Mirek never spoke about it. He lived here alone and hardly anybody visited him. He once said that you can start everything in life anew, that you can become an entirely new person. And maybe he'd started anew but I didn't ask why he'd finished with his old life. That's how it looked to me anyway. There must have been an important reason. Everybody's got problems, maybe he had big problems.'

Bartol got up and started to pace around the room nervously. Finally, he walked up to the window, stared out without seeing.

He was furious with himself; why hadn't he thought of it sooner? What the young man had said was obvious, after all. Hence this altruism, hence this asceticism. He'd experienced something in life and was now doing penance. What for? Why under a different name? He had to find out as soon as possible. There wasn't any point in looking for Mirosław Trzaska's family, Mirosław Trzaska's friends, Mirosław Trzaska himself because they'd probably never be found. They had to look for someone who knew the man before he became Mirosław Trzaska. And right away. Maybe something connected the real one to Mikulski. Yes, that would be the clue he was looking for; of that he was certain.

He turned and looked at Franciszek Konopka, who'd lowered his head again. Again, he felt sorry for the boy. He was going to carry on driving his mother and her friends to rosary-TV parties from Thursday to Thursday. And curl in on himself even more. All that would be left would be pimples, a bad bite and hens who don't give a hoot.

He reflected for a while, and suddenly the solution came all by itself. There was always a solution, so his mother had taught him. Now it could prove true.

'How old are you, Franciszek?'

'Twenty-three,' the young man replied in surprise.

'Trzaska was right, start studying.' Bartol purposely addressed the lad by his first name so as to encourage him. 'Pass your exams, then study zoology or some other –ology. Get some air.' He saw the boy come to life, only to drop his head again a moment later.

'I wouldn't know how... I've forgotten everything... I don't even know where I'm supposed to go. I don't know how to approach receptions and offices. My mother always goes everywhere.'

'A good thing she likes walking. Listen, I know somebody who'll do that for you at the beginning. She likes that sort of thing. She's got the right approach and a few acquaintances in the right places. She'd get to those offices with her eyes shut.'

Bartol went up to the jacket hanging on his chair and pulled out his wallet. He kept the business card in one of the compartments as a souvenir. At last it would come in useful. On the business card appeared: *Daniela Bartol – mother*, and their home number.

He remembered how he'd had to go to the post office to collect the recorded letter that came with it. He'd laughed. The note was just as he'd expected: seeing as he hadn't deigned to phone for a week, maybe he'd forgotten the number; if so, she was reminding him about herself and politely informing him that she'd had a hundred such business cards printed at the same time because there was a good offer and, well, just in case.

He glanced at the business card once more and handed it to Franciszek.

'This woman will help you with everything. She once taught at a secondary school and an extramural school, too. She's my mother. I'll tell her about you, but don't dare not phone. It's not worth it, I tell you, because she'll find and force you anyway. You know something about that, too. Are we agreed?'

'Yes,' replied Franciszek Konopka in a not altogether certain tone, but Bartol was convinced he'd phone.

Saying goodbye, he extended his hand.

'Well, good luck. Wait and see – you'll cope.'

'Thank you. You, too. He was a good man.'

'I'll try, just like you.'

Franciszek Konopka left the room, grasping the business card. Right after him left Bartol, who'd decided to find Lentz as quickly as possible. Lentz wasn't to waste time searching for Mirosław Trzaska's non-existent family. And Bartol wasn't to forget to phone his mother and warn her or he'd have to rush off to the post office again, or whatever else she'd come up with.

In the briefing room he saw Pilski standing, all the rest sitting. Olaf Polek was studying a stain on the ceiling; Maćkowiak had reserved another stain – this one on the wall – for himself; and Piotr Lentz was, with interest, examining his new tumour which had assumed the form of a tiny mole on his wrist, which had been growing since he was born and could grow even more at any moment so clearly had to be observed.

'I'll collect the report of the autopsy, and you produce the plan of action and deliver it,' Pilski finally said.

He tried to sound resolute, although Bartol wasn't sure whether there wasn't a hint of pity or amusement in his voice. 'Call me any time if I'm needed.'

And, as in confirmation, his phone rang. Yet again they had a chance to hear a new ringtone – this time bells chiming.

Pilski swiftly said goodbye as he tried to find the phone still ringing in his pocket. He didn't find it and gong after gong continued to resound behind the closed door.

'How's he supposed not to crack up with those bells clanging from morning till night? His Sovereign Highness, the much-needed one,' Polek summed up.

'Let him be, Olaf. He's not cracking up, he's calm. You said yourself that if prosecutors got more involved in investigations they'd be more useful in court. What do you want from him?' asked Lentz.

'That's just it. I don't want anything from him. And I don't want him to want anything from me. He's treating us like little boys. The great adviser. It's best he doesn't hang around here. Why doesn't he just get married and go home?'

'It's when he gets married that he's not going to want to rush home,' laughed Maćkowiak.

Bartol knew Polek was preparing himself for an argument about nothing, and decided to break up the banter.

'We're not going to go into the beauty of married life right now. I think we've got to search elsewhere. At least for Mirosław Trzaska's family.'

Everyone looked at Bartol.

'Don't be surprised, Maćkowiak, that you haven't learned anything from his colleagues. They all probably say he didn't have a family and the documents haven't revealed anything.'

'As I said, nothing's changed,' Maćkowiak replied. 'Everyone I've spoken to has nothing but vague recollections.'

A faint smile appeared on Bartol's face; he waited for what was to follow. And was rewarded.

'Everyone's just guessing,' continued Maćkowiak, quoting Pilski's words with vengeance. 'Assumptions which get us nowhere,.' He now spoke seriously. 'Mere gossip – he could have been an alcoholic, could have been homeless, his wife could have left him. He didn't say anything, they didn't ask anything and got used to it. Everyone's got a good or very good opinion of him. He worked exceptionally hard, apparently, and was devoted to helping others. Someone like that's a rarity. Everyone says the same thing,' added Maćkowiak. 'And they also say he was very effective, never wanted to be promoted even though he apparently received interesting propositions from town. I looked through his computer. I didn't know there were so many organisations – both governmental and others – that can be milked for money. Apart from the mail there's nothing interesting. Nor did he seek personal happiness on the internet, and apart from a couple of pages on dog shows, same thing all the time.'

'I'm not one to believe in such saints. In Calcutta maybe, but not here,' Polek summed up sleepily. 'Besides, I'm surprised Lalek left his comfort zone just like that. He suddenly fell away from that drunken piece of skirt and had a revelation. Why? Because she threw him out of a stinking dump!'

'You know what, Olaf, it's rare but this time your cynicism might be well-founded. I interrogated the son of the woman who knew Trzaska.'

'Mrs Konopka has been good enough to phone us three times already because she doesn't feel well and can't wait for her son,' Polek added again.

'She'll be all right. Getting back to the point, the lad knew Trzaska a little and had a couple of pretty interesting reflections on the subject. He never asked him about anything either, but had the impression that Trzaska had started a new life. That would fit somehow. We have to find out who he was in his other life and what sonorous name he used.'

'There's nothing in the documents about him changing his name,' said Lentz, astonished.

'And I don't think he did change it. He simply borrowed it from Mr Traska, perhaps when he was still alive, perhaps after his death. I don't think he needed to kill him. Trzaska most probably drank himself to death and was buried at the state's cost, an unidentified victim in one of our larger cities with a heated station. That's my guess, but as far as I can see it's the only way it all holds together. Acquaintances who only knew him by the nickname of Lalek didn't connect him with the surname. And our

Mirosław very much wanted to start a new life and I think he did. For a long time he was successful, until someone found him out and reminded him of the life he'd wanted to forget. I think the writing on the glasses was enough to refresh his memory.'

'All right, if he'd managed to change everything once, why didn't he hole up somewhere again?' asked Lentz. 'He probably knew nothing good was waiting for him.'

'But maybe he was waiting for it all to end. Maybe he'd had enough and didn't want to go on hiding. Maybe he wanted to put an end to his penance? We won't know until we find out who he was, and that's what we've got to concentrate on.'

'That, we can find out. I invited the woman from Staszic Street to come here so we'll soon learn a bit more. It's all a bit convoluted but if she doesn't recognise him from the photographs, you're right and that's it,' said Polek. 'Maćkowiak, you go and check our man's fingerprints. Maybe the state's already charged him before. I don't believe in such saints.'

'And you might be right, Olaf. We'll find out what he was guilty of,' agreed Bartol.

'Good. Have you got anything for me? Because I've still got hell of a lot of people to question. They're all saying pretty much the same thing at the moment but since he wasn't such a saint maybe somebody will remember something. Am I to ask about that Lalek?' Maćkowiak made sure.

'No harm in it,' answered Bartol, then turned to Polek: 'You talked to the doctor. Did he mention anything else of interest?'

'Not really anything we don't already know. Oh, he did say we have to catch that mongrel which is wandering around because it probably bit him in the ankle once he was dead. There are traces of bites, the pathologist said, an animal's bites, most probably those of a small dog, but it has to be verified. I've already phoned the local police, they're going to grab it. I'm not going to catch it. The only animals I like live in tins. Besides, I was once bitten by a dog.'

'You're scared of a little dog,' laughed Bartol. 'Anyway, the dog's called Harpsichord, pretty funny, don't you think?'

'Funny or not, I've had a hang-up since childhood. And that includes Harpsichord! Besides, I don't intend to be a dog-catcher. That lousy job's not for me. I prefer the job I've got.'

'Okay, nobody's telling you to be one. The dog probably wanted to wake the man up or knew something bad had happened, that's why it was howling. Who knows, maybe it was grieving,' Lentz reflected. 'I'll take care of it.'

'Good. The pathologist's bound to be right but it needs checking out,' agreed Bartol. 'Olaf, when you've spoken to Trzaska's former girlfriend, find other people who knew him and find out what happened to Lalek. The rest of you know what we've got to do. I'll gather all the findings and probably get it all down on paper right here.'

They talked a little longer, then Bartol was left alone. Two hours later, Lentz phoned.

'I never thought I'd see anything like it. We've got the dog. It wasn't easy but we've got it. They're exceptionally cunning, those country mongrels, but we managed,' he said excitedly.

'And?' Bartol was struck dumb; somehow he hadn't expected to be talking about the dog.

'It's a good thing it bit him. I'm with it at the vet's right now.'

'What are you going on about? What do you mean: "It's a good thing it bit him'?" You were supposed to go to the lab with it, not the vet's. Have you hurt it or something?' he asked, annoyed.

'I've already been to the lab but that's not it. Its ear was terribly grazed, I felt sorry for it...'

Bartol moved the receiver away from his ear and seriously considered hanging up, pretending they'd been cut off. But he didn't; after all, it was Lentz he was talking to, not Polek.

'And you know what? The dog hadn't been injured fighting over a bitch, there was a tattoo on its ear.'

'You're joking, the dog was a thoroughbred,' said Bartol. The conversation didn't cease to astound him.

'It's not a thoroughbred, although I do know some breeds which really do look like mongrels. Don't laugh. Maybe that's an overly long preamble to say there's something written on its ear...'

'You must be joking!' Bartol couldn't force more out.

'Why do you keep accusing me of joking? Are you mistaking me for somebody else?'

'Sorry, Piotr, I forgot about your birthday.' Whenever he was on edge the strangest things came to mind out of the blue. Like now.

'Listen, what's happening to you? We've arranged to meet this evening as it stands. I haven't been waiting around since the early hours of the morning expecting a birthday card. You must be curious to know what he's got written. You'll have to wait a bit, I'm afraid. My vet's no sadist. He wants to see to the wounds before shaving Harpsichord's ear so we can read the rest. What can be seen now is the word *Oportet*. Not the name of a breeder, as you might guess.'

'How long will it take?' asked Bartol, totally disorientated.

'Not long! I'll call you straight away, although I'm no longer sure I did the right thing.'

'How many times do you want me to apologise? It's not an obvious thing to do, write on a dog.'

'I'll be at the station in about half an hour. We'll talk. Maybe I'll be able to find out a bit more by then and you'll have time to gather your wits.'

Bartol sat down, one hand supporting his head, the other rubbing his brow. He rubbed hard as if the massage would help.

He now recalled what Konopka had said about the dog disappearing. He'd apparently been gone for three days, after which Trzaska hadn't been himself.

Had Trzaska known what it was all about? Had he understood the message? His last days at work hadn't been different from previous days. Had he come to terms with, or simply waited for, what was to come? Did he guess what lay behind those words?

Bartol couldn't answer any of these questions. He tried to call Magda. She didn't pick up.

He waited for her to call back.

She didn't call, either then or all afternoon.

The vet also took his time. Lentz, who really did appear within an hour, had no intention of hurrying him, stubbornly maintaining that it clearly had to be this way. Bartol respected this, although he didn't quite understand. He didn't intend to argue. Nor did he say that he didn't particularly feel like going out that day. They arranged to meet.

Walking down the corridor, he passed the woman from Staszic Street. He hadn't met her before but was sure it was her. She was as sober as she could be. There was no waft of alcohol. No smell, but evidence of it was there: old, worn down shoes; a jacket neither first- nor even second-hand; bright, clumsily applied lipstick. As bright as the signs on shops selling the cheap wine which destroyed the people and tenements of Staszic Street like Russian vine.

And as he expected, she didn't recognise Mirosław Trzaska on the photographs, although the other man had been handsome, too.

They had to wait.

Luckily, Lentz didn't want greetings or presents. They were to meet at Stary Rynek in a bar on Zamkowa Street. Bartol still had time to go home, change and leave his car. He ordered a taxi and tried getting through to Magda again. She didn't answer. He was furious with her and with himself. He shouldn't have trusted her. He shouldn't have.

He took his time leaving. As it turned out, the taxi driver took even more time. It was drizzling. Cold droplets found their way beneath Bartol's eyelids and behind his collar, and the wind under his jacket. Nobody felt like going for a walk.

It was even worse in the taxi when it finally did arrive, but at least it wasn't windy. The driver must have loved his work; he talked incessantly, regardless of whether anyone was listening. And everything caused him pain: his neck, legs, life. Maybe that's why he hadn't washed his car for so long.

When Bartol finally arrived at Zamkowa Street, his mother called. He glanced at his watch, oh, well. He remembered what he'd forgotten. Now he didn't massage his forehead as he'd done all day but slapped it as hard as he could. Franciszek.

'Hello, hello,' his mother began as though amicably.

'Hi, mum,' he replied, grimacing.

'I guess you haven't guessed why I'm calling?' She couldn't see him, but from the note of satisfaction in her voice he knew her expression.

'I can but timidly imagine.'

'Meaning, those schools weren't for nothing. Praiseworthy indeed. But I'm only a modest Polish teacher, believe it or not. And if it weren't for the fact that I've been particularly sensitive to this unique stutter of yours since you learned to speak, I'd probably hang up.'

'I'm sorry. Can you help him in any way? He's got a Cerberus at home, not an angel and speech therapist rolled into one like I do. Try to understand, mum.'

'I do. Can't you guess from whom you inherited both your intelligence and wit? Occasionally, of course, because you've clearly taken a break this afternoon.'

'Thank you so much anyway. I forgot. These things happen.'

'It would be simpler if you didn't forget and hadn't exposed me to a twenty-minute conversation about nothing, just to extract what it's all about from the shy young man. The patience of this angel might run out, too. For you, of course, because the boy I'll take care of.'

'Thanks. How can I make it up to you?'

'Buy yourself some lecithin; it's good for the memory. Bye.'

'Bye.'

That wasn't too bad. It could have been far worse, and taken longer.

He entered the bar. It was crowded for the middle of the week. He saw Lentz at the counter, drinking something and sending a message. Bartol had grown unused to places like this. Crowds, smoke and, as usual, a shabby-looking counter, the more shabby the more besieged. He had no idea why Lentz had chosen this place; it was more suitable for the end of a pub crawl rather than the beginning. Everybody here could be divided into two categories: those still looking around and those no longer looking around.

As in life.

He walked up to Lentz; or rather, squeezed into the tiny free space next to him. He smiled to himself thinking that Maćkowiak wouldn't fit.

'Hi, I'm glad you've come. What will you have to drink? I'm buying.' Lentz glanced at the barman. It looked like they knew each other, which surprised Bartol a little.

'A gin and tonic for me, please,' Bartol replied, studying the slivers of lemon floating in Lentz's glass. He was pleased. It didn't look as if this was going to be a heavy drinking session; Lentz was clearly intent on weakening his organs slowly, without damaging his health.

'I've got news from the vet. The writing says: *Quam Oportet*. But that's not all, there's still more. He says we have to wait till tomorrow. Does it mean anything to you?'

'The same as all the others. Regardless of where they were written. I spoke to a girl this morning who was supposed to check but she hasn't ru...' He hadn't finished the sentence before he heard a familiar tune. He looked at his phone.

'Incredible. Talk of the devil. I'll just take this, ok?'

'Of course.'

'Hello,' he answered in a slightly formal, perhaps even offended tone.

'Hello, hello. I see you called. My phone was off. I didn't want to get distracted, it was going well. I spent practically the whole day buried in old books. Where are you?'

'Zamkowa Street.' He didn't know whether he'd done the right thing. Lentz, seeing his embarrassment, nodded and shrugged, easy going.

'Maybe I could drop by, leave you what I've written. Are you alone or with a girl?'

'A friend.'

'Sorry, I'm nosy. A friend, why not? It's none of my business.'

'A colleague from work!' Bartol was embarrassed again. 'Drop by if you can.'

'A colleague from work, why not? I'll be there in fifteen minutes, I'm not far. So long.'

Bartol looked apologetically at Lentz. He wasn't sure whether he was pleased with this turn of events; he quickly finished his drink.

'Don't look at me like that. I wasn't intending to confide in you, I simply wanted to go out and chat. You were around, that's all.'

Bartol wasn't sure it was true but didn't want to labour the subject. He was even a little pleased; he didn't exclude the possibility that, in view of potential pancreatic cancer, Lentz might leave him his old clock.

Fortunately, they didn't have to wait long for Magda; she was there ten minutes later.

He noticed her first. And not only he. A number of men raised their eyes from their tankards and, with the expression of experienced tailors, measured her from head to toe and up again. With satisfaction. She looked different again. Tight jacket, thin colourful scarf wrapped rakishly around her neck, windswept auburn hair, and a flush. He didn't have to wonder long whether he was the only one to think she didn't look bad.

More and more people fixed their gaze on the girl as she cast her eyes around. He wondered whether he, too, didn't stare like that at times. Be that as it may, he didn't like it. He got up and leaned over so that she could catch sight of him more easily. It helped. She waved and briskly walked over, without looking around anymore. Several men followed her with their eyes then lost interest as soon as she reached her destination. Two men were competition.

'Greetings, gentlemen. I'm Magda.' She extended her hand to Lentz without undue ceremony.

'Piotr. What will you have to drink?' He smoothed his bald pate. 'I'm paying. It's my birthday today. Twenty-eight,' he added, pleased with his joke.

'Shame, because I'm looking for someone over thirty. Happy birthday. I hope I'm not interrupting a private party. Besides, I thought we'd arranged to meet.' She looked at Bartol.

'I phoned,' he replied. 'Piotr's also in on the investigation. It's worked out well that there's the three of us.' He smiled, his eyes on Lentz. He certainly looked like someone who had nothing wrong with him or ever had.

'I'd like some tea, please. I'm a bit cold. Perhaps with a drop of rum. I'd prefer to sit at a table – it's crowded here – but it doesn't look as though one's going to be free for some time. I've brought a file with me, I've noted down a few things...'

'You're right. Let's drink up and go somewhere quieter,' Lentz said unexpectedly and peered strangely around the pillar. He quickly pulled out his wallet and paid for what they'd ordered earlier; he didn't even attempt ordering any tea.

Bartol had no idea what was happening to him.

He didn't have to speculate for long. Before he had time to turn and see for himself, he heard Polek's laughter in chorus with the giggling of a young lady who, as it turned out, was snuggling up to him in more than mere friendship. Fortunately, Polek didn't notice them, either then or as they left. He was too engrossed in creating his new image, which involved going back some twenty years – no easy task while holding one's breath.

Bartol followed Magda and Lentz.

He stared at the ground and not only because the cobblestones of Stary Rynek glistened dangerously, warning of their slippery surface. The whole way, he mulled over what he'd seen. Polek must have gone mad. Perhaps he'd reached the age when guys still want to prove something to themselves – that was none of his business – but since when was he so stupid as to prove it in a bar where he could come across his own daughter?

Bartol knew Polek's wife well, certainly well enough to foresee what would happen if she were to find out. She'd thrash him, wring and wash him right out. And finally she'd probably throw him out on Bartol's doormat with the note: bastard to bastard.

He knew she didn't speak well of Bartol since the slip-up with the pregnancy. He didn't feel like fighting it; besides, it accorded with that twisted logic women have.

She'd pushed for the introduction; they could have made such a fine couple – her colleague from work, her husband's friend. She had such good intentions, had organised it all so well and now resented it hadn't worked out so well. But that wasn't her fault.

Obviously.

Polek's daughter was at an age when she'd stick up for her mother out of sheer spite. She'd been unbearable of late, and Polek would never live this down.

Bartol knew he had to talk to him. But how?

With relief, he set the problem aside for later. They'd reached Żydowska Street and sat down in a little bar-cum-café. It was warm with small armchairs, a chocolate colour scheme and smooth music. All this put together started to have a soothing effect.

He walked up to the bar to order something and instinctively looked around. The first thing which occurred to him was that here, on the other hand, he could come across Polek's wife. Almost all the tables were taken up by women of a certain age who talked gracefully about how to trim the wings of forty-year-old Pegasuses and how to choose the right colour of napkins to go with the tablecloth. At least that's what he thought.

He shook all these thoughts away.

'It's a good thing we moved. The atmosphere's a bit lighter here. It was dark with all that smoke and people at the other place. All nervous with the chase. While here, they calmly exchange various bedroom experiences, official and unofficial, of course.' Magda, laughing, was the first to speak.

Bartol and Lentz didn't laugh nor did they say anything.

'But to the point.' Looking at them she instantly turned serious. 'We've got three sayings.'

'Four,' corrected Bartol, slowly setting their thoughts along the right track.

'How come four?' An entire stave of wrinkles appeared on her forehead.

'The last victim's dog had the words *quam oportet* freshly tattooed on it.'

'All that! On a dog, how's that? What's this about?' Her surprise didn't surprise either of them.

'No, that isn't all. We're going to have the rest of the sentence tomorrow. Let's start at the beginning. What have you discovered so far? That's probably easiest.'

'Maybe you're right.' The highly wrinkled brow slowly unwrinkled. 'So, from the beginning. The first body had two sayings attributed to it. Right, so there ought to be two by the second one, that figures,' she thought out loud. 'Do you have the photographs?' She glanced at Bartol and nodded. 'You don't, too bad. One way or another I suggest that both the first and second dictum found by the first corpse refer to hope. That was my first association, too, and probably the best. I also took other meanings into consideration but kept going back to the same idea. Rightly so, I think. The caption *Expecto donec veniat* appears in the book of Juan de Boria in *Empresas Morales* published in Prague, 1581, with the following commentary... I've got it written down here somewhere.' She took a while flicking through her papers, finally found the right place and started reading: '"Hope should be cultivated in the belief that misfortune will not last long and the longed-for happiness and peace which will be solace for misery will come soon." Admittedly, Boria suggested the symbol of a locust to render the meaning...'

'And what's a locust got to do with it?' asked Bartol.

Lentz didn't ask anything, just sat eyes wide open.

'In this case nothing. That's not the point. It's the commentary that counts, but the images can vary depending on what model the artist followed. It's not as complicated as it seems.'

'I believe otherwise,' answered Bartol, resigned. Too many impressions for one day, he felt.

'Well, then here's a brief lecture,' said Magda. Lentz merely lowered his head and finished what was in his glass. 'A certain preacher, Christoforo Giarda, wrote something like this – and it's worth remembering.' She picked up one of her pieces of paper. '"All knowledge concerning learning and virtue is useful to man, but knowledge concerning the invention and shaping of symbolic images infinitely exceeds any other because thanks to this gift"' – she started to enunciate each word more slowly – '"the spirit, banished from heaven to the dark cavern of the body and in its deeds tied to the senses, can gaze at the beauty and form of virtues and learning removed from all matter though still generally described in its form." Beautifully put, don't you think?' She looked at her listeners and, seeing their dull expressions, didn't wait for an answer. 'Besides, he believed that the entire universe was a library of symbolic images ordered by the Creator... But to the point, the genesis of many symbols which accompany various concepts is extremely interesting and, to a greater or lesser extent, complicated. Nevertheless, not long after printing was invented, people decided to set all this in order because, as time went on, they couldn't get the hang of it all. On a French illumination from 1450 Prudence has the attributes of a coffin, coin, sieve, mirror, spade and scythe. A bit much, don't you think? You don't know what it means.'

They agreed with her. This time it was Bartol who finished his glass. Nobody suggested another round, afraid, perhaps, that they'd start to understand.

'Vasari, for example, wrote a whole book explaining what he himself had painted earlier. Finally, someone decided to see to it and a certain Andrea Alciato published his *Emblematum liber* in 1531. He was almost immediately taken to be the father of – and authority on – emblems; symbols to you. Then, in 1593 the work was completed by Cesare Ripa who wrote *Iconology* and depicted practically all commonly used abstract concepts. Other, less significant books were written, like the one in which I found the maxim, but the idea's generally the same – drawing, symbol, caption and explanation. It's a set of instructions that can be used to put forward an idea in a way everyone can understand and know what the artist wants to say by his work... Besides, the artist wasn't the most important thing here; what was important was what was intended to be portrayed. I won't delve into the details but let's put it this way: you couldn't, in principle, freely interpret what was painted in a church or municipal council. It had to be edifying and comprehensible. I think I'm expressing myself reasonably clearly?'

There was a moment of silence. Neither of them said a word. She looked at each in turn, nodded and started again.

'In your field, for example, what do you think a woman holding scales represents?'

'A balanced woman,' replied Lentz confidently.

'Yes, and with a heart – kind-hearted! A woman with scales and a sword personifies Justice. You'd better not think, just listen.' She sighed deeply. 'Right, let's take it slowly. Hope, in paintings or sculpture, for example, is represented by a woman with an anchor against the background of a seascape. I'll tell you how well it's been explained.' Again she glanced at her notes. 'I won't read to you about the anchor because that surely is a simple association, safe harbour and so on, but he wrote well about the seascape, too: "Sailing on a dancing, surging sea is not easy because man crosses the boundaries assigned to him; yet, armed with trust, he can behold the Kingdom of Heaven" – that's how Cesare Ripa explained it, among other things. So that when someone painted a young woman with an anchor and a seething sea in the background, someone who was illiterate, for example, understood perfectly well what he saw – you have to hope and trust in God that you'll return home, for example. That's why for someone who knew how to read and was a more sophisticated client, it was enough to have one symbol like, for example, those sunflowers, and a note which broadened the idea. When reading *Expecto donec veniat*, he could have recalled the story of Job who lost everything, asked himself why it was happening to him and so on but trusted in God and everything ended well. I don't intend to play the smart alec or try to convince you that it's interesting, but the man you're looking for seems to know all this. And as I was saying... aha, he's addressing a sophisticated client who's going to understand – unless he's doing it only for himself and doesn't care whether anybody reads it or not. But I don't think so. Why bother? I think he's concocting an ideology and the recipient of his work, if I can put it that way, is important. I've no clue what his principle idea is, but he does want to depict some sort of idea.' She broke off.

'And what's a locust got to do with it?' asked Bartol unintentionally.

'The bug's pestering you. It's got nothing to do with it. The same words and sunflowers are bound to be somewhere in another book. It rings a bell, but I haven't found it yet. The meaning's much the same: with time the locust will fly away and the earth will give birth anew, in the same way as sunflowers bow to the sun in farewell, but you have to have hope that dawn is finally going to break and they'll raise their heads in greeting. That's why I think it's a question of hope here. Besides, that's what the dictum *Dum spiro spero* says. A naked body and the caption "While there's life there's hope", although in our case the context is grotesque. Here, I've no doubt whatsoever. It's harder with the other body. There, I'm finding it more difficult, glasses are...'

She stopped. They weren't the only ones to turn their heads. Two girls had entered the bar, laughing exceptionally loudly. They must have made a mistake; they didn't suit the place. After a quick inspection and a giggled and gabbled appraisal of the situation, just as they'd made an abrupt entry so they made a loud decision to leave. A couple of people smiled pitifully.

'Well, you know how the virtue of Moderation is represented, don't you?' asked Magda. 'A woman adds water to wine with no implied meaning, simply to dilute it and temper the strength of the drink. A drink. It couldn't be any simpler. The symbol might well have been more widespread. The girls were a bit tipsy, weren't they?'

'They certainly were. Is there something about wine and drinking in the Bible, too?' asked Lentz.

'There certainly is! In numerous instances. Besides, practically everything's there. I even remember a sentence from Sirach's Book of Wisdom: "what life is then to a man that is without wine? For it was made to make men glad." Drunk in moderation, of course. Times change but problems don't. But let's get back to the spectacles and their writing: *Speculator adstad de sui.* I didn't find the maxim anywhere. I asked a couple of people but with no results as yet. I'm also finding it difficult to translate unambiguously. Literally, it could be taken to mean "the observer stands next to his own men", but could also be with his own, perhaps not stands but supports. I'm not sure. Spectacles represent the sense of sight so it can only refer to sight; but it could also mean the eye, for example, the Eye of Providence, God. Do you have any more details, some sort of context perhaps?'

Lentz spoke first.

'Maciej hasn't got the photographs, as you may have gathered. The second victim was sitting at a small table with his hand on a Bible. Next to it stood a cross. He was also the owner of the dog with a fresh tattoo on its ear. Part of the writing goes *quam oportet*. We don't have any more at the moment.'

'Don't have any more,' repeated Magda. Without waiting for an answer, she spoke to herself. 'Don't have any more,' she repeated again, frowning.

'Don't have any more at the moment,' Lentz said in a slightly irritated voice, looking at Maciej. 'Let's give the vet time. It hasn't healed that quickly, the wounds need to be cleaned!'

'Sorry, Piotr, that's not the point. Of course I'll wait. "Don't have any more" rings a bell but I've no idea why. You go on celebrating, I'll go home,' she added, quite unexpectedly, and got up from the table.

Both men were so astonished by her sudden decision they didn't have time to react appropriately. Paying no attention to them, Magda approached the coat rack and took her jacket.

'Please phone me in the morning, Maciej, when you find out some more. I'll carry on looking. Remember the photographs,' she said, wrapping the long scarf tightly around her neck and taking a hat from her bag.

'Wait, we'll order you a taxi, it's late,' Lentz declared.

'No need. I'll be home in fifteen minutes. The whole way's brightly lit, so no fears. I think best when I walk and I've got a bit of thinking to do, but thanks for the concern. And happy birthday again.' She walked up to Lentz and kissed him on the cheek, clearly embarrassing him. She extended her hand to Maciej.

'Call when you can.'

'Pick up when you can,' Bartol concluded in an offended tone. She was supposed to have dropped in for a moment but he guessed the moment had long passed.

'Okay,' she agreed, laughing. 'See you tomorrow, probably. Maybe I'll find something. I've confused you enough for one day.'

'Sort of, but it was still nice meeting you,' said Lentz.

'Bye.' Maciej didn't add anything; they already knew each other.

She turned as she opened the main door. Maybe she knew they were staring at her. She waved goodbye. Her hair looked radiantly red in the street light, so much so that Bartol almost saw sparks fly. At least that's what it seemed to him.

They didn't say anything at first; then, after a while, the conversation was still heavy going. They didn't even mention Polek, as though nobody had seen anything. They merely exchanged a few observations and both agreed that somebody like Magda could prove useful.

They didn't quite understand what she'd said even, though both admitted they enjoyed listening to her. Perhaps it would lead to something, and that was that.

They ordered one more drink, downed it quickly and left.

Nothing came of further celebrations.

Bartol got home, washed, went to bed but couldn't, for a change, fall asleep. The day seemed horribly long. He felt exhausted yet sleep eluded him.

All sorts of thoughts ran through his head, bouncing off each other with fatigue and helplessness.

The woman from Staszic Street, Lalek who had another life – a pity it wasn't his own – spotty Franciszek, the small lettering on Magda's t-shirt which he never managed to put together to form words. For some unknown reason he added his own eventual presence at the baby's delivery and completely lost the desire to lie there with eyes closed.

He got up, poured himself some vodka again, and again there was nothing but water. This time he downed it quickly. It helped a little. On the way back to bed, he glanced at the phone. There was a message. He read it several times: 'It'll be *non plus* on the ear. Goodnight.'

It took him a while to figure out the message was from Magda and referred to the mongrel's ear, but still he couldn't understand anything. The only thing he managed to work out was that he wasn't going to work anything out. Trivial, stupefying thoughts, such as whether or not to wear the blue sweater the following day, encouraged sleep to come – not instantly but at a slow crawl Because it had to come in the end.

As it was he woke up a couple of times in the night and between four and five didn't sleep at all. When he'd almost decided to get up for good and have an early start, he was overcome with drowsiness. He laid his head on the pillow and thought he didn't sleep. The alarm went off but a drowsy thought that he shouldn't worry, that it would ring again, flashed through his mind.

Something rang but it wasn't the alarm; it was the phone, and it didn't give up easily. It rang three times in a row. In the end it stood him on his feet.

His mother.

'Yes, hello.' He tried to sound alert but didn't manage to deceive her.

'Well, well. I thought you'd grown out of it. I still can't understand how you got through primary school when it started at eight. I hope you're grateful to me for waking you up.'

'Yes, very. I was lucky to be part of the baby boom and – just for the record – often started at eleven as far as I remember. I'm in a bit of a hurry right now, mum. Did you want anything?'

'Me, no, I'm just your wake-up call!'

'Mum...'

'Listen, I can't visit your girlfriend today so please phone and see if she needs anything. She's on leave and mustn't tire herself. Do some shopping or whatever, but get yourself involved!'

'All right, but can't we go together? You somehow manage to communicate with each other while I... You go.' The minute he said it, he regretted it.

'I'm phoning to tell you I can't.' The tone of his mother's voice now shook him awake, which didn't stop him from asking foolishly:

'But why?'

'Come on, are you really still in primary school? I can't and that's that. Women's business.'

'What?' He still wasn't in control of what he was saying.

'Which version do you want to hear? The one which will put you off your breakfast or the detailed one so you won't be able to look at food until supper?'

'All right, mum, I'll phone, but today I might have a lot of...'

'Try. And call me in the evening to tell me how hard you tried. Get up and don't sulk. Go and look how beautiful it's outside. Bye.'

'Bye,' he said to the phone, then to himself: 'Of course it's beautiful, from the very morning.'

He muttered under his breath: 'Women's business, end of conversation.' When he'd once told her he was going out with his friends and it was men's business, what did he hear? 'Since when has drinking and boasting been business?'

He looked out of the window. Nothing really had changed; the trees were bare, the grass was the colour of rotting grass, but the sun was indeed shining and that changed a great deal. Maybe that's why he got himself together with exceptional speed. Once he was in the car, the phone rang again. Fortunately, it was Lentz this time.

'Hi, I've got everything that's written there. Can you call Magda? You know what it says?'

'*Non plus*. Am I right?'

'How do you know?' asked Lentz, completely baffled.

'I'll be at the firm in half an hour. I'll tell you then.'

'Ok. See you.'

'See you.'

He phoned Magda, or rather tried phoning her again; she didn't pick up. He wasn't even surprised or very annoyed. He'd obviously have to get used to it. But a moment later he couldn't help but be surprised. She didn't call back; instead she sent a message: 'Was I right?' He wrote back that she was. Silence at her end; that was all. He merely nodded in disbelief. Surely she wasn't counting her pennies? Yet if this wasn't thrift, what was it?

He decided not to give it too much thought, at least not for the time being; the weather was fine and set both humans and traffic in a good mood. The traffic jams were the same as the day before but everybody was driving as if more smoothly and politely. He arrived at headquarters in relatively good time, and the moment he entered was taken aback. He wasn't so late as to deserve a thunderous: 'Finally!' from Polek, and expectant looks from the rest of th team.

'It's a good thing you're here. We've some interesting stuff. We need to plan the day because there's going to be a lot of work,' Maćkowiak joined in.

'All right, I'm sorry. I overslept a bit but let's not exaggerate. So what's all this interesting stuff you've got?'

'Hyper-interesting stuff. We were both right. One: one,' said Polek excitedly. 'That saint of ours wasn't so saintly. We received information yesterday that our Lalek disappeared about ten years ago, hardly anyone remembered him in Warszawa. He was collecting empty bottles and cans in train compartments and didn't get off on time – which happened often enough apparently – then disappeared somewhere along the Warszawa-Rzeszów line. Nobody looked for him nor did he turn up of his own accord, the poor guy. As you can guess, he didn't report his documents missing. We can't exclude his having sold them for a bottle. But there's more. We're leaving the best to the end, Sleeping Beauty.'

'Olaf!'

'All right, all right, listen to this. We now know who our Mother Theresa of Poznań was. And this is where you were right.'

'What? He had a record?' asked Bartol.

'And whow. Not just any felony. You're in for quite a surprise. Murder, sir.'

'I wasn't expecting anything as big as that despite everything!' He was thrown – completely.

'And that's still not all. He'd already previously wanted to outsmart ordinary mortals and be nearer to God,' said Polek with undisguised irony, and paused meaningfully.

'What do you mean?' Bartol had never liked being kept on edge, and even less so of late.

'Maciej, he used to be a priest and went by the name of Father Jan Maria Gawlicki.' Lentz, who probably didn't feel like dramatic pauses at that moment either, anticipated Polek.

'What!' Bartol was truly worked up. The rest must have already cooled down because they seemed unimpressed. 'What did he do?' he asked.

'You've been sleeping for a week!' Polek spoke again. 'The information's already ten minutes old.'

'All right, so what's there in your papers?' Bartol wanted to sort out the confusion mounting in his head as soon as possible. Something like this he had not expected.

'Not much as it is,' began Maćkowiak. 'He did sixteen years, that's all, was released and that's the last that was heard of him. Until now, of course. Maciej, this was the end of the sixties, the beginning of the seventies. The authorities had loosened things up a bit but let's not blow things out of proportion. Militia weren't the only ones involved in a case like this. Special services must have taken it over straight away. That's probably why we didn't come across him right away but had to dig around a bit, and that's probably why his files aren't up front. Maybe we'll find them, maybe we won't. Maybe he started to collaborate. Maybe he had some sort of information. Who knows, and who's going to tell you now?' he concluded in a resigned voice.

'We'll try, but we mustn't expect miracles. What we've got to do now is check whether Father Gawlicki had any family. That way we'll be all the quicker to discover his sins,' said Lentz.

'You're right, that's where we need to start,' agreed Bartol. 'One thing's for certain: he knew his Latin,' he said to himself.

Before long, they realised that, despite the incredible complexity of the case, there was a chance of their finding out much more that same day. Admittedly, Jan Maria Gawlicki had committed his crime in a small town in the Lubuskie district and served his sentence near Rzeszów but, by some miracle, his sister, Maria Anna Gawlicka-Sęk, lived somewhere between Konin and Kutno, not more than a two-hour drive away.

Nor was there any difficulty in finding out whether she was at home. Her full address and telephone number appeared on the pages of dog shows, canine associations and beneath the descriptions of numerous breeds.

They began with Lentz phoning about a Caucasian Sheepdog puppy. There weren't any such pups but there were some Labradors; in those, too, he showed interest. Bartol had initially intended to go with Polek, as he usually did. He wasn't looking forward to discussing what he'd seen the previous evening, but silently banked on the conversation cropping up of its own accord and on his being able to keep his colleague in check a little before the wife did.

After an hour it happened that he wouldn't have to keep anything in check; Polek declared that – categorically, absolutely and exceptionally – he wouldn't be able to go. Bartol was relieved, but intuition told him the relief was only temporary.

He went with Lentz.

They hadn't even left Poznań when Magda phoned. Bartol slipped off onto the lay-by to talk. He turned the speaker on, wanting Lentz to hear what Magda had to say. He feared he wouldn't be able to repeat it all to him later.

'Hi, I'm doing well for the time being. I guessed right, didn't I?'

'Hi. I'm full of admiration. Are these sayings pretty common in some circles?'

'No, but you can thank Piotr for me, they're his words: nothing more – *non plus*.'

'You can thank him yourself. He's right next to me.'

'Many thanks, Piotr. Could even be we're a couple of hours ahead on the job.'

'I didn't do anything, but am glad to be of help.'

Bartol noticed that saying this Lentz fidgeted nervously, ran his fingers through what was left of his hair, rubbed his nose nervously, and even blushed a little.

'So the whole thing reads: *non plus quam oportet*. It's from Saint Paul's Letter to the Romans, chapter 12, verse 3. You don't have to take it down, I'll print it out for you. The longer translation goes: "Do not think of yourself more highly than you ought, but rather think of yourself with sober judgment, in accordance with the measure of faith God has given you." End of quotation. Those are words addressed, in fact, to the first ministers of Christian society. Their equivalent, in our times, being priests.'

The men looked at each other. Bartol was the first to speak.

'Listen, Magda, you don't write newspaper articles, do you?'

'Quite the contrary, unfortunately. I only read them unless you've got something interesting, then maybe I'll switch jobs.'

'This isn't much of a laughing matter.'

'Sorry, of course not.' Her voice sounded genuinely apologetic.

'We've just learned,' Bartol continued, 'that the last victim was a priest. We didn't know that yesterday.'

'See. It's all starting to make sense, and I'm certainly on the right track to make sense of it all. Drop in this evening, or tomorrow. I'll prepare all the possible interpretations that come to me. You might find them useful.'

'We certainly will, I know that already, and thank you in advance. I'll drop by today if I can, if not tomorrow. See you.'

'See you. Bye, Piotr.'

'Bye.'

'It's a shame I can't make any sense of it all. Do you understand anything?' He turned to Lentz.

'She's great, Magda,' said Lentz, rubbing his nose nervously again.

Bartol had expected a straight answer, that no, he didn't understand anything. This answer he didn't like. He didn't know why the subject of women and Lentz had never existed before, and everyone had long grown used to that. He couldn't remember anyone commenting on the fact that despite his undisguised bald pate and his forty years of age, Lentz was still living with his mother, nor did anyone joke about the fact that he had a little white dog (although it was possible that Bartol was the only one who knew). A girl had, admittedly, once told Bartol that had Lentz been taller he would be handsome and was, in fact, interesting. And she'd even tried to get Lentz interested in her, but to no avail. Bartol hadn't heard of anyone else trying. Why was Lentz suddenly so worked up?

They didn't speak for a long time. Lentz reclined his seat a little and closed his eyes. It looked as if he intended to doze off; that's certainly how it was supposed to look.

One way or another, Bartol wasn't very surprised. He did the same sometimes when he didn't feel like talking. Especially when he was in the car with Polek and wasn't driving. And whenever he travelled in this direction. When they were in the vicinity of Konin, Polek would always, but always, partition Poland for the fourth time into Greater Poland and the rest. He did this with such conviction and determination as though he were going to climb out of the car at any moment, plant a border post and stand guard. He loved convincing himself and anyone who was at hand that the wind of better times did not blow from the east, that the only uprising which had won in the country – the Greater Poland Uprising – won precisely because it was in Poland and nobody interfered, and so on. It was impossible to listen for more than five minutes.

The journey went well. There was little traffic, the sun shone all the way and it only clouded over and rained once they'd reached their destination.

A signpost on the main road indicated immediate left and informed that it was only eight kilometres to Grabno. If it wasn't for the muddy road winding through the willows, it wouldn't have been far. No doubt, some other season this would have been a scenic country track, but not now.

The windscreen wipers not only swept the rain aside but also had to clear the mud which splattered beneath their wheels as they drove through puddles much deeper than they appeared. Bartol had slowed down to almost twenty kilometres an hour when beneath the wheels he sensed tarmac, which began or maybe ended right in the middle of a field. There was no reasonable explanation why precisely here, precisely now, halfway down the track.

He didn't give it any more thought; they were at their destination. They decided to ask the people at the bus stop where Mrs Gawlicka-Sęk lived.

They halted. The face of the man approaching the car wasn't friendly. He must have approached out of curiosity or perhaps because he was closest.

Lentz lowered the window.

'Good morning, we're looking for Mrs Gawlicka, perhaps you could...' – he didn't finish.

'Not again! Give us a break with that dog-woman. Any more of you around?'

It seemed to Bartol as though the man slobbered as he shouted.

'Kowalik, give the men a break. They've come a long way,' said a woman in a brownish-grey autumn coat, an amusing contrast to her pink umbrella with its stain-remover logo. 'Long way? Then they should take her with them,' grunted the man.

'Stop it, I tell you. Go to the end of the village, turn right at the little shrine, then...'

'Then they'll hear for themselves' – the man broke in again, and turning to the police officers, immediately added: 'Can't you see the bus is coming?'

They did see and pulled away, without even having time to thank the woman with the pink trophy umbrella.

'I don't think everyone likes Anna,' said Bartol.

'I can guess why. Might have seen it coming. You're going to have to go by yourself, I'll wait in the car,' announced Lentz.

'What are you talking about?' asked Bartol, annoyed.

'Listen, I like animals, which is why I even stopped eating meat. Although Sunday's not Sunday at home without roast duck and dumplings...'

'You said you were on a diet, as far as I remember.'

'Because it's better for my image. Enough, there's no point in discussing it. Go on your own,' concluded Lentz.

He said no more. Once again Bartol had the impression that, by some strange law, the more time he spent with Lentz the less he knew about him. He wondered for a moment whether that didn't apply to everyone whom he'd recently come across.

He reached what he thought was the end of the village and turned right at a small shrine full of dirty, plastic flowers. Presently they did, in fact, hear not so much the barking of dogs as angry growling which grew louder as they approached the old, square house surrounded by a hideous wall of ready-made concrete blocks. Bricks and columns. If he could, he would willingly have prohibited the production of such ghastly enclosures. He also counted on people finally getting bored of them, but they didn't. This construction appeared relatively new even.

'Are you sure you aren't coming?' he asked one more time, no conviction in his voice.

'I'm sure,' Lentz replied, with conviction.

Bartol approached the gate, wondering whether to use the doorbell. He wasn't sure anything could be heard apart from the dogs growling, barking, snarling, howling and emitting a whole range of noises he couldn't even describe.

He did use the bell, although it proved unnecessary; someone was already opening the gate for him. It caught him by surprise; he hadn't seen anyone approach. The woman was a head shorter than the enclosure. She seemed too small for her enormous, sleeveless, quilted worker's jacket and too small for the dog which stood near her, reached to her waist and must have weighed more than her – although she, too, was not the slimmest.

Bartol couldn't move a step. The dogs started barking even louder, if that was at all possible.

'Don't be frightened. Leo, home!' The huge, ginger creature cast its hostile eyes at him, turned lazily, wagged its tail the size of a grown man's arm, and meekly stepped into one of the pens. One of a hundred pens, so it seemed to Bartol. They were all over the yard, everywhere. In each, a few dogs of different hues, sizes and degree of rage.

'Have you come for a Labrador or a Leonberger? I can't remember,' the woman asked with reservation.

'I'd like to talk first.'

'My dogs have the best papers, they're champions, but do come in if you want a look.' Without waiting for an answer she made towards the front door. Opening, she added: 'I don't intend to bargain, if that's what you've got in mind.'

Bartol followed her in, accompanied by five or six other dogs, eager to make the most of the opportunity.

It stank outside, but the stench indoors was beyond description. An old domestic stench mixed with a new one emanating from huge pans in which something he couldn't even call dog-food was boiling. It reeked of urine.

'Please sit down. Would you like something to drink?' The woman removed her quilted jacket, which didn't smell all that sweetly either.

Bartol didn't know where to sit down. Everything must have been sticky. Small cages for small dogs and containing small dogs stood in the room. The food in the corridor began to boil well and good. The thought of something to drink almost made him gag.

'No, thank you.' Finally, he sat down, trying not to touch anything with his hands.

The woman left.

One of the small dogs, probably the smallest he'd ever seen, started to furiously throw itself at its cage, barking, or rather squealing like a toy, and clearly addressing him.

Maybe it had seen someone put puppies in their pocket during a visit like this; the pups could be mistaken for a fair-sized key ring.

Bartol turned his head, hoping that if he stopped looking at it the thing would finally lose interest in him. But no. Bartol got up and turned his back.

He stared at a shelf on the wall laden with cups, medals and photographs of medallists. He studied the photographs for a long time before noticing one pushed far back, a faded picture in an old frame. A small, laughing young woman astride a horse, its bridle held by a well-built, squinting boy. They could have been siblings.

'Well, go ahead, what sort of dog were you thinking about?' she asked as she entered. She tried to smile but it was obvious she didn't like talking, at least not to human beings.

'I haven't come for a dog,' began Bartol.

She made no attempt to be pleasant anymore.

'So what are you doing here?' she shouted and, after a while, added: 'You don't look like the district guard either.'

'But that's warmer. I'm from the police. Was Jan Maria Gawlicki your brother?'

The woman instinctively fell into the armchair and didn't say anything for a long time. It was as though the dogs had stopped barking, too.

'Yes. Anna Maria Sęk, maiden name Gawlicka,' she replied. 'Has something happened?'

'Your brother was murdered three days ago. Can you tell me when you last saw him?'

The woman got up without a word, walked to the door and opened it wider; two of the larger dogs understood her unspoken command and slowly left.

'More than thirty years ago,' she answered after a long pause. 'At first I didn't want to see him. Then he me,' she added, gazing at her skirt as though she had just noticed the huge stain on it. She started rubbing the stain off with her hand as though only now, as she looked into the past, did it start worrying her.

It wouldn't come off; it was too old.

'I divorced my husband, you know, moved house – ran away really – but kept my name... So that one day he would walk in like you and say: I'm here.' She broke off once more. 'From what you say, I take it there's nothing for me to wait for?' she added without looking at him.

Bartol didn't reply. Besides, she wasn't expecting an answer.

'What really happened, over thirty years ago?'

'Don't you know?' she asked in a dispassionate voice.

'I'd like to hear it from you.'

'You'd like to hear it from me? It's me who'd like to hear from you what really happened.' She started rubbing one hand nervously against the other, again without looking at him. 'Please tell me... how did he die and... live.'

'Well, he probably knew his murderer, which is why my talking to you is so important. How did he live? A good life probably. He'd been doing social work for the past ten years under a different name. He helped a lot of people and a lot of people are grateful to him. They speak well of him.'

She remained silent, staring blankly at one of the – surprisingly – empty cages.

'So he'd found his calling... He always did say he'd find it in the end... That I shouldn't worry.' She smiled at her memories. 'He always used to pull me by my plait, to frighten me...' Her hand tried to find the plait. But didn't. 'He didn't have a vocation then. Couldn't find it,' she added after a while. 'It wasn't what he'd dreamed of. It was our mother's dream. She prayed five times a day for him to become a priest. And her prayers were finally answered. Sure, God listens to a mother's prayer.' Saying this she laughed - horrifically somehow. 'Then, after it had happened, she never left the house, prayed for a quick death and He listened to her again. She was lucky; she didn't have long to wait.' The woman's face turned hostile again; it wasn't a happy memory. Suddenly she got up as if she'd returned to reality. 'I'll go and turn the kidneys off. They must be done by now.'

She left. The dogs started barking again. The fresh stench no longer steamed and slowly started to carry and cover the walls and clothes with one more layer.

'Please tell me what happened?' Bartol asked quickly, seeing her come in.

'He wasn't suited to it,' she spoke calmly now. 'He liked life. He liked women and they liked him.' She broke off. 'But our mother probably loved him more and it was probably out of love that she didn't want to hand him over to another woman. Maybe if our father had lived... He'd somehow given up on it... I think Jan even liked this unavailability of his at first. For a time.' She broke off again. Bartol couldn't hurry her, although he very much wanted to. He was worried he wouldn't be able to wash the smell off.

'I didn't see her. We visited his parish a couple of times, my mother and I, but I never saw her. Later they merely said she was pretty, that she'd got married at an early age so as to leave home because they were poor, that her husband was strange, that she laughed at him saying he had nothing in his pants... Apparently everyone in the village knew and in the end he found out, too... that what he didn't have in his pants she'd found beneath the frock of a priest... You know the rest better than me.' She broke off for good and started stroking a spotted dog which had laid its head on her lap.

'Please go on.'

'We lived ninety kilometres away.' She stopped. The dog, grateful for being stroked, licked her hand. 'Far enough not to know what was happening, but near enough not to be able to go on living there. I was a teacher in a primary school and was scared to enter the classroom after break. The children wrote all sorts of things on the board. They hadn't thought these things up themselves, they barely knew how to write... Our mother died... First I went to Konin, then came here. Perhaps you'd like something to drink after all? You must be cold ,seeing as you haven't taken your jacket off.'

'No, no thank you!' He didn't want to but must have shuddered at the very thought. The dog which had licked her hands started licking its balls again.

'Hmm, you're disgusted. One can get used to it.' She smiled. 'Cleanliness disgusts me. You can't see the dirt under it.'

'Please tell me what you know.'

'Who knows what happened apart from them... Apparently someone saw the husband spying through the window first. He knew they were there together. Then nobody saw anything anymore. Strange, isn't it? Some say he attacked them... Others that he was defending himself, that she'd concocted the whole thing... My brother didn't kill anyone. He told mother it wasn't him... After all, he wouldn't have lied... I don't know why he took the whole blame on himself afterwards. I don't know... He didn't want to see me... My letters came back...' She broke off and began to breathe deeper, sniffing. It seemed she was going to start crying; but she only wiped her nose with the sleeve of her sweater and pursed her lips.

'What was the woman's name? Do you know what happened to her afterwards?'

'Don't you know?'

Bartol didn't answer.

'Her married name was Elżbieta Garnczek. I don't know her maiden name. They also disowned her. Nor do I know what happened to her. My brother got sixteen years, she got six for complicity. I'd even thought at times that she'd waited for him and they'd run off together somewhere but from what you say... she didn't. When and where is the funeral?' she asked suddenly.

'Here's the number to call.' He pulled out a loose page from his notebook, which he'd prepared beforehand. 'As far as I know, it's all being arranged by his colleagues from work. They think he didn't have a family. Please get in touch with them.'

She stared at the piece of paper a long while.

'Poznań?'

'Didn't I tell you?'

'I never asked... He was so close by...' Again she hid her nose in her sleeve. 'I visit Poznań at least several times a year, during the show, and sell dogs at Sielanka sometimes... And we never saw each other... He just didn't want to...'

'I'm sorry, but I've got to ask. Where were you three days ago?'

'Here. People know I don't go anywhere. If I wanted to go I'd have to ask the neighbour's son to look after all this or they'd poison some of my dogs again... People are jealous around here. It didn't bother them until I bought the village administrator's car for my son because the man couldn't pay his instalments. He told everyone how much I'd given him... Ever since then they won't leave me in peace.'

'And where does your son live?' Bartol asked automatically.

'Also in Poznań...' She smiled to herself. 'He wants to get married but he's a prosecutor and doesn't make much money.'

'And his name's Gawlicki?'

'No, Pilski... After my first husband.'

Bartol was dumbfounded.

He began looking around restlessly. Fortunately, her eyes weren't on him. The spotted dog had once more laid its head on her knees. Bartol couldn't make out anything pink in the house. Nothing that would be in character with Pilski. He chased away another dog which had started fawning on him, and sprung to his feet. The dogs started barking like crazy again. Anna Maria Gawlicka, as if torn from her numbness, began to bustle around the room nervously.

'I'm very sorry about your brother. I'm sure you understand that we'll have to get in touch with you again. Please call when you come to the funeral, that'll be easiest. We'll take your statement.'

'I didn't say I'd be at the funeral!' she said firmly. 'He didn't want to see me...' she added much more quietly.

'Perhaps he lacked the courage. His computer showed that he often visited websites of dog shows. Maybe he didn't make it on time.' It suddenly puzzled him why he, or anybody else, hadn't put two and two together sooner. 'Please think about it. One way or another we'll stay in touch.'

Gawlicka nodded half-consciously and walked him to the door. He no longer paid any attention to the growling, barking dogs.

Lentz was leaning against the car, smoking. They took their seats.

'Open the window, you don't exactly smell nice. I've already had the pleasure of meeting breeders like that. So, are you impressed?'

'Extremely impressed. Let's go.'

Lentz smiled to himself and turned on the ignition.

'Didn't I tell you?'

'No, you didn't tell me,' Bartol cut him off. He wanted to be alone for a while.

They left Grabno. Lentz didn't utter another word. Nor did he say much when Bartol summed up what he'd learned. It seemed that the romantic story of the forbidden love between a priest and parishioner, which ended with the hardly romantic murder of a cuckolded husband – regardless of who had committed the murder – had also made an impression on him. Lentz was surprised and horrified, although he wasn't one to be easily surprised let alone horrified, especially where human passions were concerned, be they love or money. Apart from the passing fascinations for his imagined ailments, he generally approached everything with indifference and rationality. But this story appeared increasingly irrational to them both. Everything pointed to it not having ended many years ago in some village called Great Mocznowo. On the contrary, the drama continued, with a temporaru pause, at Mirosław Trzaska, or rather Jan Maria Gawlicki in Poznań, and, for some unknown reason, at Antoniusz Mikulski; some unwritten law said that this was not the end and no-one knew in what corner of Poland that end would come. On all this, they agreed.

Bartol didn't say anything about Pilski; he simply said that there was still something he wanted to verify. He had no idea why he acted like this.

It had stopped raining, the air was clear and the road dry, yet they passed two accidents. As if to confirm that this wasn't such a coincidence, Bartol noticed two new crosses by the roadside.

They didn't discourage anyone. Including Lentz, who drove too fast and too erratically. He pulled over, approached, overtook overtaking cars, like nearly all the other drivers, as though he were twenty and had three lives ahead of him. As though in a computer game. As though a child, at least that's what his mother said.

Somewhere halfway through their journey, they had to break abruptly and practically pull over to the hard shoulder, otherwise a mad young woman in a large four-wheel drive would have collided with a Fiat 126p head on. She, in her four-by-four cross-country truck, would perhaps have made it to her town; the other driver, in his little town car, would probably not have reached his village.

For most of the way, Bartol dozed a little or pretended to. As soon as he opened his eyes, he saw more of the same, all at the same game. As though it were a national sport, continuous championships, for life or death, or disability.

He didn't feel like commenting, preferred not to look. Briefly, he wondered why he hadn't noticed the crosses on the way there, when he was driving, but couldn't find a logical answer.

It was no different in Poznań. There, too, many drivers were willing to overtake in order to stand at least one car closer to the traffic lights, as though they'd get trophy points. He felt tired and annoyed by the whole expedition, and the day hadn't yet come to an end.

As soon as Lentz pulled into a petrol station to tank up and buy some cigarettes, Bartol phoned Pilski.

The prosecutor was at home. He had some time, but not much; he asked questions. Bartol couldn't answer any of them or say how much time he needed, but he was insistent. They agreed to meet.

Bartol left Lentz at headquarters and drove to the appointed address. He found it straight away. This time everything was in character.

Grape-vine, a new, low-rise block, ugly yet squeezed in among old tower blocks, acted as darling of the estate and pride of its owners.

As he passed garages, sunken into the ground floor, Bartol wondered in which of these stood the village administrator's car. He pressed the intercom and before hearing the door open gazed up. The higher apartments had fairly large balconies. Perhaps that, too, was a gift from medal winners of various breeds. But no. The apartment was on the second floor where there were no balconies; even so, as he climbed the stairs decorated with glass bricks on the half-landings, all the pens in Anna Maria Gawlicka-Sęk's yard appeared in front of his eyes; he could even smell them.

Pilski was already at the door. In a tie and pink shirt. Clearly this was what he also wore at home.

'Hello. Something important must have cropped up, seeing as it couldn't wait till morning. Please, come in.' He opened the door wider with a welcoming gesture.

'Thank you. I didn't want to wait till tomorrow.' Bartol didn't know how to begin the conversation. He hadn't thought of anything yet. He removed his jacket and stepped inside.

'Would you like something to drink?'

'Coffee, please. Black, no sugar,' Bartol replied.

Pilski seemed a little surprised. He'd probably expected Bartol to present him with a brief justification for detaining someone or something like that, certainly not a chat over coffee, but he didn't say anything and went to the kitchen.

Bartol looked around in amazement. He knew Pilski was getting married, yet everything pointed to him living alone. He had no idea why he had this impression but knew that he didn't have to go to the bathroom to make sure. The apartment was well set up, although Bartol was certain no woman had stayed there for a long time. Somebody had obviously tried to furnish it well; it was somehow even too correct, as in a furniture catalogue, no needless details, no dried or fresh flowers, no candles, small or large, no framed photographs and other knick-knacks. Once he spied the bike through the bedroom door which had been left ajar, he no longer had any doubts. A not-particularly-romantic bike in the bedroom and a fiancée who'd taken over six months to decide on the colour of the lettering on wedding invitations did not go hand in hand.

Pilski returned with a mug of coffee and, as he sat down, gestured for Bartol to do the same. Then glanced at his watch. Not randomly, it seemed.

'I can't say how long this will take. I just didn't want you to be caught unawares tomorrow,' began Bartol. Pilski gazed at him with increasing distrust. 'So, without needless preliminaries: a little after you left, we established that the victim's name was not Mirosław Trzaska. He'd borrowed somebody's ID and had been successfully using it for some time. His real name was Jan Maria Gawlicki.'

He couldn't describe or decipher the expression on Pilski's face. Nor did he have much time to do so. The bells on the prosecutor's phone started to chime. Pilski got up and went to the other room without a word. He didn't close the door. He didn't seem to care whether Bartol heard him or not.

'Yes... yes... yes... no, I can't... I know, choose it yourself, I can't talk now... But you've already chosen the suit! A different idea... then change... But I don't know what the dress looks like, damn it! I know I'm not supposed to know! I can't talk now... I don't know... I'll call later, I'm working...'

He came back.

'I'm sorry. People get married severral times, I've already had enough of this once. She might have come round if I hadn't picked up, and brought her mother with her. I apologise once more. I'll turn the phone off...'

'It's all right,' answered Bartol.

He watched Pilski closely. Before, it had looked to him as if Pilski had turned pale; now he appeared on edge. It was hard to say whether it was because of what Bartol had told him or because of his conversation with his fiancée. Bartol had heard him talking to her numerous times, but he'd never heard him raise his voice like that.

'I thought for a moment it was a coincidence, but since you're here, it seems unlikely,' the prosecutor said after a while.

'Right,' agreed Bartol. 'I spoke to your mother earlier...' Now he was sure the man had turned pale, and on top of that had started pacing nervously around the room. But not for long; the regular ringtone of a land line resounded in the other room. Pilski just looked at Bartol and, without a word, went to pick up the phone.

'Yes, I'm at home. You're calling that number! Yes, I'm working from home... I told you I'd call back.'

Bartol heard the receiver being slammed down. Pilski returned to the room, did not apologise a second time.

'You were there?' he asked, as he walked in.

'Yes, today...' answered Bartol.

Pilski didn't say anything for a moment, just wiped the dust from the coffee table, dust which wasn't there.

'She breeds dogs...' he tried nervously to explain. 'She's achieved a lot...'

'Yes, I know, I saw the medals,' interrupted Bartol. He tried to express a touch of acknowledgement and a lot of indifference, like someone who was rarely surprised. He knew this would be better. It seemed to him that Pilski was suffering, was greatly put out that someone had entered the world of which he didn't want to boast, one he took advantage of but from which he wanted to escape – through aluminium skirting-boards, designer lamps, pink ties and all the rest.

'I never met her brother...' Pilski began after a pause. 'But I was... no! One thing at a time, please...' he sat down, resigned.

'As I said before, we established that Mirosław Trzaska's the name of a homeless man. We had problems establishing who the victim was... As it is, we went to visit his sister...'

'Who did you go with?' Undisguised nervousness returned, as though Pilski could see the shame, the dirt, as though he stank, didn't fit in.

'Lentz,' replied Bartol and saw the relief. Up to now he hadn't been sure whether Pilski cared in the least about Polek's jibes; he didn't seem to pay any attention to them; now he knew.

'I'm sorry, please go on,' the prosecutor said in a calmer tone.

'I spoke to your mother,' Bartol tried to emphasise the fact, 'and your name happened to be mentioned. That's why I'm here.'

'Thank you for not putting it to me at headquarters.'

'I won't say that's what I had in mind but, above all, time's of importance. We have two murders committed by one perpetrator. We don't know whether the victims have been randomly picked. At the moment we can't rationally connect them, we're working on it. Be that as it may, one of the victims is your uncle. Can you tell me anything about him?'

'As I've already said, I never saw him... before. She told me the story, but not until I was at secondary school. She was convinced that he didn't kill the man. She had scruples that

she'd misjudged him, that everybody had misjudged him. I
believed her at the time. I even had some juvenile plans to go
back to the case once I'd finished my studies – for her – that,
seeing as he was innocent, I'd prove it...' He broke off. 'Some
such nonsense.'

'And what, did you work on it?' asked Bartol.

'No, not really. I only checked that he'd pleaded guilty and
been released from prison, and that's where I left it. I used to
be an idealist for a while, until I realised that in fact everybody
was innocent – in their mother's, their sister's and, above all,
their own eyes, that it was senseless to dig it all up again... since
he himself didn't want to turn up... I tried to explain to my
mother that it wasn't as easy as all that, that he needed time,
and she began to ask less and less frequently. Besides, I got a
bit scared... Perhaps it's a good thing, it would have all come
out into the open now...'

'What would have come out?' asked Bartol.

Pilski took a long time answering.

'I also looked into the whole affair about the woman called
Elżbieta Garnczek, nice maiden name – Ogrodniczak – but
her company's name tops it all – Elizabeth Garden. I won't
pretend I wasn't fascinated for a while. She got six years for
complicity; her lover, meaning my mother's brother, took the
entire blame for the crime on himself, which you probably
know. Her sentence was suspended after three years, which
didn't surprise me at first. It was worse when I read why – not
only was it for good behaviour, but also for taking good care of
a child which had been born just before the verdict had been
announced. Not bad, eh? That was too much for me.' He broke
off and looked at Bartol. 'Perhaps I had the same expression
as yours when I read all this. For a long time I didn't know
what to do. The child could have been my cousin. theoretically,
but only theoretically because the woman was married at the
time and...' He didn't finish because something ginger had just

flitted between Bartol's legs, which, as usual, didn't fit beneath the coffee table. Bartol jumped, knocking the glass surface with his knees. Coffee spilt and trickled.

'I'm sorry,' was all he said. Out of the corner of his eye he glimpsed the ginger bushy tail of a cat in the doorway.

'It doesn't matter. You could well have got a firight. I've got a cat to even things out, an alley cat at that. He likes creeping up like that, although he doesn't usually leave the other room when strangers are here. I'll just wipe it up.' He left and returned a moment later. He looked grotesque with an enormous rag in one hand, a mop in the other, and – on top of it all – a tie with pink circles.

Pilski swung the wet mop quickly and efficiently, concentrating on the huge coffee stain. Bartol sat down, unable to concentrate on anything. He hadn't suspected a cat to be in the apartment, hadn't suspected that Trzaska *aka* Gawlicki could have been either the father of a child born behind bars, or perhaps the murderer of its father, that Ogrodniczka meant Garden.

He stared blankly at the disappearing stain.

'Going back to that woman,' Pilski went on once he'd deposited the cleaning implements in the hallway. 'She must be quite interesting, I guess.'

It seemed the unexpected effort had greatly calmed him down; he spoke in a matter-of-fact tone.

'What's your guess?' asked Bartol.

'A few years after leaving prison she was accused of procuring. The case was dismissed and in the mid-nineties she founded the Elizabeth Garden Fun Factory.'

'You know quite a bit about her.'

'I told you it interested me exactly ten years ago. I couldn't find anything about my uncle. It looked as if he'd disappeared so at the beginning I searched for something about her. I stopped precisely when I read about the child. At that moment

I decided to let it go, and that's what I did. I haven't thought about it for the past five years.'

'Something happened five years ago?' asked Bartol.

'Don't catch me out on every word. That's exactly what I wanted to tell you and had in mind when I said she must have been interesting. I was driving with an ex-girlfriend to Szczecin and some twenty kilometres before the city I noticed a huge wholesale outlet with the sign: 'Elizabeth Garden Fun Factory'. From outside it looked like a modern warehouse with professional electronic equipment. It stood out a great deal from its surroundings: lots of aluminium, neat car park, trees, lawns and so on. Had I been alone I'd have stopped to see what it was, but I wasn't and had to wait until I got back to Poznań. I returned and had a look. There were some electronics, true enough, but not many. It's one of the largest sex wholesalers in Poland, certainly this part of Poland. Mrs Ogrodniczak is a very wealthy woman and the entire strange business belongs to her. That moment simply confirmed that I'd done the right thing not to delve into it all. I never thought I'd ever hear about them again. I often think the wrong things of late.' He paused. 'Does she know that the murdered man's her brother?'

'Of course,' said Bartol. 'I also told her about the funeral. And I think she's going to have to come to Poznań. Can you tell me anything else about this Ogrodniczak?' He wanted to return to their earlier conversation.

'No, I've told you absolutely everything I know. I had no intention of getting involved. I was plain scared of what I might come across.' He fell silent. 'So there's still the funeral.' Again he paused. 'Please don't say anything to her about the child, and certainly not that I knew. I don't know how she'd take it. I've got to sort everything out in my own mind.'

At that moment, the doorbell rang.

'So must I. I'll go now. We'll be touch.'

'Right,' replied Pilski, getting to his feet. He went to the hall and, without checking who it was, pressed the intercom.

Bartol also got up.

'I'd like to ask one more thing, where...'

'I was driving all day with my fiancée. The colour of the car and flowers has to go with yet a different dress. It must be the sixth shade of white. Then I stayed the night at... Besides, you're bound to meet her. If I don't open she'll probably climb in through the window,' he added with resignation.

'And did Mikulski also figure in the story?' asked Bartol, putting on his jacket.

'No, he definitely didn't, otherwise it would have rang a bell. The surname might not be particularly remarkable but it's certainly the first time I've heard of anyone being called Antoniusz, well, apart from that other Antonius. I've got one more favour to ask. I'm going to back out of this case, go on leave, but I'll be at your disposal. Please don't – as far as possible, of course – associate me with the case... At least so that some of your colleagues... For various reasons... You understand?'

'I can't promise anything.'

'Nor do I ask you to promise anything. Just give me some time to get used to the situation, that's all. I've been planning a wedding, not a funeral.' He didn't wait for a reply only walked to the door.

Bartol took his leave. He was already on the ground floor when a girl, stiletto heels clattering and jewellery clanking, passed him. She could barely raise her eyelids, heavy with make-up, to throw him an uninterested glance. All her attention was focused on a fingernail, glittering with sequins, which apparently wasn't glittery enough. It occurred to him that this had to be Pilski's fiancée who, at the last moment, had resisted climbing in through the window. She looked the part.

Right in front of the stairwell he saw a Mercedes parked haphazardly. The passenger – bored, clicking similar fingernails and wearing a similar cowboy jacket – was a woman resembling the younger one but some decades older and, doubtless for that reason, her glitter sparkled all the more against an even deeper tan.

Bartol was more than horrified.

APRIL DIDN'T FOOL AROUND; it wasn't fine and didn't stand out in any way. May, on the other hand, right from the very start tried hard not to leave newspaper headlines or television news. Everything was extreme, was the most... since records began, and even the oldest highlanders couldn't remember such temperatures, such downpours, such gales. Several places experienced tornadoes, cloudbursts, ground frost and heatwaves. Nature tried not to take too much notice and within a week everything that could flower and turn green was covered with flowers and leaves.

It was no different, it was the same in Maciej Bartol's life.

His girlfriend ended up in hospital. The pregnancy was not as greatly threatened as had initially appeared but, in keeping with May's logic, the light summer rain turned into a storm of hail and thunder.

He didn't visit her on the first day, only phoned saying that if there was no need that day he'd come the next since they had a lot of work. She believed him. Polek's wife helped him out – oh, wonder of wonders – by having already mentioned that the men were working hard on something, that her husband was coming home late and hardly sleeping. Bartol wasn't coming home later than usual, but didn't mention that. Seemingly justified, he went to the hospital two days later and brought some flowers. He didn't quite know how to behave. He tried to be calm and matter-of-fact; said that her health was the most important thing and that all the rest... he stammered – the rest didn't count.

And it was this 'rest' that caused the trouble. One stupid word. The girl started sobbing hysterically; it was impossible to calm her down. The women in the neighbouring beds, who'd previously stroked their bellies gently so as not to move unnecessarily, now looked as if they wanted to get up, crush him to the ground and suffocate him under their weight. A nurse ran into the ward, didn't ask anything, cast her eyes around and, reflecting the looks of the other women like a mirror, turned him out.

His mother wasn't phoning so he gathered she must have heard something already. He called first. She picked up and nothing – silence. When he asked why she wasn't saying anything she finally replied that a pause in music was also a sound and very expressive at that. When he asked what it was she wanted to express, he was told that she was speechless. She hung up.

Usually – even though he hadn't done anything wrong, hadn't any bad intentions, had just uttered ordinary words which somehow had been misinterpreted – he would have tormented himself from morning to night. Usually, but not now, not now that the cherry trees on the terrace among the tenement roofs were covered in pink blossom.

He saw these trees almost every evening and, more and more frequently, in the mornings, too. The first time was on her birthday. They'd been alone. He'd given her one of his treasures: an old music-box with a ballerina. He'd found it hard to part with; he'd feared she wouldn't appreciate it.

She did appreciate it; and he didn't regret it. Didn't regret it at all. He wound the ballerina up many a time.

He never came across the muscular boy again. They never talked about him, nor did she mention her former relationships; perhaps only once when she said she didn't want to commit herself because she'd made a long-term investment with a high risk factor in the past and the risk hadn't paid off. She didn't ask about his life. Which suited him.

Whether he needed to or not, he visited her. They analysed every detail and every sentence on both the pages marked by a ribbon in the Bible on which murdered Jan Maria Gawlicki's hand had rested. The pages contained two chapters from the Book of Wisdom. Everything could apply to anything, everyone and every situation: nothing but wisdom. There was also a paper bookmark with the words *Credo in unum Deum.* A toss-up according to Magda. The words of the Apostles' Creed had been mandatory since 381 AD, a little too long for them to be popular. On the other hand, if they took it that everything in Antoniusz Mikulski's case had referred to Hope in some strange way, and in Gawlicki's case everything referred to Faith, then it might fit.

He'd also gone to Gawlicki's funeral. Unlike Mikulski's funeral, this occasion had gathered a crowd, but the effect was similar, meaning non-existent.

Neither Gawlicki's sister nor his nephew had attended. Bartol had seen Pilski a couple of times since then and spoken to him, but he hadn't asked why neither he nor his mother had been present. Nor did he ask why, in fact, Pilski was getting married.

Nor did he manage to question Mrs Ogrodniczak, the chairman and sole shareholder of the Elizabeth Garden Fun Factory Company. For the past two weeks she'd been staying at a health clinic and it wasn't her custom to inform her employees of when she'd return; they expected her at any moment. Bartol also waited; he didn't want to scare her away with a sudden summons. He knew she'd left the country and hadn't yet returned.

He felt he was running around in circles again – during the day. In the evenings, on the other hand, everything spun all the faster – and it spun pink.

III

ELŻBIETA OGRODNICZAK didn't even try to fall asleep; she never could in planes. She kept touching her face, avoiding her still painful lips. She felt she wouldn't be able to laugh for a long time. It didn't bother her much. She rarely laughed.

***

Polek's wife was pleased he wasn't home. She waited for her daughter to fall asleep then started packing. She didn't have to explain to anyone why she was taking stiletto heels and a pair of practically invisible, golden thongs she'd carefully hidden earlier, to a three day training conference. She smiled at the panties and blushed again, as she had when buying them.

***

The girl stared at the child she was feeding and didn't feel anything, not even that she was feeding. She was sure that the following morning the doctor would come and say, just like her head of department had once done:, 'You're not competent enough'. Maybe she'd even ask: 'To do what?' And he'd reply: 'To be a mother'. And this time, too, she'd agree; this time, too, she wouldn't even cry.

***

A truly pissed occupant on the top floor of the tenement in Wilga had smoked almost a whole cigarette before noticing the couple kissing on the terrace. The view was obscured by branches, those of a cherry tree. He pondered a long while over how they'd managed to carry such large trees to the roof before he returned to his room and beat his own woman, out of sheer bitterness that things hadn't turned out as well between them.

**

Melka's night shift began unusually. First the man with strange glasses had appeared uninterested, then paid up front, and now he was kissing her all over for at least ten minutes. Somehow she felt ill at ease; her boyfriend, after all, was downstairs in the hotel bar. Finally, she asked the man to stop; he laughed scornfully and finished off like an ordinary client.

**

Krzysztof Bolko, the regional leader of a neither poor nor rich area near Szczecin, lay in bed waiting patiently for sleep to come. The room seemed unbearably stuffy and too bright for the middle of the night. He could have got up, opened the window and pulled the curtains to, but he didn't. He kept closing his eyes only to instantly open them again. He knew that, in the end, he'd have to turn over on his other side and part from the drowsy and soothing wall. Sometimes it worked. A bit on his back, a bit on his other side, then turned to the wall again. Sometimes, but not this time. His wife performed the manoeuvre almost at the same time. They'd have nearly collided had the duvet, which she'd unknowingly thrown to his side, not absorbed the undesired blow. For a while, he stared at her with what could have been disgust or perhaps boredom. Her nightdress, exceptionally short because of the heatwave, had ridden up to her neck, revealing enormous white knickers. Not for the first time did he have the impression that he was looking at gigantic rings of over-pickled white sausage, produced by a drunken butcher. He'd have swiftly turned over again if it weren't for the malicious satisfaction with which he watched two persistent flies which – chased away by the nervous twitches of the slumbering body – stubbornly kept landing on it again.

'So she didn't manage to wipe them all out,' he muttered to himself, smiling a touch scornfully at the recollection of how she'd raged with the fly swatter, swiping the flies just when the sports news was on, probably so that they wouldn't distract her by sitting on the television during the serial which followed the news. The loud slap of a hand trying, in sleep, to kill yet another fly which obstinately kept sitting on his wife's cheek woke him up completely.

He got up, made energetically for the kitchen then slowed his pace midway. He'd just remembered that the fridge was going through yet another family diet, grapefruit this time. He didn't even approach the fridge to check what else was there; he'd bought five kilos of grapefruits that day himself, so what else could there be? He went instead to his bag which lay by the armchair; there were some chocolate bars in the bag, slightly melted, but they were there. He ate all five. He laughed heartily to himself; one for every kilo of the nasty bitter stuff.

He adored such moments when he felt he'd outsmarted somebody or something. And maybe this hadn't been his only success that day, he thought, as he remembered the very promising applicant. Complaints all day long then, towards the end, a request concerning land available for development. And on behalf of Mrs Garden. He'd never have thought that she was so forgiving. Up until then he had, in fact, been frightened of her. He'd won the last elections loudly fulminating against the previous regional leader for having agreed to the construction of a warehouse with all that filth, when it was still in construction.

Initially, he'd pretended to a certain degree that he was trying to prevent it. The councillors, as usual, couldn't do anything but helplessly counsel, whereas he'd been vociferous while doing nothing in the hope of the case petering out in time. And it had. A beautiful complex had appeared, beautiful profits from property tax – the largest in the district, employment and salaries for a large number of people – also the highest in the region. Somehow it had all turned out. He was just as quick to explain to himself where the friendly attitude of such a woman could have come from; big money and serious people weren't as petty as the riff-raff. He thought the same of himself even though he hadn't spoken to his neighbour for ten years because the latter had sold him an allegedly good car; but that was an entirely different matter.

He'd been slightly terrified when first talking to the man. The man had been a bit strange, wore strange glasses, and a not particularly masculine little heart hung at his neck. Bolko must have broken into a sweat when he heard the client ask about land for an enormous toy warehouse. He was afraid to even think what sort of toys the man had in mind but the latter, sensing his unease, had smiled warmly and jokingly set things straight by saying he meant ordinary toys for children, teddy bears, board games and so on. They'd both laughed. The atmosphere had relaxed considerably. To such an extent that he'd very willingly offered to deliver the gift to Mrs Elżbieta – who'd just left the country – in person. So the man wouldn't have to visit her company again, seeing as he was so busy. Krzysztof Bolko didn't generally do people favours but this applicant had been so polite, so promising for the region's future and for him, that he hadn't been able to refuse. Nor was a personal visit to Mrs Garden without significance. With a present from a friend whom she'd recommended, he could even phone her at home and arrange to meet for coffee, or perhaps even something else.

'Oh, that woman is certainly elegant and must surely know something about her kind of trade,' he laughed lewdly at his own thoughts.

He went back to bed and fell asleep with a smile.

MACIEJ BARTOL had been pacing the room for an hour. Now he stood at the door, listening for footsteps on the stairs. He knew the unique rhythmic clatter of heels, knew it since birth, and was simply scared. All day long he'd devised complicated escape plans, realising they were absolutely senseless. In the morning, not only the day had attacked him with its brightness and his lack of sleep. Not only had the alarm rung, but his mother, too... had rung.

Just so, as it were. They'd been intending to go together to visit his daughter and her granddaughter anyway; his mother couldn't get over the joy of it being a girl because that was, as if, better than a grandson. He'd left a message in the evening, explaining why he hadn't been able to visit the previous day, but had the odd impression that she hadn't listened to what he'd said or, what was worse, had listened to it but in her own way. She'd said, almost calmly, that she'd first drop in on him then later they'd go to the hospital together. It wasn't until he'd simply asked why, seeing as the hospital was closer to where she lived, that all hell had broken loose. She'd replied in an entirely different tone of voice, saying she was just in the right mood to discuss the city's topography. And that even if corpses lay strewn in a row all the way along Święty Marcin Street from Kaponier Roundabout to Stary Rynek, he was to be at home.

There was little hope of escape.

The footsteps strode in, inevitably and resolutely.

'Hello, it's nice to catch you at home. I wasn't entirely sure you wouldn't find some desperately convoluted excuse.'

'You used to say I was your little hero.'

'A lot of time's gone by since you brought home that little bird with a broken wing in your scarf.'

'Mum, please stop. You know it isn't easy for me either.'

'Even though the Caesarean section spared you some trauma, I hope this is only some sort of male post-natal depression.'

Bartol stared at her dumbfounded. He opened his mouth to say something but didn't have time.

'Please be so kind as not to enlighten me.'

'Mum, you know I couldn't yesterday.'

'Then it's a very good thing you can today.' She walked through to the living room and sat down in the armchair.

Bartol thought that was the end of the assault, but he was wrong.

'And please don't explain anything, not today, not now and preferably not tomorrow.' She brushed the hair from her forehead in a specific way, as though casually, as though she were thinking something over. He knew the gesture perfectly well and knew that now she was going to say what she really wanted to.

'You know, an old saying has been going round and round in my head that explains everything. You know which one? It's the one about catarrh and love being the two things you can't hide. But maybe it's going around in my head because it's lost its way, what do you think?'

It seemed to Bartol as though she'd paused intentionally, just to see whether he'd turn pale. He did. He had no idea whether she knew anything or whether she'd played *va banque* and now, by just looking at him, had seen her conjecture prove true. He had no illusions that now she knew for certain.

The phone rang. For some reason he'd been sure it was Lentz but he was wrong. It was Magda. He had no idea of the expression on his face but he must have looked crushed because he heard:

'Pick it up or the phone's going to blush.'

'I'll pick it up later,' he mumbled and muted the ringtone.

'But don't worry,' his mother began after a while. 'I'm not going to say it's bad timing and I'm not going to think it over or ask you any questions now. There are more important things I'd like you to resolve in the way I taught you. Successfully, I hope, because I invested masses of work and time in it and, in my old age, don't want to think the time or money was wasted.'

'Well then, how many times are we going to go back to the same conversation? I accept the child, am going to help bring it up as best I can, although it all seems so abstract to me right now. But I'm not going to live with them. I'm not going to pretend my love's come to an end because love had never even begun. What else am I supposed to say? That I don't rush to the hospital because I don't know how to behave? That I see the child but don't yet know what I feel?'

'You know where the problem lies? In that she doesn't know how to behave and doesn't know what she feels either.'

'Mum, regardless of anything else, she wanted that baby.'

'She also wanted a wedding with a hundred people, a dress made in Paris and a film star like Żebrowski for a husband, all in a package. And so what? Do you know how much one imagines about motherhood has got to do real motherhood? About as much as an advert for Pampers has to do with dirty nappies. I was there yesterday. It's no better, if not worse.'

'You said she was tired after giving birth.'

'I did because she was. She's already been in hospital for a week, the baby's jaundice is almost gone but she's not getting any better. She's being discharged today and mustn't be left alone, not even for a minute.'

'So what do you propose, because I suppose you do have a solution?'

'We'll go there together and you, concerned, are suddenly going to have the brilliant idea that since she shouldn't be alone and you have so much work, she could go and stay with me for a while. I'll be delighted with the simplicity of the idea and on top of that I'll be extremely happy. It's your problem to convince her and make it look convincing.'

'Have you still got that Franciszek on your shoulders by any chance?'

'From time to time. Except that he's less trouble than you are, even when you're asleep. Besides, he'll probably prove useful.'

'You think she'll agree?' he asked after a while. He didn't expect the stage of forcing the plan about their initially living together would end so strangely.

'She's got to agree. Believe me. For the first six months I loved you differently than for the rest of your life, except in those days nobody explained this could happen. The word depression was reserved for the Żuławy flatlands. After giving birth, a woman was allowed to be tired yet happy, but I wasn't tired yet I was unhappy.'

'I didn't know.'

'You didn't have to.'

'Mum,' he said after a long pause, 'do you think it doesn't take it out of me, the fact that everything's not going the way it should?'

'Don't be all that worried. The sun also has spots. Get yourself together, we've got to go.'

She agreed. Dispassionately, indifferently, or out of tiredness: it was difficult to say.

He made two runs between the housing estate in Polanki and Ogrody. He carried and brought things although he didn't quite know what they were for. It was hard for him to believe that all this was for that tiny bundle he'd brought from the hospital. He was scared to pick the bundle up, so his reason dictated; was also afraid of staying at home too long, but couldn't honestly say why. Fortunately, nobody asked him and, fortunately, again he wasn't the centre of attention.

Once again he blocked Magda's neighbour's car when parking in front of the tenement in Wilga. The neighbour wouldn't be able to drive away in the morning but apparently he didn't get up before nine anyway so there wouldn't really be any problem. The rain was light, but it was enough to act as an excuse. Bartol left his phone number on the windscreen.

He knew it was one of many, albeit the smallest, of temporary solutions he came up with in his life and about which he tried not to think beforehand. He knew they lulled his vigilance through ostensible and blameless action; he knew and did nothing about it.

It was a near certainty that one day the neighbour would get up early and the morning would be a write-off, just as Magda would finally find out about the child, about the fact that the child was living with her mother in his mother's apartment; and this, too, would be a rude awakening.

As he was reaching the first floor, the thought occurred to him once more that he should tell her everything, but the thought was obviously too heavy and stayed on the second floor, could no longer be seen from the fifth and, as he knocked on the attic door, he forgot it had even existed.

Again he was touched by the same view. Sheets of paper spread out on the floor, next to them a couple of books, spines up, a couple put aside, one open and on it a heavy, small statue of a laughing Buddha who saw to it that the book didn't close, a glass of wine. And the words: 'It's a good thing you're here...'

For a long time he didn't even listen to what she was saying; he didn't really want to hear more. She turned away to look for something and returned with an illustration she wanted to show him. It was small. He didn't study it, handed it back to her and pulled off his damp sweater.

'Good.' She gave him a moment. 'Sit down and look carefully. Do you want something to drink?'

He didn't have time to reply. Picked up the illustration again. Studied it and froze. It was a photograph of an etching depicting a mother with a child on her knees; from behind her back peered some more children. Bartol sat, or rather collapsed ,onto the sofa.

'What is it?' was all he could manage.

'Love,' Magda answered quite naturally. 'Well, what will you have to drink? Wine?' She looked at him and smiled. 'Or something stronger? You're a little pale.'

'Make it something stronger...' he replied, slowly regaining his balance. It wasn't an allusion; probably something she simply wanted to show him.

'You're right. The air's too heavy, as if a storm's brewing... Take a look at the other pictures on the table. I'll be back in a minute.'

It still took him a long while to gather his thoughts. The illustrations showing fragments of paintings and etchings depicting mothers with one, three or a whole group of children, didn't help. Only when Magda had returned and sat down next to him, only when he'd almost choked on his gin with its drop of tonic – the way he liked it – did he start to regain peace of mind.

'Are you going to visit her tomorrow?' she asked after a while.

'Who?' This time he did choke.

'You're a bit strange today. Careful, or you'll suffocate. What do you mean 'who'? The Ogrodniczak woman.'

'Yes,' he replied still coughing. 'She's already back. I called her company. She's going to be there.'

'I don't know whether we're on the right track but it would be good for you to be prepared. Presuming that my thinking's correct, Hope and Faith have already been buried, only the greatest remains – Love.'

'Why the greatest?'

'"And now these three remain: faith, hope and love. But the greatest of these is love." Letter to the Corinthians. You've never read it,' she laughed.

'I don't read other people's letters, haven't you noticed yet?'

'I couldn't help but notice. You'd better listen then. Love can be represented in various ways. There's worldly love, sensual

love and love in general. The latter used to be represented with
a torch, basket of fruit, flaming heart but above all children.
Alciati has it that there can be no end of them, however many
will fit, it doesn't matter. Cesare Ripa states decidedly three. I'll
read it to you: "three children indicate that although single love
is a virtue, it is triple love which has power because without it
neither faith nor hope has meaning" – and, in my opinion, it
does have meaning for this person. He left it, meaning Love,
to the end, and it's not out of the question that it could refer to
this woman. She's somehow mixed up in all of this.'

'That's why I'm going there. Let's say we're right, what do
you think I ought to look for and ask about? Children? Latin?'
He felt everything was slowly returning to normal. He made
himself more comfortable on the sofa, looked and listened.

'Both one and the other, of course. Ask and look around. I'm
trying to tie it all together. I know I'm going to find a painted
or graphic representation with all this in one, and with an
inscription at that, I just know it. If not in some church then
in a town hall, if not in Gdańsk then in Paris. I've no idea why
I haven't found it yet but I will, and then we'll know what to
look for or what's been found, but make a bit of an effort now.'

'So what symbols and what sayings am I looking for and
where are they supposed to be?'

'All of them and everywhere. Note down what comes to
mind and if you see anything in Latin, even on a cake of soap,
call me.'

'What's soap got to do with it?'

'I've no idea, it just came to mind. Besides, Venus emerged
from the foam naked: will that do?'

'It could. Maybe I'll just see a heart and arrow on a wall?'

'Don't joke. Even if you see a heart-shaped box of chocolates,
take a good look at it and all the chocolates, too. Besides, do
you think a heart like that was thought up by one of your pals
at junior school?'

'No. I associate it with a little chubby Cupid and his bow. It's probably his doing.' He laughed.

'Cupid with an arrow is the notion of sensual love, sudden, at first sight, heralding a change of events, but a heart as symbol of sublime love, if pierced by an arrow, bleeds – unhappily. And if you think that Cupid is nothing but a chubby child, you are mistaken. There was a time when he used to be represented as a beautiful youth with an enormous quiver resting on naked, firm – very firm – buttocks. All he's got left from childhood are his curls. I'll show you in a moment if you like, I've got one somewhere here of exceptional beauty.'

'No, thanks,' replied Bartol nervously ruffling his fringe.

'Then take a look at all these illustrations. Love figures in all of them. I'll make us another drink. It's got stuffy with all these feelings.'

He merely glanced at the photographs; they all looked alike. Then he gazed at Magda as she extracted ice from the bag, sliced the lemon, as she walked and smiled. When she sat next to him, all he knew was that he didn't want to talk about Love anymore, unless it was about the other kind. He pushed all the papers aside. Picked up one picture, with no children in it: just a man and a woman, the latter holding a flower. He showed it to her when she returned.

'I prefer these innocent flirtations.'

'They're not all that innocent,' Magda replied. 'The covering on her head shows that she's married and that joker in the lace next to her looks to me to be nothing more than a musician. Look, she's holding a wild rose and this most surely indicates sinful and forbidden love.'

'I'd never have thought it. Then why did they paint such filth?' he asked laughing, looking at the apparently innocent scene again.

'See what an imagination they had. It's a censored version of the story of sin, as a warning, so women looking at it knew what vain sensual love looks like and where it can lead. If you like I can show you how real love, married love of course, was represented and praised...'

'No, thank you. Perhaps some more of that sensual love,' he said, slowly brushing behind her ear the strands of auburn hair which had broken loose of her grip and fallen in all directions.

She didn't say anything, which was a good sign; nothing in the vein of 'wait, let's get some more work done, I've just remembered something'.

With a touch of irony, she merely asked: 'Is this how you want to release creative energy? A brief leap into Chaos and back.'

'That's exactly the sort of journey I'm in the mood for right now.'

'And what would you like to know?'

'What, for example... does an ear exactly represent in this context?' he asked and started kissing her ear, lazily, as though there, on the inner side of the lobe, he'd be able to find the answer.

'In this context, you say...' she repeated, stretching out her words and body. 'It is, above all, greedy for flattery, or rather... lip-homage...'

He didn't wait for further encouragement.

After a lengthy interlude, she was the first to speak: 'That's not all. It's also exceptionally sensitive to vows or compliments, if you prefer...'

'About your breasts, for example?' He pulled down the right strap of her bra.

The strap didn't resist, fell gently, revealing one breast.

'For example...'

'And what, for example, does such a liberated breast stand for?' he asked, toying with her nipple.

'Well... It could signify sincerity, fertility. Or perhaps simply the jealousy of the other, imprisoned one... I don't know yet...' she replied.

'Well then, perhaps we simply have to do something about it, explain it to the other one,' he said, pulling down the other strap. 'There's no hiding the fact, it's waiting for an apology... impatiently. Shall I take care of it?' He didn't wait for her assent.

A moment later, he looked at her again; she, too, opened her eyes.

'What's waiting for an explanation now?' she asked.

'The hair grip.'

'Both my naked breasts are smiling at you and it's my pinned-back hair that's putting you out,' she laughed, her eyes on his imploring face. 'All right, unfasten it.' As clumsily as he'd pulled the grip out of her hair, so very accurately did he throw it into the wastepaper bin.

'We didn't like each other at first sight,' he declared, spreading her hair as it tumbled over her shoulders.

'See,' she said, winding a strand around her finger, 'and I thought that loose hair as a symbol of power to magically enslave men was a bit of an exaggeration.'

'Not in the least... Now just the dress... I ask it...' The dress consented with unwitting encouragement.

'And the feet?' he asked, seeing them instinctively rub against each other.

'That's for the prince... I've no idea what he did with the slipper during his tedious search for Cinderella,' she answered, unbuttoning his shirt, then belt, then trousers. 'What can that be compared to?' she asked herself.

'Aren't there any symbols for it anymore?'

'Come on, there are masses. In fact everything that's hard and erect.'

He eased her onto her back and started kissing her stomach.

'You've reached the seat of ecstasy and sinful desires.'

'And where will I get to in a minute?'

'Could be... the pomegranate, or fig maybe...'

'I've never tasted one but it's probably my favourite fruit...'

Again he didn't get enough sleep, and again didn't regret it.

Much to his own surprise he left Poznań exactly as he'd planned although not everything had gone according to plan. He'd just been about to phone Polek when the latter had called informing him that he wasn't going anywhere, that he was having problems with his family and would Bartol cover for him should the need arise. Bartol agreed without asking any questions but knew the unwelcome conversation no longer wished to be postponed, and at most could wait until the following day and not a day longer.

That's what he decided, and then focused exclusively on the purpose of his journey.

For two weeks he'd been gathering information about Elżbieta Ogrodniczak. At moments he was fascinated, at moments horrified. He didn't know what to think of the woman. She kept slipping through his fingers, refused to be pigeonholed; as if she were made of pigeonholes: locked, left ajar, open, ones which could no longer be closed.

He had no idea who he was going to meet.

A hard, efficient chairwoman who employed seventy people and had long ago erased her twentieth birthday, one she'd spent behind bars?

A clever tart who had stopped earning with her body soon enough and had started using her head in order to run an exclusive dating agency long before that's what they were called, and ended her career running a legal, profitable business in a related field?

A young woman for whom three years in prison had not been enough to form a bond with the child to whom she'd given birth there?

The woman who'd later had a pair of twins of whose fatherhood many a prominent figure in the country had been suspected, a woman who'd never confirmed or denied anything, brought the children up alone for twenty years just to bury them later in the same cemetery as the one into which they'd crashed their light sports aircraft?

He knew about this from the newspapers; from newspapers, too, he'd cut out two photographs of her. There, in the third row at some gala event, the photographs too small to read anything from her face.

He was scared of the conversation.

During the entire journey, he prepared himself, thinking almost exclusively of Elżbieta Ogrodniczak, his thoughts escaping to Magda only briefly. Even more briefly, to his child. When almost at his destination, he started running through his conversation with Pilski and covered nearly a whole kilometre before realising he'd passed a factory. He turned back.

It could easily be mistaken. The building looked like a warehouse or production plant of some highly specialised equipment. Silver, corrugated, modern, surrounded by a neatly trimmed hedge, neatly planted trees, neatly parked cars. Nor did the large letters EGFF clarify anything. He didn't find the sign marked Elizabeth Garden Fun Factory which Pilski had mentioned but, as he parked, sensed it was the right place. As soon as he entered, all certainty vanished.

A door of steel and glass opened. Immediately behind it, on the right, he saw a row of desks on which stood computers behind which sat women wearing headphones. The women simply registered his entry with their eyes and continued to tap away on their keyboards. On the left, he saw a hall with rows of shelves. He didn't know why he walked towards them. From a distance, the twenty metres of shelving looked crammed with shampoos and conditioners. He was wrong; side by side stood lines of vibrators. Pink ones, green ones, ones made of flowery glass and some whose function he couldn't quite figure out. It was the same with what looked like a shelf full of pharmaceuticals. They seemed to be medicines but the images on the packaging suggested, in a more or less explicit way, what they were used for. A raging bull, a wild horse, golden rain. The swan on the packaging of some syrup – for potency no doubt – seriously interested him because although the swan's neck was long and thick he couldn't work out a connection.

Just as he was thinking he'd have to ask Magda what a swan like that could signify, a young woman approached offering to help. When she heard that he wanted to talk to Mrs Ogrodniczak, she retorted that, unfortunately, Mrs Ogrodniczak wasn't in. His hint that he was from the police was met with a shrug: so what, the head wasn't in anyway.

After long negotiations with one of the managers in a beautiful office and another in an even more beautiful office, he was connected to the boss. He briefly told her why he was there. To his amazement the woman invited him to visit her at home – if he'd be so kind. He would be so kind.

The house stood nearby.

Still a little bewildered by the unusual products, Bartol arrived at the given address. He'd presumed the architecture would be modern and now quickly decided never to presume again. Passing through the open gate, he drove in a small circle and parked in front of a small house stylised on a traditional Polish manor.

A tiled roof, brick, wooden shutters. Flowers beneath the windows; he'd no idea what they were called but knew they suited the place. The same as the ivy which wound its way around the pillars, sheltering the front door with a green parasol of not yet fully opened leaves but which, when open, would shroud the door completely.

From these entangled creepers emerged a woman. He hadn't noticed her before while she, snuggled up to the pillar, must have been observing him for some time.

She now walked towards him. Slowly. Dressed entirely in black. Black, too, were the enormous glasses which covered half her face. The sweeping long skirt, tightly fastened at the waist, undulated. He didn't know whether it was because of the wind which he didn't feel or because of the flowing, determined movements which betrayed the self-confidence he sensed.

'Good morning. Maciej Bartol, I take it?'

'Yes.'

'Elżbieta Ogrodniczak. Please come in. I think we'll sit outside. It's a beautiful day.' Without waiting for him to agree as to the beauty of the day, she opened the door wide and walked ahead.

The tone of her voice was in equal measure pleasing and brooking no argument. He followed her.

He knew she was almost as old as his mother but she didn't look like his mother, even from the back. Her tight blouse clung to a body which could have belonged to that of a ballerina who, despite her age, had not forgotten how to keep a tight rein on herself. Not a gram of fat, not a millimetre's deviation from the vertical. The long skirt, fastened tightly by a wide belt, emphasised her narrow waist even more. Black hair, also disciplined to lie smoothly against her head, was pulled back close to her nape by an elastic band.

It hadn't been the wind: the skirt undulated as it floated through the living room. They stepped out onto the terrace. The woman stopped, turned towards him and with a slight, barely perceptible gesture, indicated a large wicker armchair. He sat down, or rather sunk into it.

'What will you have to drink?'

'Water, if I may.'

'You may,' she replied and retreated into the house again. He wasn't sure whether it was a good thing that the interview wasn't taking place in different surroundings. These here intimidated him. He felt as if he were inside some magazine: *Idyllic Life* or something like that. Lilacs of all shades and colours blossomed; behind his back he heard the murmur of water flowing, probably over pebbles; on the coffee table was spread a tablecloth embroidered with flowers.

Mrs Ogrodniczak returned with a jug of water, half full of ice beneath which swam green leaves, as if part of the green-patterned drinking glasses. He hoped the leaves wouldn't fall into his glass; he loathed mint and other such extras. They didn't.

She sat down.

'I'm listening.' Her face didn't betray any emotions: there was no half-smile, no grimace, eyes still hidden behind the sunglasses. It troubled him.

'Due to the circumstances I'm compelled to talk to you about matters concerning the past,' he began timidly and broke off for a second.

:'You already told me that over the phone, please go on.'

'Jan Maria Gawlicki has been murdered...'

'How?'

'At home. We suspect it's the same murderer who'd previously killed Antoniusz Mikulski in a similar way.' He couldn't be sure but sensed that something stirred the stony face. 'We're searching for a connection between the two men. Does anything come to mind...'

'No, nothing comes to mind.' And silence.

He now knew one thing: he couldn't conduct the interview this way. So he started anew; beginning in the simplest way.

'I have a favour to ask of you. Could you please remove your sunglasses while we talk? I find it hard to speak to you without seeing your face.'

'Of course, if it'll make it easier for you.'

It didn't. The entire surface around her eyes was one yellow-green-red bruise. He was taken aback. He knew from somewhere that she'd been to some exclusive renewal clinic but he'd never expected anything like this.

'It takes a long time to heal sometimes,' she explained, sipping her water and half-closing her blood-purple eyelids. Satisfaction with the effect she'd achieved was the first emotion he heard in her voice.

'Mrs Ogrodniczak, we have reason to believe that if we don't apprehend the person who committed these crimes, another may be committed. One of our hypotheses assumes that we need to look for clues in the past, Mikulski's as well as Gawlicki's. Hence my visit.'

She said nothing for a while; only what could have been a half-smile appeared on her face and swiftly disappeared.

'Am I a suspect?'

'Probably not, certainly not directly. We've checked, you weren't in the country at the time.'

'And now you've checked for yourself?' Again she slowly half-closed her swollen eyelids.

'No, I wanted to talk about the past.' He didn't add that it was perhaps also to warn her about what might lie ahead. He had no idea which way the conversation would turn.

'Well then, you might be lucky.' She lost herself in thought. 'We'll talk. Go ahead and ask.'

'You were once in love with Mr Gawlicki.' The moment he said this he knew he couldn't have got off to a more idiotic start.

'Why do you suppose that? I never loved him, I loved my husband.'

He might have expected it. He was wondering how to begin again but this time she was the first to speak.

'I was nineteen when I got married. I was the happiest girl alive, just as it should be. Everyone envied me. He was different. Beautiful, gentle, fresh. Never stank of vodka, never shoved sweaty hands under my skirt in an alley, roughly, just to grope. Never. It's just that, after the wedding he didn't do so either...' She paused, then continued: 'I didn't know what the problem was at the time. He held me like before, touched me like before, smiled like before but that wasn't enough. I didn't fully realise just to what extent it wasn't enough. Then came sweet words and taunts in turn, laughter and tears, every day and every night. I couldn't leave him - and not only because it was unthought of in those days. I loved him, loved him and thought all this had to change, that there was a way. Where did I get the idea of jealousy? The naivety of a twenty-year old girl, no doubt. Why Gawlicki? Out of the blue. He asked for it, came of his own accord, not once, not twice. He was good-looking and, in a sense, free. Did I hide it? Just enough for my husband to notice. For it to shake him a little. And it did. That's what I thought when I saw him eavesdropping through the window. I wanted to see him suffer. I left Gawlicki naked in the bedroom, silently ran round the house and saw... him suffering, glued to the window, staring... with his hand down his trousers... What did I feel then? Infinite hatred, despair, helplessness. I started to scream, he took fright, pushed me into the house so that the neighbours wouldn't hear. I hit him, scratched him, he merely protected himself. In the end I stopped, from sheer powerlessness or tiredness, I don't know... He started to calm me down and I was almost calm until he said that everything was all right, until he put his arm around me... that arm, until I saw Gawlicki in the door, until I felt his sperm trickling down my thigh, until I saw him look at him like that...' There was a long silence. 'I don't know how a brass figure of Our Lady with Child had come to be in our house, but it was there – at hand. I don't know why I kept on suffocating him when he fell, I don't know why Gawlicki stood and didn't do anything. He didn't understand what was happening and probably never came to understand. He said he loved me, and made love to me. He didn't know why I'd thrown myself at my husband, thought he was the reason. But Gawlicki didn't mean anything to me and I didn't care what he thought. At first, he testified to the truth, that he hadn't done anything. But later, when he discovered I was pregnant, he blamed himself entirely. I said it wasn't the case, but the militia at the time took a definite fancy to his version. A priest, and Our Lady's head imprinted on the victim's skull – I think they were delighted. Nobody was interested in what I had to say. The testimonies didn't tally so they made me an accomplice and put all the blame on him. Besides, I wasn't interested in what was going to happen to him or to me. I only wanted to turn back time. So that my husband could hold me again, just as long as he was there. But he wasn't. I hated Gawlicki as if it was his fault. I also hated his child as if it wasn't mine and gave it away. I never saw Gawlicki again. You're going to ask whether I've got any regrets? Yes, I only regret that the regret came so late, probably too late.' She stood up. 'Now you know everything. I don't care whether you believe me or not. I'm going to the bathroom to rinse my eyes. You'll never know whether that's because of the memories or as a preventive measure following surgery. You may still ask a few questions but not too many, I feel extremely tired.' She left.

She was right, he didn't know why her eyes had become redder: from the sun, tears or general exhaustion. Whether he believed her or not wasn't really all that important. Coming here, he knew that, like it or not, he'd hear only her version of events, one he'd never challenge – because how, with whose help? As it was, he didn't have a clue why she'd bothered to tell him all this. She didn't have to, and he'd never have forced her to do so. She'd wanted to tell him, but why? He had no intention of pondering it over. As soon as she reappeared, he simply asked: 'Why did you tell me all this?'

'I wanted you to know.'

'That much I know, but why?'

'Now that, I won't tell you.' He had no idea what the grimace on her face implied. 'Perhaps I'm getting sentimental in my old age.'

'Have you had any contact with Jan Maria Gawlicki's and your child?'

'No... Never... after I gave it away, never... At first I didn't want to be a mother and wasn't, then I wanted to be and was... And no longer am... You know that both my sons were killed?'

'Yes, I know.' He was sure now that tears, for a brief moment, appeared in her eyes, appeared then disappeared.

'So you also know what my punishment is, my penance. Please don't pester me anymore. I don't know who could have killed him. Maybe you have to search closer to the surface.'

'Maybe. Some Latin maxims were found beside both corpses. Have you by any chance received any flowers or other trifle with a saying attached?'

'So you think I'm not a suspect but in danger?'

'Not necessarily, but we can't rule anything out.'

'No, I haven't received anything. Now please go.'

'Here's my card. Please call if anything troubles you.'

'Troubles... I no longer know what that means. I'll see you out.'

He stood up, angry at himself; he hadn't played his cards right. Maybe what she said about what had happened so many years ago was true, but he was now certain she was hiding something from him. He made use of the bathroom; purposely spent a long time in there and flushed the toilet several times, so that she wouldn't be waiting for him at the door when he left. It would give him time to look around a bit. It worked. She wasn't there, but nor did he find anything which aroused his suspicion. He didn't see any writing on the soap; there were no heart-shaped chocolate boxes or photographs of mothers with children. He didn't see any photographs of children either.

She was standing at a desk in a small study right next to the front door and staring at an angular mirror lying there. She turned abruptly.

'All right? Have you finished?' He had no idea whether she was asking about the bathroom or knew he'd been snooping around.

'Yes. That's a beautiful mirror.'

'Yes, it is beautiful. I brought it back from China. It gives a perfect reflection.' She walked up to him, closing the door behind her.

'If I have any more questions, I'll take the liberty of calling.'

'See you.' He didn't know whether she was throwing him out with these words or really thought they'd see each other sometime. Her face had turned to stone again, the contours of her eyes turned bluer.

Up until Polek's phone call, Maciej Bartol had only one plan – to find himself at Magda's place as soon as possible and tell her everything. Bu Polek had phoned asking what time Bartol would be home; and as soon as he'd received the answer announced he'd wait. Where? On the staircase. He wasn't going to talk over the phone. It so happened that Bartol didn't have the slightest wish to talk to Polek, to agree on his alibi or anything in that vein, but he couldn't turn him away. He assumed, at first, that it would take five minutes then, seeing the sloshed Polek waiting on the doormat with an overnight bag, changed his mind and called Magda that he wouldn't be coming that day.

It was Friday, the thirteenth to top it all, but this he hadn't expected.

Only a month ago Polek had maintained that he had a grown-up daughter, yet now he was screaming: how could she do it to a little girl? For a while, Bartol couldn't understand what he meant. During an ordinary morning row, apparently, Polek's wife had suddenly announced that, in that case, she was getting a divorce, that he'd just helped her decide and that their child was already an adult and would understand. Because she deserved something in life too. Because the fucking mountaineer – as Polek put it – would see to it. Why mountaineer? Because apparently he'd told her that, for him, she was the Mount Everest whose summit he wanted to conquer. It wouldn't have occurred to Bartol that Polek's wife could be any sort of summit for anyone at all, but he refrained from saying so. For a good half hour Polek named all the mountains and mountain ranges he knew before deciding that he'd make Karakorum of the mountaineer's arse then repeated it over and over again. At a certain point, Bartol couldn't take anymore and admitted Polek was the one he'd seen groping a young lady, so where was the problem? To which Polek simply replied that that was neither here nor there because he was only conquering the Table Mountain.

So Bartol decided not to say anything and allow Polek to moan and get drunk as quickly as possible. In fact he didn't see any other solution for the evening. He poured himself small tipples, poured Polek measures twice as large, but the outcome was quite the opposite. Tiredness caught up with him while Polek blabbered incoherently yet coherently enough to inform the neighbours of his passion for geography.

Before Bartol had heard, for the hundredth time, that the Mariana Trench was the place where all women should be put, and how could she throw him out of the house – that in fact he'd been the first to say he was leaving – but she should have made him stay yet didn't, and that the most important thing was to have friends with whom one could conquer mountain peaks – a litre of time had gone by. He fell asleep in the armchair, Polek on the sofa. The latter snored terribly.

In the morning, Bartol had a headache and Polek wasn't there. On the table was a note: he'd forgotten his toothbrush.

Bartol didn't know where to start the day. What he'd most willingly have done was go to see Magda and tell her about what had happened the previous day, less willingly, he'd have gone to see prosecutor Pilski about the same thing. Unable to decide, he chose a third option. He went to headquarters.

Soon it was clear that it was the best solution. True enough, he didn't discover what was happening to Polek, who'd taken a day off, but he did find out that he wouldn't be talking to

Pilski in the near future. Lentz informed him that Pilski, leaving all his cases aside, had asked for a month's leave in order to take care of his mother – apparently. Nobody had believed him, either – apparently. Someone had even asked jokingly what his fiancée would say, to which he'd replied that he'd look into her grievances at a later date. Lentz summed it up in one sentence: all sorts of assumptions were being made. Bartol made his too. Pilski's version seemed perfectly true to him: he'd broken up with his fiancée – which Bartol considered the right move and had decided to take care of his mother – which was a good excuse. Lentz accepted the explanation with an indifferent expression, which meant something like 'you obviously know what you're talking about' and without any questions showed Bartol a letter lying on his desk. It was from Pilski:

> *I'm at your disposal at any time. I now have to take care of my mother. You know the address at which to find me. See you soon.*

Bartol didn't have time to properly analyse what he'd heard and read.

A phone call from downstairs threw him a little. Romana Zalewska was waiting to speak to him. He'd almost forgotten about her.

Surprise would remain on his face for much longer. The first thing she announced was: 'Because the light was on.'

Once they were upstairs, she was the first to speak again: 'I didn't think I'd find myself here again either, and as if for the same reason.'

'I'm pleased to see you again, of course, but please repeat what brought you here.'

'I know it's going to sound strange yet again, but the light was on, in the evening, a couple of days ago.'

It did sound strange. He had in front of his eyes what seemingly was the same woman: composed, resolute, even more attractive in spring, but this seemed to verge on obsession. He didn't really know what was happening to the house in Solacz. All he knew was that it was the subject of complicated, relatively rare legal procedures since no owner had been found. And that no owner had been found he knew full well, but this surely didn't mean that nobody could enter. It could have been some police experts, for example.

'You don't have to look at me so strangely. I haven't gone mad ,even though the silhouette I saw in the window also seemed familiar. Over the four days since I first saw the light' – she emphasised the last words in such a way that Bartol sat up and started to listen like he had the last time – 'I've been checking what's happening with the house and whether it could have been strangers. Maybe it was, but not necessarily. There are so many people interested in the house that even the smallest pieces of information go through the lawyers opposite, two design offices and one over-advertised advertising agency. Even I, when I enquired, started to be treated like an enemy in a battle for the property. That's why it's taken so much time. Apparently nobody had been there, or at least nobody who shouldn't have been. No burglars either, as I checked by egging on the lawyers. They raised the alarm, needlessly so according to your men. But I saw a light on in there!'

'I believe you. Up until now you haven't been wrong about matters concerning lights.'

'Nor am I professionally wrong in these cases. A dispersed and concealed source of light is almost my sign of identification.' She relaxed a little.

'I associate you with light, too.' They both smiled. 'I'll look into it. You mentioned a silhouette?'

'Far-reaching assumptions they sometimes say, but mine go even further, are just about visible. And I'm no longer sure if it's not a figment of my imagination, but I think – I repeat – I think I saw Mr and Mrs Mikulski's son through the window. I know he didn't come forward as a beneficiary and wasn't at Mrs Mikulska's funeral so he's probably not here. Maybe I saw a ghost, even though I don't believe in them. Either way, I had to come and tell you for my own peace of mind.'

She did, indeed, look relieved. Bartol, on the other hand, was trying hard, very hard to remain calm. He tried, too, not to show either surprise or excitement or anything at all. Slowly, everything started to fall into place. He leaned back in his chair, practically sat on his fingers to stop them drumming nervously on the table, stop them rubbing his nose, stop them making any unnecessary, treacherous moves. The police were supposedly looking for the son, but he blamed himself for having neglected this trail a little. Lentz had been right, yet again – the simplest solution.

'He's probably not in Poland. He didn't come forward about the estate. He's not obliged, of course, but as you can understand, it's quite a profitable duty.' It seemed to him that she had, in some way, been waiting for such an answer. 'But I'll try to find out who could have been prowling around the house. I never asked you before' – he now angrily crushed his hands harder, controlled his voice – 'but, as I gather, you knew him well?'

'Even if you'd asked at the time I don't know whether I'd have told you. It wasn't a relationship... there's no relationship really...' For the first time he saw her lose her self-control; the unintended cluster of words, an ordinary slip of the tongue openly revealed what she hadn't intended to say but what he'd intended to ask. 'No, the two things had simply nothing to do with each other.'

'Please don't get upset, I'm not interested in your personal life. You came of your own accord because there was something worrying you and we're here to resolve your worries. That's all.'

'I'm sorry, you're right. All in all, it's easier for me to explain my agitation now. Perhaps what I saw in the window was what

I'd subconsciously wanted to see. Then I blew it all up because if it had been Janek he, too, could have been in danger.'

'Please don't be angry, but I'm obliged to ask: when did you last see Jan Mikulski?'

'Four days ago, so I thought. I've just told you.'

'Yes, of course, but you're not sure. And for sure?'

'Ten, no, maybe twelve years ago.' She paused. It seemed she even blushed, although it was hard for blushes to break through the layer of powder. 'I know it might seem strange, maybe ridiculous, I was much older...'

'No, it's not strange and it's not ridiculous...' he said almost to himself, thinking how like Elżbieta Ogrodniczak she was. Younger but similarly tense, draped, uniformed, upright, even her hair was tied back in a similar way although with a fringe, the eyes were also somehow... It was only the two deep furrows which appeared on her increasingly frowning forehead that brought him to order.

'The fact that I'm telling you something doesn't mean I need you to comfort or justify me. Two years of effective therapy were enough for me to be able to justify everything to myself. We won't delve into it now. The short-term episode ended equally as quickly and unexpectedly as it had begun, that's all.'

He wasn't good at talking to these women. Again he was furious with himself. Try as he may, everything pointed to the fact that he could only interview women of questionable quality.

'I'm sorry, that wasn't what I'd wanted to say.'

'I know what you wanted to say.' She started to get up.

'No, you don't.' A sharper tone of voice seemed the only solution. It worked. She looked at him with a hint of interest, and sat down. 'You're an attractive woman and I guess the same must have applied ten years ago – although I'm not sure it would have been true twenty years ago, as far as I remember from your photograph as a student, that's all.' She smiled, clearly pleased with what he'd said. 'As a pure formality I just want to ask: was there a specific reason why Jan Mikulski left the country and can't or doesn't want to return?' he asked as calmly as can be, as if indifferently, as if he wasn't greatly interested.

'I don't know. Probably for the same reasons as other young men. Besides, he'd been adopted and didn't have a very good relationship with his adoptive father. But he did love his mother very much. I asked him straight out and he evaded the question, merely saying that silence is a virtue and he wasn't going to say anything because – I remember this – a wise man will remain silent until the right moment. And one day he'd explain. Some such nonsense. I had no illusions. He was young, wanted to leave and left. Mrs Bończak didn't say anybody like that had been at his mother's funeral so he's probably not back. You confirm it, so I must have seen somebody else. Probably someone's got keys to the house and as, a friendly gesture or for a couple of złotys, is showing it to interested parties. Still, I'm glad I came. You've reassured me,' she said in a relaxed voice.

Bartol's head, on the other hand, was racing, racing to his desk, racing to Lentz, racing to Magda. Everything had become clear. Of course, someone had taken care of the child, the unwanted child of a sacrilegious union, and that child was now thanking everyone for it. Only the dull repetition in his head of the words 'a wise man will remain silent until the right moment' kept him on his chair. He didn't want to note anything down; he wanted to wait. He must have had a foolish expression on his face because now it was she who was looking at him oddly. He took a deep breath.

'Yes. It's good you've come. And if, let's say, the son were to pay you a visit, please let us know. His statements could prove very helpful.' He smiled. He wanted to sound as natural as possible and ask a few less important questions so she wouldn't go away convinced that she'd suggested who the main suspect could be.

He opened his internal files and printed out Pilski's photograph. He wanted to make sure that, under the pretext of taking a holiday, he wasn't conducting some sort of private investigation again.

'Have you ever seen this man? Has he ever spoken to you?'

'No. I've never seen him.' She shrugged indifferently.

'One last question.' He reached into his file. 'You know there were a great many paintings in Mr and Mrs Mikulski's house but very few photographs. We found one in his escritoire, cut out of a newspaper. Perhaps it's of no significance, but since you're here maybe you know who it is.' He congratulated himself ten-fold for having taken a company folder from the Elizabeth Garden Fun Factory warehouse. He'd taken it out of curiosity; only later did he see, and cut out, a photograph from some anniversary celebration showing the chairwoman, again in the background, but clearly suggesting she was the subject in hand: all the rest of the people were standing either in profile or the back. He passed it to Romana Zalewska. She gazed at it with a blank expression.

'I know that for a pretty meagre contact with Mr and Mrs Mikulskis, I get around quite a bit. I don't know the woman. Because that's who you mean, isn't it?' she looked at him suspiciously.

'I've already told you, we don't know. Maybe it's someone they knew or maybe the photo just happened to be lying around, but since you're here I'm asking, that's all.'

'A domineering woman, a bit sad, not a bad figure, keeps herself upright. No, I don't know her; don't think I've ever seen her. You could ask Mrs Bończak. She once mentioned an elegant, quarrelsome ballerina. Whether that concerned Mikulski's house or some other, I can't tell you now.'

But Mrs Bończak, at a crowded stall handing one customer a pair of thongs, another customer a bra, could.

'Yes, she was there, but how do you know this?'

He tried to call Magda not once, not twice, but fourteen times. She didn't pick up. He still hadn't got used to it.

Lentz, as usual, picked up after the first ring and, as usual, without needless questions resigned himself to setting aside everything he'd been doing and concentrating solely on Jan Mikulski, taking it to be a certainty that he was in Poland and was their chief suspect. Bartol merely added that they were in for a dreary procedural chase and the most recent photograph they had was on Facebook from his last class.

Bartol didn't have time to reach headquarters and see the school photo before Magda phoned. Nor did he have time to say anything about her not having picked up the phone. She got there before him.

'I couldn't answer the phone but that doesn't matter now. Listen carefully because the phone doesn't charge itself and is going to run out of battery. How fast can you get to Gniezno?'

'I'm in the car, but...' Furious, he slipped into the lay-by. He wasn't prepared for such a conversation and had no time to say anything.

'Listen, I think I know who could have done it. In my opinion it's Antoniusz Mikulski's son, the first victim's, but let's not waste time on details now, you've got to come here anyway. I'll wait.'

'In just under an hour,' dumbstruck, he answered her earlier question and, without asking anything else, added: 'Where shall I go?'

'The cathedral. There's a large, very historical one, you'll find it. If my phone runs out, I'll be there somewhere, probably in the old chapter house. There's a baroque polychrome here...'

'Where? What?'

'In the chapter house, surrounded by the virtues – literally. The chapter house is where the chapter meets, in this case where the entrance usually is. A polychrome is a multi-coloured painting, on the ceiling in this case. Understand? Doesn't matter if you don't. Call the woman and ask whether she's found something like a platter with the writing *Omnibus omnia* anywhere near her, or two blades, knives, something like that, with the writing *Alter alterius* since you think she's the one concerned. I'm waiting.'

'Spell it for me.'

Fortunately, she managed not only to sigh with patient sufferance but to spell the Latin words before the connection broke off.

Bartol collected his thoughts before phoning Elżbieta Ogrodniczak. She was unpleasant. She said only that she had no idea who Jan Mikulski was, hadn't visited Poznań for twenty years, hadn't received any suspicious gifts and hadn't seen any Latin words anywhere near her recently, or Hebrew ones for that matter. She hoped she wasn't suspected of anything and was allowed to travel because she was at the airport. On her way to the Paris Fair. When informed that it could be a matter of her own safety, she retorted that a squadron of lawyers – who were going to get in touch with him imminently – was watching over her safety. She didn't answer the question as to when she'd return and turned off the phone.

That wasn't the only phone she turned off. She turned off her second phone – her company one, her third – the land line at home; she turned off her laptop and computer. She turned off all the alarms. She turned off the world. And waited.

She waited as she carefully dressed in the morning, like someone waiting for somebody important. She waited as she made some tea – boiling more water than needed, coffee – filling the espresso machine to the brim. She waited sitting on the terrace. A second glass of water covered with a napkin also waited. Everything waited.

She waited.

Ever since she'd received the mirror, she'd been waiting every minute, studying herself and her life in it. She searched for the eyes. She searched in the eyes of those who wanted to meet her and in the eyes of those she met by chance. She searched although she knew she wouldn't find them because all she remembered were the frightened eyes of a child, and those eyes she'd never see.

So she waited.

But when he arrived, she didn't see them either; he'd hidden them behind a pair of glasses. She remembered those glasses – the first luxury she'd owned – which he'd lifted off her the last time she'd picked him up. She hadn't been able to pull them out of his clasped fist.

She'd missed those glasses.

Maciej Bartol found himself in Gniezno much sooner than he'd anticipated.

He couldn't miss the cathedral. From afar, too, he caught sight of Magda sitting on the steps by one of the side entrances. As he approached, he noticed two old women throw her a look full of disdain. Magda half reclined with her elbow resting on the step above and her too-short skirt failing to cover the full length of her crossed legs. The women had a reason to complain. But he liked what he saw.

She wasn't paying attention to anyone, didn't see him until he stood right next to her. She sprung to her feet.

'At last. I thought you'd never come.'

'Couldn't get here earlier. Tell me what you've found.' He gestured at the cathedral door.

'What? Exactly what I wanted. Aren't you going to ask how?'

'I thought I'd ask later.'

'Where did you get that gift of spoiling the mood? Listen, because this is important and I'm not going to repeat myself. I've probably got an allergy from all those ancient papers. I looked through seventeen volumes of Dutch prints yesterday and there were still more. When I got home I saw some unpaid bills which must have got lost among the pile of cards and pieces of paper.

Don't look like that, it's not your fault. I simply realised I was wasting time. I tidied everything up, put it away and decided to take a different approach. I realised I'd reached the Monastery of Apa Jeremias in Saqqara from the fifth century because some virtues figured there, but didn't really have any idea what was in the church in Szamotuły in the sacristy, for example. Don't look at me like that. I've still no idea what's there. And it came to me like a bolt out of the blue. A restorer of old buildings. And Mikulski was a restorer, too. I thought I might find something hidden somewhere in some small town with a note saying it was going to be restored but hadn't been described yet. But no, what I found was something that had already been restored fifteen years ago. Nobody had written anything about it. And this had been found not in some little roadside church but here, in Gniezno Cathedral. But now come and see for yourself.'

She said all this so quickly he didn't even have time to think it over. And, without waiting for his reaction, she took him by the hand, opened the enormous door and pulled him into the depths of the cathedral.

He thought he'd remember something – after all, he'd been here on a school trip – but his only recollection was that of being told to stop chewing gum. He'd stopped and pretended to have swallowed it, then, when the teacher wasn't looking, he'd stuck it to the nose of some bishop and skilfully stretched it over his face. The stunt had won him recognition and respect among his friends; it had been worth it. He couldn't remember anything else.

But now he walked. Walked and looked around amazed, like a child.

At St Adalbert drowning in gold, at the twisted pillars which guarded him and looked as if they might come to life at any moment, might curl further and crush anyone who invaded the place.

At the enormous stained glass windows which seemed to change the speed of light and allow it only to spill lazily over the golden stucco work, the marble tombs, the stone floor.

At the priest who dozed in the huge confessional with an expression of bliss on his face almost identical to that of the bishops on the tombstones.

He looked as if he had only learned how to look esterday.

The cathedral was almost empty; only the subdued murmur of whispering, deadened by the measured thudding of his shoes and the clapping of Magda's flip-flops.

They came to a halt right opposite the altar, on the other side of the church. There, where there would usually be an entrance, was an enormous wrought-iron grille which didn't partition off an atrium but another room.

'And now take a look,' said Magda, opening the huge grille with surprising ease. They entered. In the light of a bulb hanging on a piece of rope, he saw an old built-in church pew, a huge candle, an old baptismal font, in the corner some banners carried during processions, and on the walls paintings depicting numerous human figures. He didn't know what they represented, just as he didn't know who the bishops in the portraits were.

'For heaven's sake, don't look around, look at the ceiling, at the polychrome!'

And he saw it.

First a host of figures, each separate in its own frame, nearly every one holding something – colourful, old, probably beautiful. Until recently that's all he would have said on the subject. He wouldn't have known more – once, but not now. Slowly, very slowly he stopped just looking and started reading.

He noticed the three most important figures almost at once. Love gazing lovingly at the children surrounding her. Faith with a cross and Apostles' Creed, which he now recognised as he read *Credo in unum Deum*. And the third, trusting and the most beautiful of them: Hope with an anchor, the only hope of a ship struggling in the seas raging behind her back.

They were the most important ones, centrally placed, but they weren't alone. They only reigned over the rest. Over Justice with pursed lips, scales in one hand, sword in the other; over the gently smiling woman pouring water into a chalice and whom he recognised as Moderation. And over others whom he didn't know.

'What do a snake and mirror represent?' he asked.

'Prudence, one of the cardinal virtues. Even the snake is seen in a positive light from time to time. The phrase "be as prudent as snakes" comes to mind but I don't know where from, but a mirror… There was a saying once: "What is contained in the mirror does not reside in the mirror". In other words, you have to look wider, not just at your own reflection. That figures. Justice is there, with the scales. As Job said: "if my foot hastened towards deception, may He weigh me on a just scale", He meaning God, and punish me if necessary. Hence the sword.'

'I recognised her. Moderation, too. I only don't know who that one is, the one dragging something.'

'It's the only man in the group. He's called Fortitude. It's a bit biased. The virtues were generally personified by women because apparently they nurture and caress but, as you see, that obviously isn't enough for Fortitude. He's dragging a shattered pillar, like Samson, and hurrying to the stronghold at the top of the hill behind him. To God, in other words – the refuge of safety. I don't know whether it's intentional but he's the only one who's entering into a dialogue with those who look at him.'

'What dialogue? I can't see any speech bubbles.'

'You won't see if you don't look. He's the only one moving. He's the only one turning round and looking at you as though inviting you, saying: follow me, don't be afraid, I'm Fortitude, you be valiant too.'

Bartol stared for a long time. All the other figures were,

indeed, either sitting or standing with no intention of going anywhere. But although he stared and stared he still didn't feel he was being invited anywhere.

'As for the other young ladies,' Magda said after a while, 'I've still got to think about them a bit, apart maybe from Silence – there in the corner.' She indicated one of the figures kissing a ring. 'I'm sure about her.'

'Is "a wise man will remain silent until the right moment" written there?'

'No.' She looked at him astonished. 'It's *Non Revelabo*, which means: "I shan't disclose". But look at the pictures in the cradles coming off the three virtues.'

He didn't quite know what cradles were but didn't have time to ask. He saw, and only then realised what he was really looking at.

'He's been here.' These were the only words he managed.

'He has indeed. The only thing that consoles me for having taken too long to look for it is that I was right from the start, apart from a few tiny details. Each of the three divine virtues is further commented upon by the symbolic images. Look at Hope. On one side she's got sunflowers, hopelessly stooping as they wait to see another sunrise. And they'll live to see it because that's what's written beneath them: *expecto donec veniat* – I wait until it appears. Perhaps the corpse lying on the other side isn't a corpse at all. Perhaps it's survived the raging ocean storm behind Hope because *dum spiro spero*, that is, as long as there's life there's hope. Maybe it'll come to life at any moment. '

'That doesn't mean much to Antoniusz Mikulski anymore. He's not going to come to life.' As soon as he said this he had no doubt whatsoever that he'd already seen a body laid out in exactly the same position and girded with a red cloth. It, too, had seemed to be asleep, but for eternity.

'No, not really. Now look at Faith. She believes in one God because that's what's written on the inscription in her hand and she's holding a cross and host. On one side of her is the Eye of God watching her, and the inscription's the same as the one we had on the glasses. Why is there an eye here and he put it on a pair of glasses? The only thing that comes straight to mind is that, in this way, he wanted to say that he's only a man, that he needs the magnification of a pair of glasses or lenses, but that he's watching all the same. Now look at the dog on her other side.'

'He even looks like Harpsichord.'

'Yes, going by what you showed me, yes, he does. And there's the text about not holding too high an opinion of yourself. But do you know what this dog and Gawlicki make me think of right now, above all? A text from the Book of Revelations about those who didn't enter the Kingdom of Heaven... It goes something like this. Outside are dogs, lecherers, murderers, blasphemers and all who love falsehood and live by it. It fits in with his character, doesn't it?'

'Very much. That leaves Love.'

'Yes. And there are two representations here, too. I've still got to check but take a look. Two crossed blades symbolise joint action. The inscription below reads: *Alter alterius*. It's an extract from the Letter to the Galatians: "Carry each other's burdens." I still don't know how this fits in but...'

'You know all those letters in Latin by heart?'

'Are you mad? I talked earlier to a clever priest here. He also told me where the words on that silver octagonal platter come from. *Omnibus omnia*. And this is what might be most important. I've noted it down. It's a Letter to the Corinthians, the bit about boundless Love. Listen to this: "To the weak I became weak, to win the weak. I have become all things to all men so that by all possible means I might save some." That's an extract for someone with a mission, isn't it? Even with a little license for devious action if that's the way you want to interpret it.'

'In the name of Love?'

'Of course. Even in the name of Love if you like, but love of yourself if you restrict those deserving to be saved to yourself. And if that's the way you're prejudiced, then everything's allowed. It could be a coincidence, but as I said before, three children in the company of Love, one on her knees and two behind her back, is a group which appears frequently. But everything's falling into place too perfectly here. Maybe the next in line to meet the son is Mrs Ogrodniczak.'

'You guessed it might be him by looking at the paintings on the ceiling?'

'You overestimate me. I told you I talked to the priests here. One very old one didn't know much Latin but had an excellent memory, especially as regards things about the distant past. I told him I was writing a thesis about the restorer Antoniusz Mikulski who played a big role in salvaging the church's monuments at a time when circumstances weren't very conducive for that sort of thing, and that I was collecting information. He didn't recall the name, but remembered perfectly well that the small son of one of the restorers got lost and spent the whole night lying locked in the chapter. He added that it couldn't be the same man I was writing about because he wasn't very nice, to anyone even his son. He shouted at the child as though he wasn't his, but the little one was very brave. The priest remembered very well because the boy didn't even cry when they found him in the morning. And this happened some thirty years ago. Maybe it really wasn't his child but that Ogrodniczak's and the priest's? That's something you need to check out.'

'Elżbieta Ogrodniczak visited the Mikulskis and apparently it wasn't a pleasant visit. It's all falling into place.'

'Come on, we'll talk about it outside. We're not going to hear ourselves speak in a minute. Judging by the din I'd say there must be two coach loads of kids, in a way that's good... Let's go.'

Only now did Bartol realise what had been troubling him for some time now. The muted hullabaloo was approaching inescapably. They managed to get out before the swarm – whispering loudly, rustling and giggling – poured into the old chapter house.

They talked a little longer and went in search of the old priest. He soon turned up and wasn't in the least surprised that someone was asking him the same thing again, as though he'd long ceased to be surprised by anything. He repeated exactly what he'd said earlier and had nothing else to add. He didn't remember the name of the restorer but did remember that the boy wore glasses and a pair of checked trousers.

They didn't find out any more.

They returned to Poznań. Magda asked for a lift to the Collegium Novum, since she'd arranged to meet an art hysterian there. Bartol didn't know why she called him that; she couldn't explain it either – apparently he was a rare eccentric.

Bartol intended to talk to Lentz as soon as possible. As he neared the crossroads which led straight up to headquarters and to the left straight to his mother's door, he remembered that he hadn't called her over the last two days. He picked up the phone, called Lentz: nothing had changed, as yet. Maybe it would be best, he thought, if he popped in for ten minutes to see her – them – of his own accord. He'd knock up a couple of points for himself, especially as it didn't look as though he'd be able to do so over the next few days. He'd explain everything neatly and that would be enough for a while. He turned.

No open door awaited him. He had to open it himself. He heard his mother walking around in the bathroom. It was very quiet. This didn't surprise him. Only two variants had come into play of late: either screams or whispers. What did, however, surprise him was an Uhlan's uniform hanging in the hall and an enormous hat on the shelf nearby.

When his mother emerged from the bathroom, he whispered: 'What's this?'

'A uniform,' she replied in her usual voice.

'That much I can see, but whose is it?'

'Franciszek's now.'

'Who's Franciszek?'

'What a stupid question! You're the one who left me with him, don't you remember?' Seeing the expression of complete incomprehension on his face, she continued: 'The son of a friend of mine who's a mathematician used to be an Uhlan. He worked his way through all the regiments, rowed with all of them, and since he's got a horse and still likes dressing up, has now become a knight. He's bought himself a suit of armour but has still got the uniform.'

'And?'

'And he's given it to Franek. They met once and liked each other and since he – Franciszek that is – also rides, in case you didn't know, nothing stood in the way of his joining the cavalry. Besides, I encouraged him myself. He takes his oath quite soon as far as I know, straight after his exam. Why, what's so surprising?'

'Why, nothing,' he replied, not understanding either her tone or their conversation. Besides, only then did he realise that they were talking quite loudly.

'Are you alone?'

'Can you see anybody?'

'Mum, what's up?'

'Nothing!'

'So where are they?'

'They left yesterday. I thought I'd told you.' Pretending to think it over, she added: 'Or maybe I didn't? I don't know anymore. Maybe because we didn't have a chance to speak?'

'What's happened?'

'Nothing's happened. She simply wanted to go home.'

'Will she cope?' he asked, still not understanding any of this.

'Why so over-protective? Of course she'll cope. She's a clever and good girl.' She paused. 'And I think Franciszek's going to help her. He proved exceptionally helpful at changing nappies when you weren't here, was even pretty good at it.' He saw her strange smile, but it took a while for him to register what she wanted to tell him.

'Mum, he's too young!'

'Too young for what, may I ask?' She shrugged. 'To be an Uhlan?'

'You know what I mean,' he practically shouted.

'You've both got similar qualifications but his motivation is as if better and more sincere. He's a good lad. And now listen to me carefully and learn, because I'm not going to live forever. It's not important what role life's allotted to us – sometimes it's not for us to decide – and there's no point in fighting or disputing it, but what is important, or most important, is to play one's role well. I also got a bit lost recently. I wanted to be actor, director, prompter, everything. It doesn't work. We're not going to discuss it now. Both you and I have got to think it all over. But not now: right now I haven't got time. I'm off to the coast today and want to take my granddaughter for a walk before I go. We'll talk when I get back.'

'Are you going with Aunt Basia?' He knew perfectly well he was enquiring about what was least important at that moment, but he did ask and regretted more than ever.

'No, with Krzysiek. And he's not your uncle and even less so mine.' Saying this, she turned and made her way towards the wardrobe from which she took two large suitcases.

This was too much. Bartol didn't say more either. He turned and left. Without a word. He didn't slam the door, nor did he shut it quietly.

Sitting in the car for ten minutes without turning the ignition key didn't help, nor twice thumping the steering wheel so hard as to bruise his hand. He regretted not having at least thrown the uniform on the floor and trampling it. He regretted not having asked who Krzysiek was so he could do the same to him.

He regretted not being able to control himself and stamping in a puddle like a little boy, for looking for a guilty party without knowing where the guilt lay.

Magda phoned; he didn't take the call. Lentz phoned; again he didn't take the call. He pulled out, but in such a way that he almost crashed into another car. In his rear-view mirror he caught a glimpse of a straw hat on the head of a horrified elderly gentleman. The man might have survived the war but he lacked the courage to off-load himself by hitting the horn. Contrary to logic, this calmed Bartol and he drove the rest of the way to headquarters calmly.

Lentz was waiting for him. In fact, he'd phoned to let Bartol know he was waiting. At first, Bartol tried to explain all about the virtues, why Moderation had a mirror and that there was a Letter to someone, it didn't matter who – he couldn't remember – but that he was weak for the weak so as to save himself at least. Seeing Lentz's face, he realised he wouldn't have understood what he was saying if he'd had to listen to himself either. He stopped talking about snakes, blades and that sort of thing, and concentrated on Antoniusz Mikulski's son. He said they'd been in too much of a hurry to bury him in some Burmese jungle and that they'd spent too long wondering what connected all the characters in the drama, and that he was, perhaps not a hundred, but ninety percent sure that the third act wouldn't take place without the participation of the vibratory Elizabeth, whatever she might say.

Lentz remained silent for a long time, then when he was about to say something, he didn't have time. Polek burst into the room and started rummaging in the drawer of his desk. He ignored them, finally found something and made towards the door. Bartol got to his feet and – very quickly, so as to make it on time although he didn't know why – informed Polek of the chief suspect in the case on which they'd been working for months. It made no impression on Polek, who acknowledged it with one sentence – so the case was wrapped up – congratulated them and wished them luck. Then left. Bartol ran out into the corridor after him. Polek turned and showed him the leaflet in his hand. A small mansion with red towers on the seafront itself.

'Łeba. That's where we're going, but don't even try to find me there.'

Bartol continued staring at him with uncomprehending eyes.

'I haven't been on holiday alone with my spouse since she's been my spouse, meaning never. But things are going to change because now, brother, I'm on an historical mission. I intend to prove that mountains suck because they only block the view. Oh, and you have to do a lot of walking when you're there, while I intend to lie around: on her, under her and on both sides all at once. Because the satnav in my head had broken down and I'd started moving around in the wrong place. So if any comrade tries to get in touch with me please say I've passed away.'

Bartol continued staring, speechless. He'd heard 'my old woman' hundreds of times, never 'my wife', let alone 'my spouse', so all he could blurt out was: 'They've given you leave? I thought you were down for August?'

'I'll get some in August, too, and if I don't I'll learn how to embroider artistic tattoos.'

'I hope you have good weather,' said Bartol. Up until now Polek had always fled from home to work, not the other way round.

'I don't give a shit about the weather. It can do what it likes. What counts is that my room's on the ground floor. Not a metre above sea level. Absolute zero. You'll manage without me. Thanks for putting me up, but I can't sleep very well when I'm alone. Bye.'

'Bye,' said Bartol to Polek's back, remembering how long it had taken him to fall asleep because of Polek's snoring. Maybe the murmur of the sea would drown his snores, he thought, and returned to the office. Rarely did he see curiosity registered on Lentz's face, but he saw it now.

'What's up with him?'

'He's taking a holiday.'

'He's got it bad with that girl.'

'Better still, with his spouse.'

'Aha.' As if to spite everything, the expression on Lentz's face returned to normal. 'Listen, I've been thinking about that woman with the warehouse. Why is she so brave, bearing in mind she might be next in line? And I came to the conclusion that her behaviour isn't any different from that of the other two. They were waiting for him. Whether they expected what was coming or not is neither here nor there. The fact is, they were waiting. Mikulski had annulled his will. Perhaps he'd changed his mind and didn't want to leave everything to dogs but to parrots, for example. But he could just as easily have thought that, since his adopted son had turned up, he'd atone for some of his sins, make up for lost time. The same applies to Gawlicki. He guessed that someone had got to know about his past, perhaps even guessed who it might be, and he, too, wanted to wait for him in spite of everything. After all, he could have fled again, become a head shepherd and raced around mountain pastures. He didn't have a lot of needs and knew how to blend in with the background. The same could apply to the woman. She's lost two sons, and when the one she lost earlier turns up at least half of the maternal balance will have been evened out.'

'You're right, yes, you're right, that must be it. Wait...' he said, although Lentz had no intention of leaving. He dialled Magda's number. And – wonders never cease – she picked up after two rings. She spoke first: 'You didn't really have to call back. Truth might still be there, maybe Wisdom, but I thought it's not that important anymore...'

'I'm not calling back. I'm phoning to ask you whether the golden octagonal platter could, for example, be a mirror?'

She remained silent for some time.

'I admire you more and more with each day. A painted mirror which doesn't reflect anything will resemble nothing other than a silver plate. Yes, if you think about it carefully, it's got to be a mirror, and nothing else. To the weak I became weak... I reflect reality to reach reality...'

'Thanks, but I've got to hang up.'

'Then do, that's perfect, because I've finished too. I wish to thank you for a pleasant and creative collaboration.'

'What do you mean?'

'In a nutshell: your sibling.'

'What are you talking about? I don't have any siblings.'

'That's just it, your non-existent sibling, which leads me to the simple conclusion that Daniela Bartol's – that is, your mother's – little granddaughter is directly related to you. I met them on a walk. I congratulated her, congratulations were accepted...'

'I'll explain everything to you!'

'I very much doubt it.' She hung up.

First he stood up, took one step towards the door, turned back, sat down, stood up again, then sat down again and looked at Lentz, who quickly pretended he was going through the papers on his desk. He clutched his head and ruffled his hair as though to make what was on his head correspond to what was inside. A muddle, chaos, mess. Uhlan Franciszek with a nappy, some man called Krzysiek, Polek at the seaside with his wife, Magda! All he wanted to think about was that, at some stage, the day had to come to an end. But when? And there was still Ogrodniczak and the mirror which he saw on her desk, which had to be *the* mirror and had to be inscribed, whatever she said. He glanced at Lentz. No, this is what he had to take care of first. The rest he'd sort out later.

'Lentz, she's already received an invitation and is waiting for him. Phone the prosecutor's office and sort out a search warrant for her house. No, it'll take too long to explain. I'll call Pilski, get him to arrange all that quickly. You phone the local boys and warn them we're coming.' The desk phone rang. 'Right, take that first.'

Pilski's phone didn't answer. Bartol dialled Mrs Gawlicka-Sęk's number. She said her son wasn't in. Bartol was just going to explain he knew that and also knew that her son didn't want anything to do with the outside world, but in exceptional circumstances Bartol was to call. And he probably would have explained, were it not for the expression on Lentz's face positively telling him that he had some important news to pass on to him – immediately. He hung up.

'They've apprehended Jan Mikulski. He's downstairs.'

'How? Who?' The speed of it all was beginning to horrify him.

'The traffic boys. Just so,' replied Lentz, shrugging. 'In ten minutes he's ours.'

In those ten minutes, with Polek's help, he found the number of Pilski's fiancée. He called. A squeaky, offended voice informed him that she wasn't engaged and didn't know anyone like that. All that Bartol had time to think was that her last visit to Pilski's apartment couldn't have been a great success.

Lentz and Bartol went downstairs, in silence. Bartol had no idea what Lentz was thinking; he didn't even know what to think himself. One thing appeared certain – all this would soon come to an end. Presently he was going to see the man who'd killed two people in cold blood, turned it into a performance, the strangest Bartol had ever seen, and been arrested – just like that – by the traffic police.

He wondered what the man looked like. It was a good thing he didn't have much time to reflect because everything pointed to his having a very limited imagination.

The individual waiting for them was neither boy nor man and wore a Hawaian shirt with a palm motif, a pair of knee-length shorts with numerous pockets, and dreadlocks instead of hair. He was chewing gum and, clearly pleased with himself, sat rocking on his chair and casting his eyes around. As they walked in, he smiled broadly and was the first to speak:

'Gentlemen, I've just had a brainwave. I'm going to write a guide to world jails. I've already gone through two European jails this week so we'll start with Europe.'

'And where, if I may ask, were you before us?' asked Lentz.

Bartol couldn't get a word out.

'Frankfurt-am-Main, the airport. It's not quite as luxurious here, I must say, but pleasant enough.'

'What held you there?'

'A dog. I was standing quietly doing nothing when it came up to me and gently laid its paws on my shoulders. I can't say it was small but it was quite friendly, so to speak.'

'Were you smuggling drugs?' continued Lentz.

'Why smuggle when you can buy them anywhere?' he replied, amused and rocking away on his chair. 'If I happened to want to make some money today I'd more than likely speculate in the price of rice by the ton, not powder by the kilo. It's more profitable. I was simply flying in from Colombia, a hospitable country where they offer you the best of what they've got. Besides, I think the hospitality's still got a grip on me. The rest must have stuck to my clothes and that's what the dog smelt, but since there were only traces there was only enough to hold me for twenty-four hours, so I didn't get to see much. Whereas I'm curious as to how long I'm going to be entertained here.'

'Is Antoniusz Mikulski your father?' Lentz posed another question.

Bartol couldn't remember ever having been so disorientated. Unless this comedian was an actor, and a relatively good one, he couldn't be the person they were looking for. The palm trees on the man's shirt undulated with the chair.

'Antoniusz? In a way, yes. He took me in; the kind benefactor. But I don't have any respect for him even though he's dead, irrespective of how he died. He didn't even deign to tell me about Aurelia's death and I practically thought of her like a mother. And now I've seen he's got rid of everything from the house which could have been associated with me. Nice, don't you think?'

'Did you come across a sealed door by any chance?'

'I did indeed, and an unsealed window vent which I'd used ever since I was little. Apparently some lawyers were looking for me, but after the way he disrespected me it's hard to believe he left the house to me. I just wanted to go in and walk around a bit. After all, I did live there for fifteen years.'

'I don't know much about law, but since Mr Mikulski invalidated his earlier will, the house belongs to you. Did you know that?' asked Lentz.

'So that's your game.' He grinned broadly and blew a bubble with his gum. When it burst, he added: 'No, I'm not the one who treated him to such an original parting. I was in South America all of last year. A great change after Asia, I assure you. So much for my alibi. As for the motive... I didn't like him much, true enough, and where money's concerned the dollar's been pretty low lately but not low enough to worry me. I'll have enough to pay for the promotion of my jail guide.' He'd grinned all along but now started laughing to himself. 'What do you think, what would I have to do to get twenty-four hours in a Czech jail? I'll probably start there, I fancy a beer.'

'I don't know. You'll think of something,' replied Lentz, also laughing. 'Do you know Edmund Wieczorek?' he asked with a secretive expression.

'I don't think so but hold on, hold on, wasn't that the name of our postman? I liked him.'

'No doubt. You can ask him, he's got a lot of good ideas.'

'So the old fellow's still alive?'

'He is, and occasionally doesn't know what to do with his time either. You'll get to like each other again.'

Lentz was clearly enjoying the conversation, Bartol quite the opposite. For ten minutes he'd thought he was done with the case, but only for ten minutes. Now he just wanted to hear anything, anything that would get him out of the place where he was stuck. Nothing came to him so he merely asked 'Did you ever get lost in Gniezno Cathedral?'

'No, not me. I was careful; after all, that house was better than the orphanage.' His laugh, this time, was insincere, ironical. It was obvious these were memories to which he didn't want to return. 'The kid before me got lost. He'd probably just taken him in as a trial run. The run didn't prove a success. He even told the kid to call him 'dad' then gave him away.' He stopped rocking in his chair. 'He was a piece of shit. I was the shrewder, but things turned out better for the lad because some aunt took him in, so my mother told me later. She was a good woman, suffered her fair share through him, too.'

Bartol didn't hear the last sentence. He'd already disappeared.

Waiting since early morning, Elżbieta Ogrodniczak asked herself whether this was, in fact, the day. The reply arrived in the afternoon, with the postman whom she glimpsed pushing something into her letterbox. She waited, walked up to the letterbox and extracted the envelope. She knew the sender. A moment later, she also knew his address. She went back and started preparing for the journey. She was in no hurry. She took a long shower, calming her body which shook and sweated as never before. She approached the chest of drawers where she kept her underwear and took her time choosing some knickers. All seemed inappropriate, bearing in mind that total strangers might shortly be looking at them. The rest was easier.

She watered the flowers in the house and on the terrace. Turned on the sprinklers.

She decided to pack. Then realised she wouldn't really need anything for this particular journey.

Finally, she closed the door behind her, slipped the keys into her handbag, only to take them out again a moment later and place them on the little wall nearby.

She climbed into the car and drove off. Only once did she look back.

The sun was setting.

Night was falling slowly, stealthily, as it usually does in summer.

Maciej Bartol's second conversation with Mrs Gawlicka-Sęk was even less pleasant than the first. He drove out to see her although he didn't expect to hear anything other than what he'd heard one and a half hours earlier over the phone. Her son, as before, apparently still wasn't in, and when asked whose son Jan Maria Pilski really was, she replied that he was hers and that she wasn't going to talk to Bartol anymore. When he said he'd find out anyway, she retorted that he could go ahead and find out, she didn't have to talk to him. She turned him out threatening to loose the dogs on him. The mention of suspicion and danger didn't help. She said she'd already once made a mistake like that and wasn't going to do so again. She'd talk to her son herself because she didn't believe a word of what Bartol said. He didn't know whether she said this because she'd long got it into her head that she was his mother and he her son, or because she'd been carefully instructed in what to say.

How efficiently Pilski could manipulate people and reality, Bartol was to experience for himself. He'd planned it out pretty well. Dressed in a pink tie, coat, Oriental-patterned scarf, he looked like the member of a club for careerists of various kinds; and the invented fiancée fitted in well. Nor did he have to invent much here: all the couple had in common was a common staircase, and he must have passed her numerous times. It wasn't difficult to imagine the sort of conversations they'd have and what a great problem the lettering on wedding invitations would create for her, not to mention the colour of the wedding dress. The idiotic ringtones announced news of idiotic things and begged to be treated indulgently, just like the scraps of conversation overheard by everyone. It was hardly surprising that the dog trader, shamefully concealed, did not fit in. Bartol himself had been caught out. He thought he'd spared Pilski Polek's teasing, and that's what he'd been supposed to think. Pilski had gained time, although God only knows what he needed it for. He could have done it all in three days, but no. Maybe the action was meant to unroll slowly, create the unease inspired by random messengers and the acceptance which comes with time. According to a formula known only to himself, he'd chosen the messengers carefully. The gigolo Rudzik had probably brought the sunflowers, which is why Mikulski kept the business card; the glasses were delivered by a woman so nondescript nobody even remembered her; Bartol wondered who the third person would be. He also wondered whether everything was going according to plan. Did Pilski want to remain in the shadows, thinking that nobody would guess what connected him with Mikulski? Who, after all, would remember that Mikulski had taken in a little boy, given him hope, then deprived him of it? Did he want to cast suspicion on the son, Jan Mikulski, so as to stir things up a little, or did he know the latter would remember? Had he expected the police to find and bury Jan Maria Gawlicki – a fallen priest who had killed faith, and not Lalek – Mirosław Trzaska? Was he waiting that long so that Elżbieta Ogrodniczak, a mother who'd bestowed her love unevenly, would know what she was paying for and be prepared?

Bartol pondered all this as he drove with Lentz in the night towards Fun Factory. He called the local police for a second time, asking whether Elżbieta Ogrodniczak was at home. For a second time, he heard that she was in Paris. This time, however, he asked how they knew – and discovered that they hadn't checked her house but merely phoned her company, where a manager had informed them that this was so – so it must be true. Bartol was furious, screamed that he could have done that much himself! The local big shot, not put off by any of this, retorted that he could indeed and could also stop bothering them because they had their own vice investigation to deal with, with the regional leader figuring in the main role, all the female staff to interrogate, and three television channels on their shoulders since morning.

Lentz drove. Without a word. In his own way, he was a little surprised by the whole situation. And not even so much by the fact that another suspect had suddenly appeared, which he acknowledged with one sentence – that Polek had suspected him all along – but by the fact that Bartol hadn't told anybody about any kinship between Pilski and Gawlicka. Lentz didn't have to add that this was going to cause problems; and he didn't. Bartol was grateful. He didn't want to think about that now; he wanted to find himself in Elżbieta Ogrodniczak's house as quickly as possible and, more importantly, find her alone. The only thing he knew was that she hadn't flown either to Paris or anywhere else.

When they arrived, only the garden lights were on. She could have turned them on herself, but they could equally well have turned on automatically with the dusk. They couldn't be sure. They drove around twice. It looked as though nobody was in. Nobody apart from the crickets which tried to drown the sound of sprinklers as they stubbornly turned and turned, watering the grass, plants and, in places, the paving stones. The men entered the porch. Bartol grasped the door handle; there was no bell. He yanked but it didn't yield. He was just about to walk around the house and enter by the terrace when Lentz showed him the keys lying on the wall. For a moment longer, he hoped they wouldn't fit. But they did.

Dawn was already breaking when they returned to Poznań. Bartol didn't want to go home; there, domestic problems which he didn't want to face, awaited him. Once more he found himself behind his desk and, having sat down, thumped it with his fist.

And so what if he'd found that bloody mirror – inscribed, so he guessed – since he hadn't thought of it sooner? He hadn't found either Pilski or Elizabeth. Neither in one house nor the other, nor even in the cathedral; he'd called there, too.

He struggled with his thoughts for a long time before falling asleep in the chair. He woke briefly and, out of the corner of his eye, caught sight of the letter still lying on his desk. He read the four sentences ten times.

*I'm always at your disposal. I now have to take care of
my mother. You know the address at which to find me.
See you soon.*

He read it for the eleventh time and still was none the wiser. The only thing he knew was that he ought to know and that soon it would be too late. Too late for everything.

In the end, he dozed off. He had no idea for how long: ten minutes or an hour, it didn't matter. He'd managed to dream of all the mirrors and hand mirrors he knew, including car mirrors, before he was abruptly woken by a thought reflected by he knew not what.

'It's there! Where it all began! Where he began! Yes, it's there!' Of this he was now certain.

He sprang to his feet. He wanted to protect her, whether she wanted it or not. He was just scared he'd be too late.

And rightly so.

'LOOK, AND I WAS SO SCARED I wouldn't be able to make you up so well. Oh, I forgot, you can't see anything anymore. Never mind, I'll look – that's what counts,' he said as he kept walking away, then approaching the armchair again. Meticulously adjusting every fold of her wide skirt. So that it lay well, broke up the faint light well.

'How beautifully you've sprawled out. A true *materfamilias*.'

He gazed, slowly tilting his head to one side then the other. She looked good from every angle.

He walked up closer.

'Well, maybe the head should be a little lower, like this. A hideous grimace has distorted your face, but that's no problem. You'll be gazing at the child with care and concern in your final moments.' He gently leaned her forward.

'Like this.

'Good, you can't see it now.

'It's a good thing I finished before she started sobbing,' he said, untangling the rope still wound around her neck.

'What? Did you think I'd be touched? How touching!

'Look! The rope's tied well. Triple twine doesn't break all that easily.

'You know what moderation, renunciation and being prepared for a journey mean. Now I'm ready, too.

'At last,' he added after a while, plunging the thin blade right into her heart.

'No need for more holes, this one's enough, just right. There, it went in smoothly. Maybe because there's nothing there, there's never been a heart there, at least not for everyone,' he laughed out loud. 'I forgot to ask, do you prefer *Alter* or *Alterius*.' He studied the inscription on the blade. 'Or maybe I didn't forget, I'm starting with you, so we'll go in turn. *Alter* for you, *Alterius* for me.'

He stepped away again, ecstatically, to gaze at his work from a better perspective.

'Of the three, you're the most important. You're my Love.

You, you, you, you, you, you,' he laughed, threatening her with his finger.

He glanced at a corner of the empty room.

'And you took away my Hope. To take in and give away like that, not nice. You're no better.' He turned in the other direction. 'You deprived me of Faith, bad man. What – screwing, screwing then no doing?

'I put you to shame with my morality, I, the discarded fruit!' he yelled, still laughing. 'Yes, it's me!

'Done. The time's come,' he said, calmly sitting on the floor next to her and pressing himself between her parted legs. Between the folds of her wide skirt, deeply, as deeply as he could.

He raised his head.

'There, I'm not standing behind your back anymore. You're looking at me now. Even gazing at me with care and concern. Because I'm all you've got left. Well, look, look.'

He rolled his sleeves up to the elbows.

'Take a look.' He stroked the laddered scars on each arm, one at a time, slowly recalling the shallow, momentary, old, still timid, now pale cuts, and the deeper, newer, pinker slashes. 'You think it hurts, hurts, no, no, it soothes, soothes. I assure you. Now look at the relief. The top level.' He laughed, severing and tearing the veins first of one arm then of the other, on a level with his elbows, at the highest rung of the ladder scarred with cuts.

He closed his eyes, laid his head comfortably on her knee.

'I told you. It doesn't hurt. It's a relief.'

'Can you hear my heart beat, it's beating fast, too loud, it'll slow down soon... There, it's already slowing down, boom, boom, boom... boom, boom. Divine rhythm... three.'

'There, I can see you... Justice of mine...
    Why are you... Why are your lips pursed so tight?
    Smile... it's for...'

ZOFIA PITUCH woke up just as tired as she had gone to bed, no differently. She bore the night shifts less and less well. It wasn't so much the dissecting of the chickens as the cold of the freezer-room, which penetrated the bones and was at its worst in the summer. She didn't even warm up waiting half an hour for the bus to Moczanowo. The early morning, too, had taken its time to grow warm.

The heat of the day, as well as the persistent flies, didn't let her sleep in. She got up and shambled to the kitchen thinking she was alone. She hadn't expected to see her daughter home at eleven o'clock.

'Samanta, what are you doing here?'

'Painting my nails, are you blind or something?' The girl didn't even raise her eyes from the table.

'No, I'm not,' replied her mother, looking at the daughter fastidiously gluing glittery beads onto her two-centimetre-long talons. There wasn't enough room for all the beads; two fingernails were broken.

'Why aren't you at work?' she asked. She wanted to scream but had no strength left.

'Because I'm not going anymore. Pawecka's bought herself a new car. Thinks she's found herself an idiot who's going to work for what she pays,' she answered, combing her outspread fingers through the air.

'Maybe that's because it's her shop,' replied the mother, although she no longer felt like talking. She went up to the kettle full of water. Turned it on and wanted to take a clean glass from the cupboard. There weren't any; she glanced at the sink.

'I don't give a shit,' the girl explained after a while. 'I'm getting ready now. Looks good, eh?'

The mother didn't know what she was supposed to be looking at. All she could see was a protruding belly, oozing out of a too-short blouse; protruding, so that the pink ring wouldn't dare lose itself amidst the folds of fat. She had no strength left;

she didn't even feel like washing a single glass ,but she did. She didn't want to waste the boiled water.

'What's that for?' she finally asked, seeing the expectant eyes of her daughter.

'What for, what for! Television's coming soon, ain't it? At long last something's happening in this shit hole. We're neighbours, like, so they might ask us questions.'

'My God, what are you talking about?' Zofia Pituch was ready to drop and, supporting herself, collapsed onto a chair.

'Found two corpses in the old cottage next door, didn't they, the one with a curse on it, the one nobody lived in. It must be important cos it's crawling with police.

'Listen, just you tell me what went on there 'cos they're goin' to ask, like, ain't they?' she demanded as she went up to the mirror.

'Dear God,' shouted the woman, and her head fell helplessly into her open palms.

'Jesus, there you go again. This really's goin' to be Great Moczanowo now! Look good, do I? Go down well on TV?'

'Dear God, dear God, dear God...'

HE'D BEEN STANDING in front of the door for a long time before she opened it; but, in the end, she opened. He bore it and also bore the way she looked at him. He said nothing, waited until she spoke first.

'Do you realise there's nothing more naff than a guy with a stupid look on his face and a red rose in his hand?'

'I do. I went for a simple symbol. Look what else I've written here.'

'Well, well. *Amor vincit omnia*. Love conquers all.' She looked at him, almost smiled but only briefly; and, closing the door, added: 'Let's not go over the top.'

He turned and said to himself: 'Things aren't that bad. It'll all sort itself out. Patience is also a virtue.' And left the flower on the doormat.

It looked as though it had been placed in a frame.

about the author

JOANNA JODEŁKA was the first woman to win the High Calibre Award for the Best Polish Crime Novel, taking the prize in 2010 for her debut *Polychrome* (*Polichromia*, 2009). Her second crime novel, *Grzechotka* ('The Rattle'), was published in 2011, followed by her third in 2012.

Polychrome is Jodełka's first novel to be translated into English.

about the translator

DANUSIA STOK is a member of The Translators' Association / The Society of Authors, and is an established translator from Polish of long and short literary fiction, TV interviews, and film scripts. Danusia has translated, among others, film scripts by Krzysztof Kieslowski and Krzysztof Piesiewicz, works by Mariusz Wilk and Adina Blady Szwajger, novels by Marek Krajewski, Andrzej Sapkowski and Agnieszka Taborska and has compiled, translated and edited *Kieslowski on Kieslowski*.

also available from stork press

Madame Mephisto by A. M. Bakalar
ISBN Paperback: 978-0-9571326-0-3
ISBN eBook: 978-0-9571326-1-0

21:37 by Maruisz Czubaj
Translator: Anna Hyde
ISBN Paperback: 978-0-9571326-8-9
ISBN eBook: 978-0-9571326-9-6

Illegal Liaisons by Grażyna Plebanek
Translator: Danusia Stok
ISBN Paperback: 978-0-9571326-2-7
ISBN eBook: 978-0-9571326-3-4

Freshta by Petra Procházková
Translator: Julia Sherwood
ISBN Paperback: 978-0-9571326-4-1
ISBN eBook: 978-0-9571326-5-8

The Finno-Ugrian Vampire by Noémi Szécsi
Translator: Peter Sherwood
ISBN Paperback: 978-0-9571326-6-5
ISBN eBook: 978-0-9571326-7-2

Mother Departs by Tadeusz Różewicz
Translator: Barbara Bogoczek
Editor: Tony Howard
ISBN Hardback 978-0-9573912-0-8
ISBN Paperback 978-0-9573912-1-5
ISBN eBook 978-0-9573912-2-2